YOU CAN'T ESCAPE FROM MARS!

By
E. K. JARVIS

I0616915

ARMCHAIR FICTION
PO Box 4369, Medford, Oregon 97504

*For more information about Armchair Books and products, visit our
website at…*

www.armchairfiction.com

Or email us at…

armchairfiction@yahoo.com

LANDING ON PHOBOS WAS TABOO...

For space jockey Jerry Utah, putting the new spaceship through its testing phase was nothing unusual. But, when he unexpectedly saw a beautiful woman's face through the viewport, he lost control and crashed—on Phobos, a moon no one was welcome on. There was something was wrong on this tiny Martian satellite— and Utah was in a perfect position to find out just what it was. The Martian Priests, who ruled the Red planet itself, also held this little moon in a grip of deadly fear with strict customs and an iron-clad policy of no interference. But what were the priests so keen on protecting? What secrets lay hidden on Phobos' pock-marked surface? Utah knew his curiosity might get him into trouble, so instead of helping him, the Priests were going to kill him. However, something Utah said changed their minds. It would be much more entertaining for them to keep him alive...for now.

FOR A COMPLETE SECOND NOVEL, TURN TO PAGE 83

CAST OF CHARACTERS

JERRY UTAH
He wanted to get back to Mars in a hurry, but he found himself in a sticky situation that might prevent his return—permanently!

NERISSA
This young beauty was responsible for Utah's crash, and now it seemed she was going to be the cause of his death!

THE PRIESTS
A sinister brotherhood that wanted on one on their forbidden moon; and they were more than willing to kill to keep it that way!

HARRY HENRED
This rocket engineer thought he was coming to Phobos to make a lot of money, not risk his life for some silly game…or dame!

ULRUK
A High Priest with something to hide. Just what was the source of his apparently unlimited supernatural power?

KAVISH, THE MARTIAN
He was ready, fairly willing, and very able. The object of his desire was nearly at hand—if he could kill, he would have it.

CHAPTER ONE

THE SHIP was a new model, the first of a special design for use on Mars. Test pilot Jerry Utah put her through her paces, noting mechanically the details of flight not recorded by the automatic equipment she carried. She responded well to her controls, she wasn't unduly noisy, there wasn't any stray vibration present, she hit her Mach numbers like a thoroughbred. He set her in level flight, held her steady.

Below him, now thousands of miles away, the Red Planet dreamed in a thin haze. From this altitude, the canals looked like imaginary lines, and the hidden cities of the red deserts were really hidden. Rising swiftly on the horizon was Phobos, the inner moon of Mars. Since one of the requirements of this ship was that she should be able to reach the moons of Mars easily, he set her nose straight toward Phobos.

Phobos—the name had been selected on Earth, in 1877, when the satellite had been first discovered. Phobos was a root word meaning fear... He wondered why such a name had been selected for this fierce little companion of Mars? What had been in the mind of the astronomer who had picked this name?

Of all the words available to him, he had certainly selected the right one as a name for this moon.

Phobos—Forbidden World.

When the first humans arrived on Mars in 2021—a daredevil crew of death-cheaters lead by old Trask Filler—they had discovered that the Martians had already achieved space flight to their satellites. This was as far as the Martians had gone, either they had lost interest in the worlds up in the sky when they got this far or they had not been able to muster the courage to jump off into the emptiness of space itself. But they had reached their moons.

So much the humans learned soon after they landed. In the two score years that had passed since that date, the human had learned little more about the moons of Mars, or even about the Martians themselves. The Martians had declared Phobos off-limits to all humans. What was hidden on this little satellite no man knew. The Martians themselves seemed to regard the little moon with a mixture of superstitious awe and dread in which fear was the biggest emotion.

Utah watched Phobos enlarge rapidly in the plastic glass of the control cabin.

Then, as though it bad been wiped clean, the image of the moon vanished from his eyes.

The vision of a woman replaced it.

And what a woman! Full-breasted and red-lipped, with dark hair tumbling down across her shoulders. A clinging dress in the Martian style revealed rather than concealed the loveliness of a lithe body. More startling than anything else was the fact that she was human.

There was no human woman like this on all Mars. Utah, who had a connoisseur's taste in such matters, was willing to bet that no such woman existed on the Red Planet. If she had existed here, her name would be a legend among the women-hungry men who crossed space to reach this outpost of desolation in the sky. For a split second, so swiftly did the vision come, he had the impression that the woman in the glass was real. He could see her eyes looking at him, the startled lights in them, and he had the impression that she could see him. Her lips moved to form words.

He shook his head and closed his eyes, to dispel the vision. "Utah, have you gone space happy?" Sometimes men crossing space thought they saw things outside the ports of their ship that could not exist there. His first dazed impression was that he was a victim of such an hallucination.

But when he opened his eyes, the woman in the glass was still there.

Panic caught him. The vision ought not to be there. It was actually in his mind, not in the plastic, it had to be in his mind, there was no other place it could he.

"Utah, you fool!" He doubled up his fist, smacked himself full in the mouth, a backhanded blow that brought sharp pain with it and left the taste of blood on his lips. That ought to dispel the vision.

But—the vision remained.

SIMULTANEOUSLY somewhere in the control cabin of the ship a bell rang sharply—the radar warning system going into operation. For once in his life Jerry Utah—failed to hear the sharp clang of that tiny bell. His attention was concentrated on the vision.

Was this vision real? Could it be real? If it was real, how was he seeing it? He knew from time to time that very strange results had been reported in radio reception, fences had been reported as talking, iron deer on lawns, even the fillings in the teeth, all these had occasionally acted as impromptu radio receivers, startling the hearers by detecting a radio program when no receiver seemed to be present. Was this vision he was seeing actually some telecast program that was being reproduced by the thick plastic of the view port?

It could be, maybe! No one had ever reported such a thing but perhaps it could happen. If this wasn't happening, had his mind gone bad on him? Had he begun to see things that didn't exist?

The woman seemed to see him, something no telecast vision could do. She looked up at him, then past him. He saw fright in her eyes. Her lips moved, screaming words. Dimly he seemed to hear them.

"Look—out!"

For the first time he heard the clangor of the bell. He jerked his eyes to the radar screen. There, clearly visible, was the red warning signal. He lifted his gaze to the vision port.

The picture of the woman was gone from it. The plastic was undistorted. As the vision had come, so it had gone. Instead of the woman, he saw in the plastic—the jagged rocky surface of the Forbidden Moon, dead ahead of him.

It was this moon the radar screen had detected.

The ship he was flying was a jet job designed for operation either in or out of an atmosphere. He was travelling at a rate several times the speed of sound—the Mach counter stood above the three mark—indicated he was travelling more than three times the speed of sound at sea level. He jerked the controls to turn the ship, to dodge the grim rocky mass rising up so fast in front of him it seemed to be materializing there. The ship responded. G's hit him a mighty blow.

The ship had been soundly designed. It would take a sharp turn and emerge unharmed. But the human body wouldn't, even in the protection of a G-suit, it wouldn't take the pressure. Even as he twisted the controls, he knew too many G's were going to hit him.

He tried to soften the turn, fighting desperately to get the ship under control and to keep himself from blacking out. He had the dazed impression that he was a child again, playing pop-the-whip, and that he was on the end of a long, long whip—as the popper. The G's seemed to reach into his body and crush his substance molecule by molecule, missing no single atom.

He knew he was going to black out. He fought against it, knew it was a fight he couldn't win. Ii he turned the ship swiftly enough to dodge Phobos, the pressure of the turn would make him black out. If he didn't turn it, he would crash.

As the blackness hit him, he kicked off the power.

The little ship hit with a thundering roar. The ejection controls, designed to release the pressure cabin took hold. The whole cabin was ejected just before the ship itself hit. Utah went with the cabin.

Flung clear of the ship, the cabin was tossed upward in a mighty arc, from which it came floating down. It struck the side of a hill, bounced, struck again, and slid to a halt at the bottom.

JERRY UTAH did not know how he got out of the cabin. He was dazed, shocked, and blundering unconsciously, like a swimmer trying to swim to shore but not knowing quite how to do the job. Then, little by little he began to get impressions of the scene around him. Some things were right, other things were wrong.

The air was wrong. Not that there was anything wrong with the air itself—it was sweet, breathable, and maybe a little heavier than the air on Mars itself—but the fact that it existed at all was wrong.

He was on Phobos, he had crashed here. Even in his dazed state, he knew this much. But on a solar body the size of this tiny moon all of the molecules of that mixture of gases that is called air should have escaped into space ages in the past. Even Earth's moon was airless, or practically so. Phobos should have no air at all.

But it had air. He was breathing. This one fact proved there was air on the moon. Also, he could hear sharp crackling sounds mixed with a steady roar and a blast of heat, all of which were coming from the burning fuel tanks of the flier and all of which added still further proof of the existence of air.

The heat was becoming uncomfortable. It was a pressure urging him to move. But moving would require effort and it was so nice just to lie where he was and exist without being really conscious. If he moved he would become conscious and if he became conscious, he would hurt, a chain of circumstances that was all too clear to him. Therefore, don't move. Just lie still. To hell with the heat. The hell with—

He was aware of scrambling sounds near him. A voice called sharply to him.

He ignored it. The hell with it too. It wanted him to move. He wanted to lie still. It was so nice and restful here.

Something or somebody grabbed him, lifted him, began to half carry, half drag him. He tried to cry out in protest at this unwarranted intrusion of his right to rest but his complaint went unheeded.

Later he was allowed to lie down and the something or the somebody who had carried him away tried to make him comfortable. Quite a lot later, he opened his eyes.

He hastily closed them again.

The vision was back.

"Go 'way, witch!" He waved a feeble hand.

The vision didn't go away. It started to talk. "I'm so glad you are not dead. Please don't close your eyes. It was all my fault. I'm sorry but I didn't mean to do it."

Amazed, he listened to the voice. The words were English.

An exclamation of disgust followed. Then the voice came again. It was speaking Martian now, the language of the red deserts, at a mile-a-minute clip. Utah listened with languid interest. Ordinary Martian he could understand, if it was spoken slowly enough and he was given plenty of time between words, but this was moving much too fast for him. As best he could gather, she was apologizing for using something that she called the *uni projection,* whatever this was.

He didn't pay much attention. He was convinced this was a dream, a distorted fiction of the mind created as the brain itself was destroyed. "I'm dead," he told himself. "I died when this ship crashed. Now I'm hearing voices and seeing visions."

THIS WAS A rational, sensible explanation and he could think of no other. True, it seemed to last a long time, but he knew enough psychology to know that the brain could not be trusted to measure time accurately, it made instants into hours or hours into moments, depending on the focus of its attention. No, he was dead.

He opened his eyes again.

The vision was still there.

It didn't look like a figment of the imagination, a dream-inspired hallucination. It looked like a real woman. She was kneeling beside him. She had torn off a part of her skirt and was using it to wipe something from his face—blood, he thought. He reached out a tentative hand and touched her.

She was startled by the gesture. She drew hastily away from him like a child frightened by a sudden movement. Then, as if she sensed the uncertainty and bewilderment in him, as if she realized he was a drowning man grasping at straws, she moved close again—and allowed him to touch her. His fingers found firm flesh, warm, living flesh.

"You—you're real," he whispered. Sometimes dreams turned into reality. This one had. There was awe in him. He had seen this woman in a vision and because of the distraction of that vision, his ship had crashed. He should have died in that crash. But he hadn't. Now the woman of his vision was here with him, real, alive.

Who was she? What was she doing here on this rocky, forbidden moon of Mars? How did it happen there was enough air here to sustain life? Questions tumbled through his mind like mad acrobats drunk with marijuana.

"Yes. I am real. As real as you are."

"Who—who are you?"

11

"My name is Nerissa."

"Nerissa." He said the word as if he still did not quite believe all this could be true. "Nerissa what?"

She shook her head. "Just Nerissa. I do not have any more names. Should I have?"

"People usually do," he said. "Like me. I'm Jerry Utah."

"Jer-ry U-tah," The words came to her tongue with difficulty. She spoke a swift sentence in Martian, which he did not understand.

"I was forty to fifty miles away from this rock pile when I saw you," he said. Defiance sounded in his voice as if he dared her to explain how this could have happened.

"Yes, yes," she answered. "I saw your ship and I used the *uni projection*—"

"The what?" he said.

"It is a trick of the priests here. I have learned it from them. By using it, you can make yourself be seen at a great distance. You can also see what is happening far away. I do not understand how it is explained—"

"I don't either," he answered, whistling. He knew the Martians were far ahead of earth scientists in developing some of the more obscure functions of the mind. Perhaps this *uni projection* which she said she had used was some development of ESP powers.

"How does it happen there is air on this place?" he continued.

"Why is air here? Because we need it to breathe," Nerissa answered.

"But what keeps it from flying away?" He tried to explain what he wanted to know.

"Oh, I see," she said at last. "The priests here have some kind of a machine that creates gravity. It is this machine that holds the air here."

HE NODDED. The explanation he understood but he did not understand the whys and the wherefores of the matter any better than he understood the operation of the *uni projection*. But he saw one thing quite clearly—both the *uni projection* and the machine for creating artificial gravity meant that here on this rocky moon science had taken tremendous strides indeed.

On Mars itself they knew nothing of the *uni projection*. Nor did they know anything about artificial gravity. Martian scientific development seemed to have stumbled badly on the main planet.

But it hadn't stumbled here on this moon. Instead, it had gone forward with tremendous speed.

"How did you get here, Nerissa?" Utah said.

Her expression was troubled. "I do not know, for sure. I was brought here when I was a little girl."

"From Mars?"

"Yes, I think."

"Who brought you here?"

"The priests, I guess," A tiny tremor passed over her face when she used the word *priests*. He saw it, wondered about it. Was she afraid of the priests. Were they the rulers here? What was hidden here on this forbidden moon? Again the questions were tumbling in his mind like mad acrobats. Well, he would get them answered, he supposed, in time. He was alive and not badly hurt. What else mattered? At a sound the girl rose quickly to her feet. For a moment she seemed to search for the source of the noise that had disturbed her.

"The priests come!" she said quickly.

Utah caught a glimpse of a long file of blue-clad figures moving toward the flaming wreckage of the ship. Blue was a sacred color on Mars, a color restricted exclusively to the priesthood. "Let 'em come," he said.

"But they will kill you!" she spoke.

"Kill me?" he gasped. "In heaven's name—why ?"

"Because you landed here. This is a forbidden moon."

"But I didn't land here on purpose. It was an accident."

"That will make no difference—to them." A shudder crossed her face.

"But I couldn't help it."

"You have broken one of their laws, whether or not you intended to break the law is of no importance. Jerry, there is only one way I know to save you."

"What is that?"

"Tell them that you have come here to challenge for Nerissa."

"What?" He didn't begin to understand what she meant. She did not explain. "Just tell them what I said. If they ask you questions, pretend to know nothing. They must not see me with you. I'll see you some other time, if I can." She dropped from the rock, slipped into a crevice between two huge boulders and was gone from sight.

Utah got stiffly to his feet and awaited the approach of the column of blue-clad figures.

CHAPTER TWO

THEY DIDN'T see him at first. They circled the burning ship, spread out from it to begin a search of the vicinity. He could have run from them, but running would get him nowhere. The girl, Nerissa, might have helped him hide, but she had chosen to do otherwise. She had no reason to help him. So far as he could see, there was no good hiding place on the whole of Phobos.

The surface was tumbled, broken rocks, utterly inhospitable to life of any sort. If the Martian priests lived here, they had their quarters underground. Food must be brought here from the mother planet, no food could be grown in this rocky soil. There was no vegetation. Not even wild goats could find a living here.

Utah waited for the priests. No sense in going to them, let them come to him. A priest caught sight of him, a voice called out a harsh command in the guttural language of Mars. The priests came trotting toward him.

The men of Mars and the men of Earth looked a lot alike. Martians usually had bigger chests than humans, a development brought about by oxygen needs in the thin air of the Red Planet. They were usually not quite as tall as men but they were heavier built though the heavy build did not mean they were stronger than humans. Physically, the two races were about on a par. Martian skins were the color of old copper, again the result of the thin air blanket over the planet, which let through to the surface an excessive quantity of ultra-violet radiation.

These priests were typical specimens. They surrounded him with a ring of glittering hostile eyes peering at him out of hawk-nosed faces, making him think of vultures surrounding a victim as they waited for him to die.

One, with the bright yellow hood that marked a low order in the hierarchical rank, spoke to him.

"What are you doing here?" The language was Martian, but he had been on the Red Planet long enough to understand what was meant. He explained. They looked curiously at the wrecked ship, this was probably the first ship of human construction most of them had ever seen though they knew that humans were on Mars.

"The crash was an accident," Utah said. "If you will help me get back to the planet, I will be very grateful."

Surely, in spite of what Nerissa had said, a request for help would not go unheeded. After all, he had done nothing wrong by any reasonable standard of conduct. And nobody would refuse to help a man in trouble. Or so he thought.

But on this moon of Mars, the code of conduct was different.

Yellow Hood shrugged, a gesture, which said he wasn't interested in helping anybody, and as for the fact that the human had arrived here as a result of an accident, they had their own rules on this moon.

"Kill him," Yellow Hood said. The order was given with utter indifference, as if the life of a man meant no more to him than the life of an insect.

From under the blue robes knives flashed.

Utah was unarmed, if he had been armed it would have made no difference. Before he could have drawn a gun, they would have had a dozen knives buried to the hilt in his body.

Nerissa had been right when she had said they would kill him! Was she also right when she said she knew of a way to save him? If she was wrong, he was a dead man. He lifted his hand, spoke rapidly.

"I wish to challenge for Nerissa."

THE EFFECT of the words was almost magical. The lifted knives stopped moving. Startled eyes were turned toward him. A look of astonishment appeared on the face of Yellow Hood. "You wish to challenge for Nerissa?" he spoke.

"Yes," Utah answered.

"What do you know of Nerissa?"

"Nothing."

"Then why do you wish to challenge for her?"

What was it the girl had said? If they ask questions, tell them nothing. Utah shook his head. "I do not understand the question," he answered.

It was an answer that was not satisfactory to Yellow Hood. The Martian asked other questions, popping them out in guttural bursts of harsh sound. To all of them Utah made the same reply—a shake of the head and the repeated statement that he did not understand. Yellow Hood gave up.

"Very well. According to our custom, anyone who comes here to challenge, must be accepted. You will get your wish."

The tone of his voice said that he didn't think that the wish would do this human much good in the long run. Utah took a deep breath, drawing the thin air of this moon into his lungs as if he was grateful that he was still able to breathe.

In point of fact, he was grateful. When the knives had flashed, he hadn't expected to do much more breathing of any kind.

They marched him away. He caught a glimpse of a smooth field where the Martians landed their own unwieldy spacecraft. No hangers, no repair shops were visible. Runways led underground. Apparently the craft were stored under the surface. He was taken underground too. A door was opened. Yellow Hood motioned for him to enter. As he hesitated, Yellow Hood literally kicked him through the door. He sprawled into the room.

Three humans and one Martian looked down at him. The door slammed shut. Torches set in wall sockets flared in a smoky room. Skins were piled in a corner, bedding material. There were no beds, the bed had never been invented on Mars. There was a table, with stools around it.

The three humans looking down at him from these stools were unshaven. Their clothes were wrinkled. They looked as if they had been here for weeks. For a moment they stared at him as if he wasn't exactly welcome here, then as his torn clothing and battered, bloody face made it obvious that he was hurt, they rose as one man and came quickly toward him, to help him if they could.

The lone Martian in the room remained on his stool. His attitude plainly said that he wasn't going to get up to help any damned human who had ever lived.

"Can I help you, old man?"

"Say, you look like you've been in a smash."

"Can we do something for you?" the third man said.

Utah got slowly to his feet. These three humans looked like refugees from a graveyard, they looked like living allegories of want, privation, hunger, and despair, but they had offered to help him. He liked that. "I look a little worse off than I actually am," he answered. "As for doing something for me, if you could arrange to cut the throat of that priest with the yellow hood—"

"Sorry." The tallest of the three laughed bitterly. "I'd like to oblige you. Fact is, nothing is needed worse around this joint than a wholesale throat cutting, but this pleasant activity is forbidden to animals like us. Anyhow, in this case, you'd have to get in line. Say, don't I know you? Aren't you Jerry Utah?"

UTAH STARED at the tall man. Something about the features seemed familiar, where had he seen this man? "Harry Henred!" he exclaimed. He remembered now. An altercation in a dive near the spaceport. A couple of Martians had resented this tall man. There had been a slight rhubarb. Nothing serious, nothing that a knife in the guts wouldn't cure. The two Martians had obviously intended to provide exactly this cure for the tall human when Utah had stepped into the fracas. The result had been a couple of Martians with very sore heads, and two humans who were very firm friends.

Utah's hand shot out and he grinned all over. There was no one in the whole solar system that he would rather have seen here than this tall ex-spaceman. The two men shook hands. "Meet my pals," Henred said, nodding to the two humans. "Sam Bywater and Kelso Mead."

Utah found himself shaking hands with the two men. Bywater was short and squat in stature and built on the general lines of a gorilla. He looked as if terrific strength resided in those hunched shoulders. Kelso Mead was more slender but the look of the coiled snake was somewhere about him. Both seemed very friendly but both of them also seemed to size him up, to look him over carefully, as if they were measuring him as a potential antagonist and were trying to determine his strength and his weakness.

"He's a bad customer in a close fight," Henred drawled, to the two. "That I know for certain. Split-second reactions, wallop of a mule in either fist."

The two grinned—uneasily, Utah thought. He glanced at the Martian, who remained sitting on the stool. "What about him, hasn't he got a name?"

"Yeah, but he's too busy to be polite."

"Busy doing what?"

"Figuring out the best way to cut our throats," Henred answered. "Isn't that right, Kavish, old pal?" he said in the Martian tongue.

Kavish, the Martian, curled his lips in a thin snarl but did not bother answering.

"What are you doing here, Jerry?" Henred questioned. "Did you sucker in on this deal too and come here to play games with us?"

Utah told them what had happened. When he had finished, Henred spoke dolefully. "So you told 'em you had come to challenge for Nerissa? Then you *are* going to play games with us. Welcome, pal, to our select little group." His grin was sardonic, a bitter wretched grimace that twisted his face out of all resemblance to the human.

"I don't get it," Utah said.

Henred paused and seemed to grope for words. "Jerry, what do you know about the customs of Mars, especially their religious customs? I don't mean their religious beliefs, I mean the practices they have evolved over the centuries in connection with what they call religion?"

"Damned little. What have their customs got to do with us?"

"Practically everything, including the little matter of life and death. Custom is king here. We were sucked into—and you have run right straight up against—the meanest, most vicious custom ever evolved by the Martian mind—and believe me, that's a broad statement."

"You talk like an expert," Utah commented.

"By profession, I'm a space ship engineer," Henred answered apologetically. "But I've kinda made a hobby of studying customs. Do you know anything about the Chinese?"

"Not much. Why?"

"Because the Martians and the Chinese have much in common. They're both old races with long histories. The longer a race continues to exist, the more it tends to become fixed in a rut. It develops fixed fashions in clothing, eating, how to greet a superior, how to talk to an inferior, and how to worship God. Every detail of the life of an individual from the cradle to the grave becomes ordered for him—by custom. In time, customs assume all the force of law, and the individual who violates custom is very severely punished, by death if the infraction is serious—and often even if it isn't serious. Custom thus becomes a sort of protective coloration, a method of recognizing members of your own group."

"What does all this have to do with us?"

"I'm coming to that. What we have run up against is a mixture of primitive belief and strange custom. Once this custom we're facing had some kind of a value, but it has long since outlived its usefulness. However, it continues to exist and is as strong today as it was when it was first invented."

HENRED took a deep breath and pulled a package of cigarettes from the pocket of his rumpled jacket. "To understand what we're up against, you've got to understand how it originated. The first part is concerned with the primitive Martian belief that this moon was the home of their gods. Did you know the Martians worshipped this moon?"

"No, I didn't."

"Well, they do. And they worship it because they believe their gods live here."

"But they have space ships that can reach this moon. They ought to know that no gods live here," Utah objected.

"That's exactly the point. The Martians discovered how to build crude space ships. But they never ventured any farther into space than their moons, this moon particularly. Why?"

"I don't know."

"Because the priests seized control of space flight as soon as it was invented. They grabbed the first space ship the Martians ever built. They announced that the space ship was a sacred vessel, that it was to be used to transport priests to and from the home of the gods, this moon. Nobody but a priest has ever been on Phobos. They fly regularly from this moon to Mars. They tell the people on the planet that they come here to learn the will of the gods, that they visit the gods here, and when they return to Mars, they announce to all the people the will of the gods. They've built up one of the tightest monopolies that ever existed anywhere in the solar system and they use this black traffic in superstition to clamp a complete control over the whole planet."

Henred's voice had risen, anger was audible in his tones, anger directed at all forms of superstition. "The Martians are a quiet, peaceful people. Their biggest defect is that they are willing to believe almost anything. For centuries their priests have told them lies and they have believed the lies. The priesthood, with its fountainhead right here on this moon, has every man, woman, and child on the planet by the throat."

He had been speaking in English but the Martian, Kavish, must have understood at least part of what he was saying. Kavish rose to his feet, a snarl on his face. "Sacrilege. Silence, blasphemous dog, before the gods strike you dead."

"Set down before I knock you down," Henred answered. The lanky engineer cocked his fist.

Kavish's hand went inside his robe, came away empty as he reached for a knife he did not possess. He sat down hastily. "If I had a knife you would not talk like this."

"You'll get your chance with a knife." Henred answered. "Just be patient until the time comes."

"But what does all this lead to?" Utah questioned.

"This is all a part of the background," the engineer answered. "It doesn't mean much until you get the rest of this sweet little story, which concerns itself with another custom."

"Go on."

"This custom is the yearly challenge for the vestal virgin."

"Eh?" Utah said, startled. For the first time, he caught a glimpse of what was coming next. He didn't like the looks of it.

"I see you're beginning to get the idea," the engineer continued. "A part of the priestly hierarchy includes a group of women who are presumed to serve the gods but who probably actually serve the priests far more than the gods. These women are taken as children, infants, in fact, and are brought here and raised by the priests, a new one every year. Each year one reaches the age of marriage. Any Martian who wishes to do so many challenge for her, although another custom restricts the number of challengers to five." He looked meaningfully at Utah. "That's where you came into the story, Jerry. When you arrived here, saying you wished to challenge for Nerissa, you brought the challengers up to the proper number—five."

Utah's breath whistled in his throat. The story sounded utterly incredible but he had been long enough on the Red Planet to know that the incredible happened here. There was certainly no reason why Henred should lie to him. Nor did the engineer look like a man who was lying. Nor did he appear to be out of his mind. "But Nerissa is human," he protested.

HENRED smiled wryly. "That fact made it a little hard for the priests this year. Their vestal virgin was a human woman. No Martian wished to challenge for her, except our friend, Kavish here." He nodded sardonically at the Martian seated on the stool, and got a scowl in reply. "That's where we came into the picture. Since they had a human woman and since only one Martian wanted to risk his valuable neck for such a doubtful prospect, they decided they would open the lists to humans, I don't know whether they went around and tried to get volunteers or not. If they tried that, they failed. At any rate, since they couldn't get volunteers, they pretended they had some very special jobs to be done. They offered fancy wages—two thousand dollars a month, gold. They were pretty vague about what was to be done in return for this money, but they succeeded in sucking in Sam Bywater, Kelso Mead, and yours truly. No doubt they were trying to dig up a fifth man when you arrived and solved the problem for them. So here we are, Jerry, the five of us, challenging for Nerissa." The engineer laughed, a sound with no suggestion of mirth in it.

Utah lit a cigarette. In his mind was the thought that he had been through enough for one day, that he deserved a chance to rest, to relax his nerves. He shook his head, "I thought, when I got out of that crash alive, that I was the luckiest fool in the system. I'm not so certain now. How do they work this challenge thing?"

"I'm not certain," the engineer answered. "No doubt they will brief us later. In essence it's all very simple. The one who remains alive gets Nerissa."

"Huh?"

"He also gets to be a member of the priesthood," the engineer continued.

"But which one of us will remain alive? I mean, how do they determine that interesting little fact?"

"They don't determine it," Kelso Mead spoke for the first time. "We determine it."

"Eh ?"

"The one who succeeds in killing the others gets the girl," Henred said laconically.

"That's what I was afraid of," Utah sighed.

CHAPTER THREE

"BUT WHAT happens if we decide not to play?" Jerry Utah questioned. He had eaten, he had bathed as far as the facilities of Phobos permitted—about a pint of water was allowed for such nonsense as keeping clean—and Henred had patched up his cuts, spreading the wonderful soothing salve of the Martians on them. He felt much better, though he didn't see what good feeling better was going to do him.

"I don't know what happens if we decide not to play," the engineer answered. "They won't take us back to Mars, that I know. I yelled no dice and demanded to be taken back home. All I got in answer was a shrug. Anyhow I think we will play." Grimness crept into his voice as he spoke.

"What makes you think that?"

"Several reasons. One is plain survival. If you and I were put into a locked room and given knives and told that the one who came out of the room alive would be given almost anything he wanted, but that if one of us didn't come out within an hour, both of us would be killed, what would we do, Jerry?"

"I'm dammed if I know," the pilot answered frankly. "I like life."

"So do I," Henred answered. "We all want to live. Four of us have got to die. If we don't kill each other, the priests will kill us. With that kind of a prospect in front of him the meanest mouse of a man who ever lived would fight. And we will fight too, Jerry, much as we would like to do something else. Also, there is the matter of the reward to the winner. I assure you that Nerissa is only part of that reward, maybe the smallest part. Another part is wealth."

"Who the hell cares about money?"

"The wealth you will get here isn't money, it's things that money can't even buy. First is luxury. The finest clothing, the finest foods. Second is power. If you win this rat race, you've automatically got a chance to succeed to the position of high priest of all Mars. Let me tell you, Jerry, that is a position of real power. Within the framework of custom, the word of the high priest is law. Millions of Martians do just exactly what he says. The will to power is a basic human impulse, Jerry. Deep down in their secret hearts most men would like nothing better than to have the power of Ulruk, the high priest of Mars. Thus—we fight. If not for power, then for the chance at life itself."

Utah shook his head. "There may be something in what you say, but I'll be triply damned if I do it."

Henred shrugged thin shoulders. "In that case, Jerry, all I can say is that it was nice to know you."

"You're going to fight?" Utah demanded.

"Not if there is any way to dodge it, but I know myself well enough to know that when the pinch comes, I'll fight. The only alternative—and this means a hell of a lot more fighting is to cut the throat of every priest on this moon."

"Then let's do that," Utah said, enthusiastically.

"Jerry, are you out of your head? There are thousands of them!" Henred answered, appalled. He brightened as another thought came to him. "Not that I wouldn't like it, but I don't know any way to get the job done."

THEY WERE a wary, restless, worried lot of humans held prisoner in this locked cell on Phobos. Somewhere on this mad moon death lay waiting for three of them, and each knew it. Perhaps death lay waiting for four of them. The Martian Kavish obviously thought it did. In his mind he was quite certain he could destroy these four humans, when the time came. He made no effort to conceal his opinion of them. "Vermin from across the sky," he called them. They took his insults calmly though the glitter in Henred's eye indicated he was storing away these insults, for future reference. Utah promised himself that he would remember them too. Deep in his heart he cherished the hope that the Martians, if properly approached, would release him, and the others as well, with the possible exception of Kavish, who obviously did not want to be released. With this thought in mind, when the door opened and priests bearing food entered, Utah demanded to be taken to Ulruk.

His demand produced dismay on the part of the priests. They had no precedent for this action, no one in the position of these men had ever demanded to talk to the high priest which was perhaps the reason Utah had his request granted. He was marched to Ulruk.

The high priest received him in a small room hung with draperies. Smoky torches provided light—the Martians knew that better systems of illumination existed, but custom barred their introduction. The room was heavy with smoke and thick with choky incense. Ulruk was seated in a heavy chair. Guards with spears held ready to thrust stood on both sides of the chair. Utah did not doubt that other guards, with more effective weapons, were hidden behind the draperies.

Ulruk was a skinny gnome. He was old, old, old. His skin was withered and wrinkled and only his eyes were alive. In them was malevolence. Looking out from the wrinkled face, they saw nothing but only served to reflect the evil glittering behind them. This Martian had outlived life itself. All that kept him alive now was hate—of all things living.

The red-hooded priest—a member of the upper tier of this hierarchy—who had conducted Utah to this reception threw himself flat on the floor before Ulruk, and motioned the human to do likewise.

Utah stood very firmly on both feet. "To hell with it," he said.

From the floor, Red Hood made frantic gestures to him to obey.

"To hell with you too," Utah said.

The spear points were dropped and were pointed at his stomach. The muscles of the guards tensed to lunge. Utah lifted his hand.

"If you kill me now, you will have to find another sucker for your games," he spoke. "Only four will be left. And that will violate custom." Four lifted fingers emphasized his meaning.

Ulruk looked startled. He spoke a single low word to the guards. The spears were drawn back. The glittering eyes looked wonderingly at Utah.

"I demand that I and the other humans here be returned to the surface of Mars," the pilot said. This was no time to cringe or fawn and to attempt to placate fate. A hard-driven bitter bluff might work. He was certain that nothing else would work.

"You *demand?*" Ulruk spoke in Martian. He was startled. There was no doubt about that. This was probably the only time in his life that any two-legged creature had dared to stand in his presence.

"That is what I said," Utah answered.

THE HIGH priest held a small golden ball in his hands, the sacred religious symbol of all Mars, the sphere, the only perfect geometrical figure. He toyed with the sphere, clasping and unclasping his fingers around it. He said nothing. The only sound in the stifling room was the frightened breathing of the red-hooded priest on the floor and he seemed on the verge of death from pure fright.

Then, very slowly, Ulruk began to laugh.

At the sound, Utah got sick at his stomach. He knew he had lost.

"It will be a great pleasure for me to watch you die in the maze or on the sword-point of a challenger," the high priest said. "You will fight very hard to keep from dying. And that will make the sight all the more pleasant."

Again the laughter rose in the stifling room. Abruptly it ceased.

"Take him away," Ulruk spoke, to the red-hooded priest who had brought the human here.

Utah knew he had gotten his audience, he had tried to run his bluff, and it had failed.

"You will sing a different tune when the space ships begin to drop H-bombs on this rotten moon," he said.

Ulruk laughed again. "In what century do you think this will happen?" he questioned.

It was a question that had only one answer. The human race had a foothold in space. They could cross regularly between the Earth and Mars, between the Earth and Venus. But it would be many a decade before they had anything that remotely resembled a space navy, before they could drop H-bombs, or any other kind of bombs, on any planet or any moon. And Ulruk knew it as well as he did.

With spear points at his recalcitrant back, Utah was marched back to the cell where he and the others were held. Henred smiled wryly when he was told what had happened. Bywater cursed. Mead was silent. Kavish grinned. "You are lucky you came away from the presence of the great one alive. Under any other circumstances, you would have been so much dead meat. Because of your blasphemy, cutting your throat will give me even greater satisfaction."

"When do they put this show on the road?" Utah asked.

"I don't know," Henred answered. "They haven't bothered to tell us. Are you in a hurry?"

"I guess not," Utah said.

He went to sleep that night with mixed memories tangling in his mind like tomcats fighting on an alley fence. There was the memory of his crash. Something deep down inside of him was still in a state of shock because of this crash. The memory of Nerissa lingered in his mind, strangely sweet and strangely bitter. She had been responsible for his crash. Yet she hadn't intended to harm him. And when he had crashed, she had tried to save him. What was inside this human girl marooned here among the savage priests of Phobos? Did she know she was the prize of the fierce competition to be staged here on this moon? What did she think about it? What would happen to her if Kavish won the competition?

Even asleep, Utah did not want to think about that.

Another memory, perhaps the bitterest of all, was the memory of Ulruk's laughter. That bit deep. Around him Henred, Bywater, and Mead twisted restlessly in their sleep. Only Kavish slept soundly, and he snored like a dothar, the Martian camel.

THE NEXT day the men were still restless and uneasy, watching each other warily as they were trying to detect hidden weaknesses, ways to strike when the time came. But the next night was different. Again Kavish snored like a camel with a full stomach but Utah awakened.

At first he thought he was having a nightmare. He lay very still on the folded skins that served to make the stone floor into a bed, staring at the image that seemed to hang in front of his eyes.

It was the girl, Nerissa.

She was there in the room, hanging in front of his eyes, as clear and as distinct as a picture.

He realized it wasn't a nightmare. It was the *uni projection*.

It didn't exist in the air in front of his eyes, it hadn't existed in the plastic panel of the control cabin. It existed in his own brain, created there by some form of telepathic control exercised by Nerissa herself.

He sat up quickly. The image moved as he moved. It seemed to be at a distance of about two feet from him. It kept that distance.

The face of the girl showed fear.

"Please! Don't move or the others may awaken." Her voice was a thin whisper drifting out of nowhere, an electric movement in his brain cells. He knew he wasn't hearing with his ears and wasn't seeing with his eyes.

In other circumstances, he would have marveled at the illusion of reality created by the *uni projection*. It was so nearly perfect that he was almost certain the girl was here with him. He sat very still in the dark room that was lighted only by the dimly flickering torches in their wall sockets.

Henred twisted in his sleep, Kavish snored.

"I slipped sleepers into the guard's drink," her whisper came again. "I am just outside the door. Come quickly. But don't make any noise."

Mead rolled over in his sleep and cursed. Utah sat very still. The *uni projection* vanished. Mead lay back down again. Utah got very slowly to his feet, moved toward the door.

It was open an inch.

Outside, under the light of a wall torch, a guard who had fallen from his stool snored noisily on the floor. Waiting outside was the girl, Nerissa. She took his arm.

"Come quickly!"

He followed her away from the door, to a side passage where there were no lights. Words tumbled from her lips. Part of them were English, part Martian.

"I have given sleepers to the guards at the hangers. They *finduck* like that stupid one back there. We will go there *malverno*. The ship you will fly. You will take both of us away from this place."

Utah felt his heart jump. Here was help from a source he had not anticipated, real help. She knew her way around this mad moon. She could take both of them to the hangers.

Even if the ships kept there were of Martian design, he could fly them. He could fly anything that had an engine in it that had a pilot's seat. Once they were away from this moon, they were certain to reach the surface of the planet in safety. There, among their own kind, they would find help. True, they would be in danger as long as they were on Mars, but an

Earth-bound space ship could take them away from the Red Planet forever.

FOR A moment, he treasured the mad thought of stealing an H-bomb on earth and bringing it back here and personally delivering it to Ulruk. It was fantasy, and he knew it. There was no way he could steal an H-bomb. They were too well guarded.

Nerissa pulled at his arm. "Come," she urged.

Utah started. And stopped. "Just a minute. I'll get the others," he said.

"What others?"

"Henred, Bywater, and Mead, the three other humans."

"Are they your friends?"

"Well, not exactly—"

"Then leave them there. We have no time. The guards will rouse from the effect of the sleepers."

"But we can't just go off and leave them."

"Why can't we?" Both anger and perplexity sounded in her voice, anger because they were being delayed, perplexity because she could not understand the cause of the delay. "What are they to us?"

"Nothing. But Henred is a good joe. And the other two are human. I'm not going off and leave a human being in this kind of a stinking mantrap if I can help it."

"But—"

"There are no 'buts,' Nerissa, I don't get your objections. The ship can carry five as well as two—"

"But taking them with us means taking extra chances. They may make a noise at the wrong time. Also, we have no time."

"Then we'll just have to take extra chances," he insisted doggedly. He saw she didn't understand. For a moment, dislike of her rose in him. She was a heartless, unthoughtful witch. Let Kavish have her. She deserved exactly that. Then he remembered she had been raised from childhood here on this moon. She didn't know any better, she hadn't had a chance to learn. The dislike of her began to ebb.

"Wait here, Nerissa. It won't take a minute."

The guard still snored at the door. Utah went silently back into the big room. Henred awakened at the touch of a hand on his shoulder. "What is it?"

"Get up. We're getting out of here." Kavish snored on. Mead and Bywater woke up. They moved softly to the door.

Kavish's snore died in a gurgle and he sat up. "What's going on here?" he grumbled.

In the dim light from the dying torches, his chin was not a clear target. But such as it was, Utah used it as an aiming point. With every erg of muscle energy in his body behind it, Utah's fist connected with the Martian's chin.

Kavish went over backward, knocked cold by the blow.

They waited just long enough to tie and gag him. At the door, they had a gag around the guard's mouth before he knew what was happening. Tied hand and foot, he was thrown bodily into the room he had been assigned to guard.

Henred took the knife the guard had carried. Utah took the short spear. The four of them moved quickly to the dark passage where Nerissa nervously awaited their corning.

"Hurry," she whispered.

At a trot, she led them through dark, silent passages carved out of the heart of this mad moon.

CHAPTER FOUR

"I WANT you to know that I appreciate this," Henred said.

"Me too," Mead and Bywater added, in the same breath.

"We're not out of here yet," Utah answered.

"And we won't get out if all of you don't shut up," Nerissa spoke.

She was moving through a winding passage. Occasional wall torches provided the only light. Many of the torches had burned down and had not been replaced. In consequence, for long distances, there wasn't any light at all. But she seemed to know exactly where she was going. The general direction she was taking seemed to be downward.

"It would be quicker if we went a more direct way, but there is less chance of being seen."

They passed a stairway that led downward. From the stairway came a faint hum, as of powerful machinery operating far away.

"What's down there?" Utah questioned.

"The gravity machines, at the core of the moon," Nerissa answered.

"I'd like to see those machines," Utah said.

"So would I!" Henred spoke quickly. "Those artificial gravity machines are the most important thing on the whole damned moon!" Excitement sounded in the engineer's voice. "Jerry, if we could get down there—"

"Shh!" Nerissa whispered.

A file of blue-clad priests had appeared on the stairway. Slowly and sedately, they were marching downward. "They go to take care of the machines," Nerissa whispered. "Come." She moved forward again, hurrying as if unnamed and unguessed fears were driving her.

Suddenly she stopped moving.

"Listen!" she whispered.

From somewhere in the distance came a chant, the whisper of a chorus of voices.

At the sound, Nerissa's face went paper white. "Ulruk and his singing slaves!" she whispered. "They have discovered you have escaped. They are coming after us."

"Then let's move, fast, to the hangers!" Utah said.

"We can't escape. There is no way to escape from Ulruk and his singing slaves."

"But they're a long ways off. Come on."

She stood stiff and still under the light from a dripping torch. "When you can hear the sound of the singing, it is already too late. They are too close for you to escape." She seemed to be speaking with difficulty. The words came from her lips slowly, with each syllable stressed. Her breast was heaving as if she was having trouble breathing.

"What's wrong with you?" Utah spoke. As the words left his mouth he was aware that he too was speaking slowly. He caught a glimpse of Kelso Mead. The spaceman was stretching his neck and apparently trying to move. Henred and Bywater also seemed to be in trouble.

"When you can hear the sound—you can no longer move," the girl spoke.

"Can't move!" Utah thought the words would explode from his lips. Instead they came slowly, in a whisper.

"Something—wrong with me," Henred muttered.

"I'm caught," Bywater whispered.

"What in the hell—" Utah took a step toward the girl. Or he intended to move toward her. He discovered that his legs would not obey his will.

A PARALYSIS was settling over his muscles. Breathing was becoming difficult. Sweat poured out of him as he strained. His feet seemed to be glued to the floor.

"What—what is this?" he whispered. Ghastly fear was in him. Nothing in all his experience had prepared him for this sudden paralysis. True, he had heard the stories they told around the spaceports, stores of the Martian legends about this moon, and of the all-powerful high priest who ruled it. But he had regarded the legends as fables, fantasies of the

Martian mind. While he knew the Martians regarded this moon with a mixture of superstitious awe and dread, he had assumed that the powerful hold of custom accounted for their reactions. Was there something more on this moon than superstition?

"It is the power of Ulruk," the girl whispered. "He comes. No one may move."

Down the corridor the chanting grew louder.

"The singing slaves carry him," the girl whispered.

"But how—did he know—where we were?" The words were jerky on Utah's lips.

"He—sees anything he wishes. It is like—the *uni projection*. He saw us that way."

"But I didn't see him."

"He is more skillful—in the use of—the *uni projection* than I am. He sees without being seen."

"But why can't we move?"

"Because he wills us to stand still."

"But how does he do it?"

"I do not know. He has great powers." She was shrinking in abject fear as the chant grew louder. All her life here on this moon she had been subjected to the will of the high priest. This conditioning was coming out strongly now. Or perhaps she really believed that Ulruk was actually all-powerful.

For the first time Jerry Utah understood why she had been so afraid when she had dared to release them, why she had urged them to hurry, why she had seemed in such desperate haste. She had known that this might happen.

"What will Ulruk do to you—for helping us?"

"Nothing. I am sacred to the winner of the challenge."

The chant had grown to a full-throated roar. There was no question that the chanters were coming straight toward them. The walls of the corridor reflected vaguely the light of torches. Torch bearers came into sight. Spearmen followed them. Following the spearmen was a large canopied sedan chair. It was borne by sixteen Martian slaves, eight on each side.

Riding in the chair, clutching in his fingers the golden ball that was the symbol of his authority, was Ulruk.

JERRY UTAH made one last desperate effort to break the bonds of paralysis that held his muscles.

Nothing happened. If he had been chained to the floor he could not have been held any more effectively. He couldn't even lift an arm. All he could do was stare from startled eyes that he could not even blink at the incredible procession drawing steadily nearer.

Was this priest actually in possession of tremendous powers that enabled him to see events at a distance, that enabled him to freeze men motionless? There was no doubting the truth. Watching the procession approach, Utah understood the frantic fear of the red-hooded priest when he had refused to prostrate himself before Ulruk. At the time, he had thought that custom and superstitious fear had been involved, but now he saw that back of the custom, back of the fear and the awe, there was a hard core of real power.

There was a reason why the priest who ruled this moon also ruled Mars and the reason was more than superstition. It had its roots in incredible power, which hid behind custom and superstition, which used these two forces as shields to mask its real strength.

Power was here on the moon of Mars, power which until now no human had ever guessed existed. Hidden power, secret power, cunning power. But power as real as the explosion of a hydrogen bomb.

What was this power, how was it used, how was it projected, how was it controlled? Again like mad acrobats drunk with marijuana, questions were tumbling over each other in Utah's mind. He did not question that most Martians thought this power was supernatural, they had little choice except to think this, and little chance to find out otherwise, but he came from a race that had spent centuries trying to find out what was hidden behind the veil of superstition. The Martians might not ask the questions, and might not try to answer them. But he would ask them, he would try to find answers to them. He was a man. His most precious heritage was the open, inquiring mind of his race, the mind that accepted as grist to its mill every fact that came to it, grinding up the facts in an effort to find the kernel of truth hidden behind them.

Ulruk might be able to reach out with an invisible force and paralyze his body. But how did this force work, what was it, how was it controlled, what were the limits of its application? There was an answer somewhere, an answer that could be expressed in terms of formula, just as the thrust of a rocket engine could be expressed in these terms, the lift of the wing of a ship designed to operate in an atmosphere, the burning characteristics of a fuel. There had to be an answer. All of science said there had to be an answer to every question. The trick was to ask the right question.

In his case, the trick was to ask the right question, and to stay alive while he did it. For all he knew, he might not be alive at the end of the next five minutes. One of those spearmen advancing toward them might run him through with the point of the blade he carried.

He ignored the spearmen. If they killed him, they killed him. He watched Ulruk. The spearmen were singing slaves, taking orders, able to bring death, but of no more real importance than the spears they carried, and not to be given more consideration than a weapon without a hand to hold it.

Ulruk was the source of danger.

The high priest riding in the sedan chair looked utterly relaxed, as if nothing could threaten him. Only the hands clutching the golden ball were tight and nervous.

AT THE sight of those restless hands something clicked in Utah's mind. It was a hunch, a feeling, an intuitive grasp of a pattern. Deep in his mind he had the suspicion that even if he knew nothing about the real nature of the power Ulruk possessed, he at least knew the switchboard through which it was controlled.

The golden ball. Inside that religious symbol, inside that perfect geometrical figure, manipulated by the pressure of Ulruk's fingers at various points, was a remote control device that reached out to some hidden generator in some secret control room here on this moon.

Ulruk's power was controlled through the golden ball.

But even if he had guessed the truth, what could he do about it? Even if he had the ball in his hands, how could he use it? He did not understand the system of switches, he did not know the nature of the force or how to focus and control it.

All he knew was the control point. That was something. But it wasn't much.

The spearmen stopped. The slaves stood still. The chanting went into silence. Ulruk looked down at the helpless group before him. Amusement glittered in his eyes.

"Were you going somewhere?" he asked softly, in Martian.

Utah, trying to answer, found he lacked even the power to move his jaws. This was one time when he would not tell Ulruk or anybody else to go to hell.

In the silence the only sound was Ulruk's gentle laughter.

"You're going back where you came from," Ulruk said.

Little by little the paralysis began to lift. With spears at their backs, they were marched away. Nerissa came with them for a distance, walking with a sagging droop to her shoulders as if all her hopes were dying here, then spearmen were detached to escort her elsewhere.

The last sight they had of her she was walking down a corridor with two brawny spearmen following behind her.

Somehow she found the strength to turn and wave at them.

It was the gesture of parting.

Back at the cell from which they had escaped, two new guards were on duty at the door. They were very much alert and they looked as if they had no intention of ever going to sleep during the remainder of their lives.

A group of blue-clad priests were emerging from the cell. They were carrying a heavy object. At the sight of their burden, Utah understood why the two new guards looked so very alert.

The burden of the priests was the body of the former guard. He was still bound, still gagged.

They hadn't bothered to remove his bonds before they slit his throat—as a penalty for allowing himself to be duped into taking a drink containing what Nerissa had called sleepers.

The humans stared at the sight. "Maybe they slit Kavish's throat too," Henred suggested hopefully.

They entered the cell. Kavish himself looked up at them from a stool. He grinned at them. "I knew you would be back," he said. "Nobody ever escapes here. Nobody has ever tried to escape, up until now." The tone of his voice said they were stupid idiots for making such an attempt.

"Ah, go to sleep," Utah said wearily.

Kavish yawned. "Twelve zonars from now, we go to the arena for the challenge," he said.

The four humans stared at each other.

Kavish rose from the stool and moved toward the sleeping skins.

"I want to be well rested when the time comes to kill you," he said.

Rolling himself up in the skins, he went to sleep.

CHAPTER FIVE

IT WAS A weird and incredible scene that took place twelve zonars later. The four humans and the single Martian were led from the cell under close guard by blue-clad priests. They were marched down toward the center of the moon, their way lighted by flaring torches. When they reached their destination, they found themselves in a single long room, out of which opened five doors. The doors were closed now. Each had a walled runway leading to it. Once you were in the runway, you had to move toward the door directly ahead of you. There was no other way to go.

The blue-clad priests ordered them to strip.

"Well, here goes nothing," Henred sighed, beginning to remove his rumpled clothes.

They got new outfits here in this place, sandals, a round shield about a foot in diameter; a short sword about three feet in length, a belt with a sheath that contained a knife with a needle point and a razor edge.

"It is for the grace stroke," one of the blue clad priests explained, indicating the knife.

"How long will this farce continue?" Utah asked.

The priests shrugged. "That depends on you."

"How does it depend on me?"

"It will continue until only one is left alive. We do not know how long that will be. Many zonars, perhaps."

"But what about food? What about water?"

"Food and water will both be found where you are going," the priests answered enigmatically.

"What happens if one of us gets hurt bad but isn't dead?" Kelso Mead questioned. The spaceman was already showing signs of violent internal strain, a pulse was jumping in his forehead and his hands were shaky.

The priest shrugged. "The grace knife is provided to solve that problem," he answered.

"But suppose nobody survives?" Utah questioned. "It could happen that way?"

"Oh, in that case customs provides that the girl becomes the bride of the high priest," was the answer.

"You've got an answer to everything," Kelso Mead spoke. "What's your answer to this?" From his belt, he snatched the grace knife—plunged it up to the hilt in the priest's heart.

The Martian went down, coughed, spewed blood from his mouth, and died. Like a wild animal Kelso Mead backed away, the red knife in his hand, his teeth bared in a snarl.

Utah expected that Mead would be speared instantly. But no such thing happened. The priests presented the points of their spears at Kelso Mead. Faced with the glittering points, the spaceman was backed into a runway, held there by three priests who kept their spears ready. But no attempt was made to harm the spaceman or to avenge the death of the priest.

"Any questions?" another priest asked.

"No," Kavish answered. "We are ready." He trotted into one of the runways stood waiting before the closed door, shield on his left arm, sword blade glittering in his brawny right hand. Kavish was ready, willing, and eager. He was a war-horse hearing the sound of trumpets, scenting the blood of the fallen, and eager to be at the scene of battle.

Henred shrugged. Signs of strain were also visible on the face of the tall engineer but from some hidden strength of soul, he found the courage to grin. His sword came up in a salute to Jerry Utah. *"Morituri te salutamus,"* he said wryly.

IT WAS THE ancient salutation of the gladiators to the Roman emperor before games began being repeated in another form and with another purpose here on this moon of Mars. Utah's sword swept up in an answering salute. "You're a good guy, Henred, I wish we could stand shoulder to shoulder against these priests instead of against each other."

"So do I," Henred answered. They spoke in English. The priests, who did not understand, stared curiously at them, thinking that perhaps this was the way these people from across the sky prepared to die.

"Into the runways," a priest spoke.

There was a runway and a door for each man. Jerry Utah moved into the nearest passage. The door was in front of him. Behind him were the spears of the priests. The man who stood here—or the Martian—went through this door when it opened, or met death at the hands of the priests behind him.

Standing there, waiting for the door to open, he wondered how many Martians had stood here during the centuries that had passed since this rite had been established here. There must have been many. What had happened to them? Four out of five died. The one who survived—and this was a grim test of bitter survival—might become a high priest of Mars. On the walls were names, scratched there by sword points as the Martians had waited, dozens of them in the crabbed Martian script. One name caught Utah's eye. Ulruk!

The high priest had come this way.

Creaking on un-oiled hinges, the door opened in front of him. The instant it opened, the priests behind him advanced toward his back, their spears level. Utah took a deep breath—and stepped through the door.

He found himself in a vast open area that seemed to stretch away for miles into the distance. The light in here was dim, on either sidelines of torches set in the walls receded away and away, until the eye no longer distinguished the individual lights. The whole vast amphitheater had been hollowed out of the interior of the moon. And it had been constructed to represent the Martian idea of heaven—a vast oasis.

Like the desert-dwelling Arabs of Earth, the Martians, living among the torrid dust of the red deserts, where water was scarce and vegetation scarcer, where life was bitter and harsh, had conceived of heaven as a land of flowing streams, of green trees, of fountains spurting waters into the clean cool air, of green grass, and bright spots of meadow.

Here in the interior of this moon, they had created a replica of their idea of heaven. The flowing streams were here, rounded hills, green meadows and trees, though how they got the vegetation to grow without sunlight was a miracle in itself. But it was here.

Here also was sudden death.

UTAH HEARD the door swing shut behind him, never to open again until the next man or the next Martian came this way. A distance of ten feet separating them, the four men and the single Martian stood side by side. Henred was on Utah's right, Bywater on his left. Then came Kelso Mead—then Kavish.

And Kavish was ready. With a fierce cry, he swung his sword in a short arc and brought it down on the head of Kelso Mead, a savage blow that split the spaceman's skull down to his shoulders.

Kelso Mead died without a sound. The spaceman never knew what hit him or that he had been hit. He crumpled and went down, falling on the strip of grass that came up to the edge of the wall. No grace stroke was necessary. Nor did Kavish attempt to give one. Snatching his sword free, he struck at Bywater.

But that burly spaceman had seen what had happened to his companion. His left arm came up. The Martian's sword rang on the metal of the shield. Bywater lifted his sword. He knew nothing of sword fighting but he was prepared to do the best he could. A single blow from his powerful arm would split a man from chin to groin. Kavish darted back from the threat.

For an instant, the Martian stood balanced on the balls of his feet like a cat ready to spring. A fighting snarl was on his face. He had tasted blood and he liked it. Utah sprang to the right side of Bywater, Henred moved up on the left.

The Martian snarled and backed away. Turning, he slid out of sight, vanishing into the recesses of the mighty arena.

"Things happen mighty damned fast around this place," Henred muttered. He wiped sweat from his face, looked down at the body of Kelso Mead. *"Morituri—*So long, Kelso. Maybe you had it coming for knifing that priest, but according to my way of thinking, you deserved a chance, which you didn't get. Do you think Kavish went yellow all of a sudden?" His eyes sought the direction where the Martian had disappeared.

"I don't think so," Utah answered. "I think he just realized he couldn't take on three of us so he decided he would try to catch us one at a time."

"I'd as soon be loose in a den of rattlesnakes as be loose in here with that Indian running wild," Bywater spoke. "He aims to do us in."

"Did you expect him to have any other aim?" Henred questioned. Acid crept into his voice, a reflection of the torment going on inside him. "What kind of a fool are you,

Sam! He's going to try to kill us. He has announced his intention often for even you to get it."

"Well, you don't have to get hot about it," Bywater answered angrily. "All I said was—" He gripped the sword and the shield and was apparently about to strike at the engineer.

"Cut it out!" Utah spoke sharply. "This is no time to turn loose your tempers, this is a time to be calm. There is just a chance, if we work this right, that we have a way to get out of here."

"How's that?" Henred spoke quickly.

"By sticking together," Utah answered. "If we stick together, we can lick Kavish—and maybe all the priests on this damned moon."

"Have you got something on your mind you're not telling us?" Henred asked. "Some idea, some plan—"

"Nothing but hope," Utah answered. "Are you willing to stick with me, to fight with me, to stand side by side with me no matter what comes?"

"You know I'm willing," Henred answered. "But what about Sam?"

"I'll stick," Bywater answered.

THEY MADE their compact then and there and they shook hands on it. In the face of a common danger, they were uniting in a protective device as old as the human race. It was this ability to unite, to co-operate, to stick together in family, clan, and national group, that distinguished the human from the animals.

"What's first on the schedule, Jerry?" Henred said.

"We'll scout this place, we'll find out what is here and what it looks like, the sources of food and water that the priests said could be found here. We'll try to learn everything there is to know about this arena, then we'll make our plans."

"It sounds as if you are considering a long stay here," the engineer spoke.

"Maybe, maybe not," Utah answered. He moved away, keeping the wall always to his right, saw something lying in the grass, moved around it. "But I hope we won't stay here as long as he did," he said, pointing.

What he had seen in the grass was a mouldering skeleton, a relic of some long-gone struggle.

"One of the four who didn't make the grade," Bywater spoke. The burly spaceman was nervous, apprehensive. He was constantly turning his head as if he suspected that Kavish might be creeping up behind him.

They circled the cavern. Counting his steps, Utah estimated that it was almost two miles in circumference. The walls were stone. There were doors at intervals but each door was tightly closed. When they came back to the body of Kelso Mead, they knew they had circled the place.

"Hello, what's this?" Henred spoke.

A trap door had slid up in a section of the circling wall, revealing an opening behind it. Cautiously they approached it. The opening was actually nothing but a hole in the wall.

It contained food, the rough Martian bread, cuts of meat, cooked, savory and steaming. It contained a single small can of water. And another jar, which held spiced Martian wine.

At the sight of what was contained in the hole, Sam Bywater moved hastily forward.

"Wait a minute," Utah said sharply. "How do we know this stuff is all right to eat? It may be poisoned."

The burly spaceman stopped in his tracks. He turned a startled face toward the test pilot.

"The food is excellent. So is the water and the wine," the voice of a priest spoke from an opening in the backside of the hole. "You have nothing to fear from eating it."

Behind the hole was a priest observing them. They could not see him but they knew he was there.

"He says it's all right," Bywater urged. "And I'm hungry."

"Me too," Henred said.

"There's a catch somewhere," Utah insisted. He moved forward to the hole, examined the food containers. Suddenly he saw the catch in the whole situation.

"How often will this food be supplied?" he spoke to the priest behind the wall.

"Once every 18 zonars," came the answer.

Utah began to laugh. "Is there any other source of food or water in this place?"

"None," the unseen priest answered.

Utah's laughter took on a hysterical note. "Eighteen zonars is roughly the equivalent of twenty-four hours in our system of time measurement. There is enough food and water and wine here for one man. There isn't enough for two or for three or four. Just one man can eat and drink."

Henred and Bywater stared at him.

"Don't you see what is going to happen, in the long run?" he continued. "There is only enough food and water for one man. There are four of us here, including Kavish. We're faced with the choice of fighting each other for food and water—or starving to death!"

CHAPTER SIX

"WHAT ARE we going to do, Jerry?" Henred asked.

"We're going to split this food and water four ways," Utah answered. He had taken the food from the hole in the wall and the trap door had closed. Now he grimly set about the task of dividing it. Astonishment on their faces, the two men watched him. Henred licked his lips.

"Four ways?" he said.

"That's what I want to know too," Bywater spoke. "Why *four* ways? There's not really enough for one."

"You are forgetting Kavish," Utah answered. The jerk of his head indicated the maze of shrubbery that grew in this fake oasis. "He's out there somewhere, probably watching us."

"And waiting for the chance to stab us in the back!" Bywater exploded. "Why should we do anything for him?"

"He's just as hungry as we are." Utah answered.

"I don't give a damn how hungry he is, I hope he starves to death. He killed Kelso and he'll kill us, if he gets the chance."

"Sure he will," Utah answered.

"And you're still going to give him something to eat." The face of the spaceman was becoming convulsed as anger began to rise in him.

"I am." Utah answered.

"By God, you're not going to give him any of my share." The sword that Bywater held came up, he slashed out with it. Utah stepped quickly backward.

Henred stepped in and caught Bywater from behind. "Cut it out, you idiot!" the engineer growled.

"Let go of me! This damned fool is trying to give away food that rightfully belongs to me."

"I know it. Did it ever occur to you that he might know what he's doing?"

"No. What is he doing?"

"There is one thing I might be doing," Utah answered. "Kavish is a Martian. The priests who prepared this food are also Martians. How do we know that these Martians aren't sticking together?"

"I don't get it," Bywater answered sullenly.

"Maybe the Martians may want Kavish to win this competition. Maybe they're trying to help him. Maybe this food is poisoned."

"What?" Consternation showed on Bywater's face, "I—I hadn't thought of that."

Utah stepped close, kept his voice low. "I'm not saying it's true, I'm saying it *might* be true. I'm as hungry as you are but I'm willing to wait until Kavish eats his portion. Then I'll feel I'm safe in eating mine."

PICKING up the dishes that held the food and the containers that held the water and wine, he carried them into the green growth. Henred followed him. "How are we going to offer this to Kavish?" he asked.

"We're going to put it down and let him come for it. It's almost certain that he is watching us. Kavish!" He lifted his voice in a shout, waited for an answer.

"What do you want?" Kavish's voice came. But the Martian himself remained concealed.

"Here's your share of the food and water," Utah said.

"What?" Kavish sounded as if he did not believe his ears. "You mean you're giving me something to eat?"

"Sure."

"I don't believe it. I think you're just trying to trick me."

"Think what you please," Utah answered. "We're leaving it here. You can eat it or you can leave it alone." He moved away, Henred following.

"Actually what are you doing?" the engineer questioned.

"I'm casting a little bread upon the waters," Utah answered.

"That's what I thought," Henred answered. "You're trying to make friends with this Martian killer."

"He is no more of a killer than you or me, he is what custom and belief have made him. If I can make friends with him, we might have four on our side."

Henred's eyes lit up. "I like you, Jerry," he said. "I like the way you do business, I like what's inside of you."

"Thanks."

They moved away. Later, from a distance, they watched Kavish come out of hiding. He ate the food they had left.

"Well, we know we can take a chance on it," Henred said, watching.

They moved back to the doors where they had left Bywater.

The burly spaceman was gone. Their share of the food, which they had left behind, was gone too. Bywater had eaten it, then had hid from them. Henred cursed beneath his breath, all the violent oaths that a space engineer might know.

"The pressure got to be higher than he could take," Utah said simply. "He was hungry and scared. He ate because food meant security to something inside of him. With a full stomach, he wouldn't be quite as scared as he was when his belly was empty. Then he hid from us because he was afraid to face us."

"That pressure doesn't seem to be getting you."

"Me? I'm a test pilot. Or I was. We get so used to looking death in the eye that a little thing like an empty belly doesn't bother me." Utah shrugged, a careless gesture, which said what the hell? "Anyhow, we'll get something else to eat eighteen zonars from now."

"Yeah, and we'll have to fight both Kavish and Bywater for it," the engineer answered. "They'll be here looking for their share."

"That's the purpose of the food that is being provided, to make us fight each other, in case we show reluctance. The question is: Are we going to stick together, the two of us? Or are we going to let them trick us into fighting?"

"I'm going to stick with you," Henred answered.

IN THE HUGE cavern, there was no sound. If they were being watched—and Ulruk had indicated he was going to watch—there was no sign of it. The two men stayed close to each other. In the dim light coming from the torches on the circling walls, wearing loin cloths and sandals and nothing else, carrying shields and swords, they looked like two warriors out of Earth's dawn history—or like gladiators out of the days of Rome's decadence. They saw nothing of Kavish or Bywater but both were there somewhere. Hours passed. Nothing happened. Both were tired and sleepy, the fatigue of pure nervous strain was beginning to tell on them.

"This thing can go on for weeks," Henred said. "What are we going to do? We've got to sleep sometime!"

"I imagine sleeping was a problem that worried a lot of Martians in this place," Utah answered. "We'll take turns standing guard." They didn't have a coin to flip, instead they drew straws to see who slept first.

Henred won. He selected a place where a tree grew close to the wall, forming a natural shelter, laid the sword handy, curled up and went to sleep. Utah found a spot from which he could watch in all directions and prepared himself to wait for whatever might happen.

It wasn't long in coming. First, there was movement in a tangle of shrubbery, the slightest possible movement as though a shadow was coming to life there. Utah saw the moving shadow but not by the shift of a single muscle anywhere in his body did he indicate that he was aware of it. If the shadow was either Kavish or Bywater, he was ready— he hoped.

Then, without warning, the shadow was blotted out—by the *uni projection* with the face of Nerissa squarely in the middle of his vision. He stared at her, startled.

She looked at him, then past him as the sleeping engineer.

"Quick, stab him while he is asleep!" her voice whispered the words in Utah's mind.

"What?" the startled pilot gasped. He simply did not believe he had understood correctly.

"Kill him quickly before he awakens!" the Martian words whispering in his mind told him he had heard correctly.

"Do you mean you want me to stab a man while he is asleep?"

"Of course. It will be easy."

"I don't doubt that. The point is—"

"Then I will help you destroy the other two," the voice whispered eagerly in his mind.

Aghast, Utah stared at the face in the projection. It was all in his mind, he knew, and the words seemed clear enough, but he simply could not bring himself to believe that Nerissa would make such a suggestion. "You don't know what you're saying, you don't mean it."

"But I do mean it!" Doubt showed on the projected face. "What is wrong with you? Don't you know a chance when you see one?"

"The chance to stab a friend in the back is not the kind of chance I want," Utah answered. "Didn't you ever hear of ethics?"

"Ethics?" Confusion showed on the face. "What's that?"

"If you don't know what it is, I can't tell you." Disgust was rising in him. "Get away from me. And stay away."

"But you don't seem to understand—I am one of the prizes you will get if you win. And to win, you must kill these people."

"You're a prize I don't want and wouldn't have even if I won."

As if this was a totally new idea, the face in the projection looked startled. "Do—do you mean that?" the whisper came.

"I never meant anything more in my life."

AN IMPRESSION of disgust showed on the startled face of the projection, disgust which said that this man was an obvious fool to put friendship ahead of his own personal interests. The projection vanished. Utah was left shaken and trembling. While Nerissa had grown up here among the Martian priests, which meant that exceptions had to be made for her, it still seemed that she should have some conception of right and wrong. She should have been born with some figment of a conscience. But apparently she hadn't.

The whole situation made him sick deep down inside. He had been tired and sleepy and nervous. Now the fatigue seemed to grow stronger. He swore bitterly beneath his breath. Yet if he had been a Martian, probably he would have taken advantage of the chance to kill Henred.

"But I'm not a Martian, I'm a human." Which made a difference, at least to him.

From the corner of his eyes he again glimpsed the shadow he had seen and had forgotten. Again it was moving; and it was closer now. He could see it much more clearly, well enough to tell what it was.

He stared at it for a long time without quite believing what he was seeing.

The shadow was Nerissa.

Her face was clearly visible through an opening in the shrubbery. She was looking at him, beckoning to him to come near.

He had just seen her via the *uni projection*. Now he was seeing her hiding in the shrubbery. Which was the real

Nerissa? Or was this face apparently looking at him from the shrubbery a trap designed to lure him to his death?

Shield on his left arm, sword in his right hand, he strolled casually over to the bank of shrubs. Anyone watching him would not have known he was making a purposeful movement. When he reached the spot where she was hiding, he did not look down at her but seemed to be watching something far away.

"Jerry Utah?" She spoke in a whisper and he thought he heard it, but in this place of shadows and of phantoms who could be sure a whisper was real? Did he hear her whisper with his ears or with his mind?

Very casually, he extended a foot. His big toe, extending beyond the end of the sandal, touched warm, firm flesh. The girl hiding here was real! He felt his heart jump.

Astonishment on her face, she watched his foot recede. "Why did you do that?"

"Just a little test," he answered.

"But why should you test me?"

"Because I just talked to you and saw you in the *uni projection.*"

Wonder showed on her face. Behind the wonder came fear. "You did no such thing. I haven't used the projection. I've been right here watching you. What do you mean— You saw me in the projection?"

He told her what had happened. Without looking at her squarely and without lifting his voice above a whisper, he described the vision he had seen.

Her whisper vibrated with outrage. "That wasn't me, Jerry. That was Ulruk, projecting my image."

"Could he do that?"

"Of course he could. I just know a little about the *uni projection,* not enough for real control. Ulruk knows far more than I and he can do things I can't. Jerry, you don't think that I would have asked you to stab a sleeping friend?"

He took a deep breath. The air felt good in his lungs, suddenly the sickness was going away from his stomach. He was no longer quite so tired. "But why would Ulruk do this, what could he gain by it?" he questioned.

"He was trying to stir up trouble," the girl answered. "He urged you to stab your sleeping friend. But what if your friend was not asleep?"

"But—"

"Look at your friend," her terse whisper came. "Look for yourself and see if I am not right."

UTAH TURNED and glanced at Henred. The engineer was sitting up and was watching him. "Hello," Utah called. "How long had you been awake?"

"I've never been asleep." Henred answered. The engineer's voice took on a drawling note with overtones of satisfaction in it. "You've been acting so damned noble that I began to get suspicious of you, I wondered if you really meant it or were you trying to pull the wool over my eyes, to trick me into trusting you, so you could gain my confidence and then stab me in the back. So I pretended to go to sleep, but all the time I was watching you."

"You're sure a trusting soul!" Utah felt hot anger rise in him.

"Don't get hot about it," Henred answered comfortably. "I've run my test and I'm satisfied. You're actually one of those ring-tailed wonders that a man can trust all the way."

As the engineer spoke, anger went out of Jerry Utah. Inside of him was a good feeling, as if here somehow he had accomplished something important, something to make a man proud. No wonder the vision of Nerissa, as projected by Ulruk, had seemed so startled at his refusal to stab

Henred. Still without looking down, he spoke again to Nerissa.

"Why are you here?"

"I came to help you," the girl answered. "I came to show you a way out of here. We'll take another chance at reaching those hangars."

CHAPTER SEVEN

HENRED AND Utah moved quietly across the vast amphitheater. Nerissa kept completely out of sight. Occasionally they caught glimpses of a bush shaking but the girl herself was never visible. "Why is she hiding so carefully?" Henred questioned.

"Because she doesn't want to be seen. If she is caught helping us again, it might be the end of her. And of us too."

"Do your really think we've got a chance to get out of here?" Sweat was visible on the engineer's face and his voice was shaky. "I mean—I doubt if I could take it if we fail again."

"If we fail, we won't have to take anything very long."

"But how is she going to get us out of here?"

"I don't know. She didn't say. But if she got in here, she can get out again. What's that?"

From some spot out of their sight came the sharp clang of metal striking metal. A voice cried out in pain. Then came a grunting sound. They moved toward the source of this disturbance.

In an open spot a Martian and a human were battling. "Kavish and Bywater," Utah whispered. Apparently the fight had been in progress for some time for both contestants were moving sluggishly and both had been wounded. Grass had been trampled, the sod was torn, Bywater's right side showed the mark of a sword thrust. Blood was flowing from a wound on Kavish's arm. Breathing heavily, the Martian was tottering on his feet

Bywater moved forward, his sword lifted high. He knew nothing about sword fighting, his aim was to lift his sword and to bring it down on the head of his opponent, beating down all opposition.

Bywater's sword came down. Kavish dropped to one knee and thrust forward, his sword point grazing the edge of Bywater's shield. The point struck Bywater in the chest, penetrated until six inches of metal were visible behind the human's back.

Bywater had taken his death stroke. At the same time, his descending sword, incompletely parried by the shield, struck Kavish on the top of the head with the flat of the blade.

If the blow had been struck with the edge, the Martian would have been split apart down to his chin, but the flat of the blade only knocked him down.

Bywater fell, and died.

Kavish lay on the ground, either knocked unconscious by the blow or so badly wounded he could not rise again.

Utah's lips compressed in a thin knife line. He moved forward, Henred keeping pace with him. "Looks like your bread upon the waters did not include Sam Bywater," the tall engineer said.

Utah did not answer. As they approached, Kavish struggled to his feet. His sword point thrust into the ground, he stood leaning upon it, too weak to do more than stand, but glaring defiance at them just the same.

"All right, cut my throat!" His voice rang in a challenge to them.

"Why should we cut your throat, Kavish?" Utah asked.

"What?" Confusion showed in the Martian's eyes. It was a question he had not been anticipating and which he was not prepared to answer. "Because—" His gaze strayed to the body of Bywater on the ground.

"What happened?" Utah continued.

"He came upon me when I was asleep and tried to kill me."

The simple statement held a wealth of meaning. "And because Bywater did that, we are supposed to kill you?" Utah said.

"Well, he is of your race. Also, there is a struggle here, and the reward—" Kavish faltered.

"Maybe we're not much interested in the reward," Utah said. "Maybe, when Bywater tried to kill you when you slept, he forfeited his right to belong to our race."

Kavish did not begin to understand. "There was also the other, the Kelso Mead—"

"Mead had just struck down a priest who had done him no harm."

"After I have slain two members of your race, do you hold nothing against me?" the amazed Martian said.

"Nothing that requires your heart's blood in return. The code of the humans is different from the Martian code. I'm not saying our code is better. But some of us try to stick by it."

"You mean you are not going to slay me?" Kavish sounded as if he didn't believe anything he had heard, that all of this was some preposterous fantasy, which existed in his mind.

"A part of our code is never to strike a man when he's down," the pilot answered.

"But the struggle here—and the reward."

"You can have all the reward, except the girl. We want our lives, and nothing else."

THEY MOVED off. "You're leaving a mighty confused Martian back there," Henred commented.

"I can't help it, I'm sort of confused myself."

"I suppose you know you are using the oldest-known survival technique—which is to make as many friends as you possibly can. Because someday some friend may be in a position to do you a favor, making friends increases the odds in your favor."

"Of course I know it. All I'm doing is giving us—and incidentally me—every possible chance to survive. Sure, we could have killed Kavish. Maybe that would have been the smart thing to do. But a dead Martian, while he will never hurt you, will also never help you."

"You're taking a long chance if you expect Kavish to help you," the engineer commented.

"I know. But we're in a desperate position and we have to take long chances. All the short chances have been used up."

Nerissa, keeping out of sight, was a shadow moving through the shrubbery. They took great care never to look directly at her. Leaning on his sword point, Kavish watched them leave. His face reflected consternation.

He had just seen something that neither he nor any other Martian had ever thought could happen—a defenseless enemy spared the edge of the grace knife. There was turmoil inside of him.

The two humans followed Nerissa to the farther wall of the arena. At the foot of a large tree half hidden behind a jungle growth of bamboo, she disappeared.

"The girl is gone," Henred whispered.

"I see she is. We'll wait and see what happens."

In that hot silent smoky land there was no sound. No wind blew here, no wind had ever blown here. This place had the damp and oppressive feeling of a vast hothouse, which is what it actually was. Jerry Utah could feel his heart beat begin to build up. He felt now like he usually did when he was warming up a new ship on the runway, preparing to blast free. At such moments, tension always began to creep up inside of him, a mild anxiety state, the medicos called this condition. The anxiety resulted from the fact that he did not know whether or not he was going to be alive five minutes after he pressed home the throttle, the mildness of that state rose from the fact that he was Jerry Utah, accustomed to facing death. There was a hidden factor in him, which made the challenge of death a stimulant, lifting him to his best. If he had been anything else, deep inside, he would not have been a test plot. Or not long.

They waited, Utah feeling the continued rise of his heartbeat. On Henred's face, sweat began to appear in larger drops, a reflection of the way the anxiety state was building up inside him. Nerissa did not appear. Casually, going roundabout, they made their way toward the tree where she had vanished. Several huge roots of the tree rose above the ground like the bones of some prehistoric monster buried here.

UNDER ONE of the roots was a hole big enough for a man to slide through. In this hole Nerissa's face was visible. Utah sat down on the root directly above her. "Okay, Nerissa," he whispered. "We'll wait until we think no one is watching, then we'll follow you."

She nodded.

Utah yawned. "Your turn to stand guard while I get some shuteye," he said to the engineer. "Sure, go ahead," Henred said. Utah laid down beside the root. So far as he could tell they were not being watched. Henred, leaning against the root, was silent. "There's nothing I can see, Jerry," the engineer whispered. Utah slid into the hole. Later, Henred followed.

Nerissa was a shadow waiting in darkness for them. "I found this place when I was a child. I used to slip into the arena to play—and to watch the fights there."

"Do you think we were seen?"

"I don't think so. This is the time when Ulruk usually rests."

Again they followed her through darkened tunnels where flaring torches occasionally marked the way, through the interior of this moon of Mars, dodging priests, watching and listening. Always they were listening. But the sound of the singing slaves did not appear behind them. No sound came.

"The hangars are near now," Nerissa whispered. "We will soon be there. Are you sure you can fly the ships?"

"I'll take that chance," the pilot answered.

"What—what is it like on Earth?" the girl questioned. "I have often watched it in the sky. I knew it was my home and I—I dreamed that some day I might go there."

"I'll show you what it's like, if once we get off this moon."

The girl was excited, for the first time a glow was on her face. It showed through the dirt and the dust. With a short sword firmly gripped in her hand, she looked like a warrior queen from the days of the Amazons.

"We will get away from this moon. Look, there is the hangar."

The tunnel widened before them. A glow of light appeared. The passage emerged forty feet above the hangar floor. A long twisting flight of steps led downward.

Below them, its blunt nose pointed upward, poised ready for flight, a Martian ship lay on the runway. A blue-clad priest-mechanic was nonchalantly working with the fuel inlet pipe. The engines were not in operation, warming them would require a matter of two or three minutes. But the ship was there, ready to take off for Mars.

Beyond the end of the flight ramp, Utah caught a glimpse of a patch of washed-out blue—the sky, as seen through the thin atmosphere of Phobos. It was the most blessed sight he had ever seen.

"If we can once get inside that ship and get the doors locked, the blast of the motors warming up will keep every priest out of reach until we can take off," Henred said. The tall engineer had become wildly excited. His Adam's apple was jumping and the lines on his face were relaxing. "I can run the motors of that ship. I can run any motor that has a wheel to turn or a jet to blast. Come on Jerry, here's where we move out of here!"

He stepped out of the tunnel and on to the little platform at the top of the steps, then stepped quickly back, a strangled cry on his lips, his face sagging and his eyes wild.

Utah, coming close behind him, saw what Henred had seen—and what had been hidden from their sight until they emerged on the landing. It had been hidden because it was almost directly beneath them.

Ulruk in his sedan chair borne by the singing slaves!

"That devil knew where we were all the time," Henred whispered. "He was playing with us, like a cat with mice. He let us come on—and all the time he was here waiting for us. Jerry, our goose is cooked!" A shrill hysterical note had crept into the voice of the engineer. For a moment, he had had a taste of freedom, of life itself, and then the taste had been snatched away from him.

Simultaneously, the chant of the singing slaves began to lift on the air!

BELOW THEM, Ulruk could be seen. He was looking upward, the light of devil's lamps glittering in his eyes. His fingers moved caressingly over the golden ball he carried.

The paralysis began to come.

As he felt the paralysis begin to reach invisible fingers toward him, touching him in a thousand places with hands of icy chill, Utah forced himself forward. His muscles responded reluctantly, in another minute, in another thirty seconds, perhaps in another ten seconds, they would cease entirely to respond, but during this fractional split instant of time while the radiation from the golden ball was taking effect, he could still move, sluggishly but enough to take a few steps.

He took these steps. Straight from the edge of the landing on the steps, he launched himself outward. Like dying Hamlet leaping down upon his murderous stepfather, Utah launched himself outward and downward—straight toward Ulruk. There was in him at this moment something of the same feeling that must have motivated the prince of Denmark in that he was now beyond hope of life.

No matter what was the effect of the radiation pouring outward from the golden ball that Ulruk held, even if it paralyzed everyone within its reach except the singing slaves, who were immune to its effects, it could neither stop nor slow the plunge of a falling body.

The man who was falling downward might be paralyzed and unable to move but nothing could stop him from falling.

Jerry Utah hit on top of Ulruk, high priest of Mars. The impact of his body knocked the golden ball from Ulruk's hand. It fell to the floor of the chair. Ulruk reached frantic fingers for it.

In the moment when the ball left Ulruk's hand, the paralysis that held Utah was broken. He could move again. And there never was a moment in his life when he couldn't move faster than the high priest of all Mars.

His sandal crashing down smashed the golden ball. It burst into two parts. Like the works from a smashed watch, out of it came a multitude of tiny coils and springs, microscopic switches, a spew of parts. Like miniature lightning blue sparks leaped from part to part. Utah felt the jolt of an electrical discharge in his leg. Smoke spurted from under his foot. He turned his foot, savagely, on the remnants of the golden ball.

The high priest had claimed that his ability to strike with paralysis all who opposed him was a phenomenon of his priesthood, a miracle that he could bring into existence because he was very near to the gods.

In this moment, it was a miracle that failed. When the golden ball was smashed, the radio control that flowed through it was broken.

The broken parts of the ball crunching under his heel, Utah pulled himself to his feet. Ulruk's hate-filled eyes glittered with vast surprise.

The chant of the singing slaves went into horrified silence. The whole hangar stood as if stunned, the slaves and the spearmen stared from startled, uncomprehending eyes at what was happening. Their high priest was in danger. This was a fact they could not instantly comprehend. They had always believed him to be beyond danger. They needed time to grasp this new idea that he could be in danger.

Utah lifted his sword. If he did nothing else in his life, he intended to drive this weapon clear up to the hilt in Ulruk's heart. With the high priest dead, this priestly hierarchy might fall for lack of a leader. Greater empires than this had fallen when their leader died.

Ulruk saw the lifted sword and knew the intention of the human behind it. If his slaves needed more time to think before they could grasp this new situation, he did not. He could think faster than they, could see what was about to happen.

It was not something that he wanted to happen.

He flung himself backward over the throne chair. For an instant, he looked like an over-grown monkey turning backward flip-flops as his body whirled through the air.

Utah's sword point rammed into the back of the throne chair. He cursed and yanked it free, leaped to the seat of the chair and looked over the back of it for the high priest.

"Kill him!" Ulruk, on the floor below, shouted to his spearmen.

CHAPTER EIGHT

JERRY UTAH spun just in time to see a spear thrusting upward at him and to catch it on his shield. A second spear was coming, the spearman thrusting with it like it was a pikestaff instead of throwing it. He slashed at it with his sword, severed the point from the shaft.

At least twenty of the spearmen were below. They were between him and the ship. To hurl himself at them would have the same result as a wild and savage tribesman driving himself at a Roman phalanx—he would die on the points of thrusting spears coming at him from all directions.

If he stayed where he was, the spears would also reach him.

"To hell with you devils!" His voice rose in a shout. If he had to die here, he could at least show them how a human met his end. His yell was a scream of defiance that echoed back from the solid roof of stone overhead.

Like a gigantic bird falling, something came down in front of him, landing in the sedan chair. He jerked himself back from it, thinking he was being attacked from a new quarter. Then he saw that the falling "bird" was Henred. Released from paralysis with the crushing of the golden ball, the engineer had launched himself downward too.

From the platform of the sedan chair, two sword points faced the spearmen below. A spearman thrust upward. Utah reached out with a long arm and struck down. The spearman retreated howling, a useless arm dangling.

Henred grinned. "Two at a time, Jerry."

Two swords against twenty spears!

Then there were no longer two swords, but three, Nerissa came down from up above. But she missed her leap and went off the edge of the platform, sprawling to the stone floor below.

Utah and Henred went right behind her. She came quickly to her feet.

"Charge them!" Utah said. Where one man would have had no chance, two men and a woman might get through. "Straight toward the ship. Cut down anybody in the way."

They drove themselves straight at the disorganized spearmen. Spear points clashed on metal shields, gleaming blades turned red. Before their fierce onslaught, the spearmen broke. The three humans went through their ranks—and raced for the ship sitting with its nose pointed along the ramp that led to the far-off sky.

They made it, Utah shoved Nerissa and Henred through the open door, leaped through himself, slammed the door shut behind him, locked it, leaped toward the pilot's seat.

There was a grin on his face and a grin in his heart. He had his hands on the controls of a ship! It did not seem possible, it had never seemed possible. But it had happened! Outside was the sky. Outside was room to move in.

Far-off in the distance, hanging in the sky like a great balloon, was the planet Mars. Its thin tracery of canals was visible to the naked eye. The red deserts were sprawling blotches across the landscape.

Mars, freedom, safety! His shout was a burst of triumph in the control room. He snapped the switches that started the drive.

And nothing happened.

Henred's long finger pointing at the instrument panel was a signboard pointed the way to death.

"The fuel gauge, Jerry!" The engineer's voice was a husky, cracked whisper that had no resemblance to the voice of a living man. "They emptied the tanks before we got here. They knew we wanted a ship. They set this one here on the runway as bait for us, set it here with empty tanks!"

"Great God in Heaven!" Utah's voice was a prayer, a plea. Fiercely he jammed the palm of his hand against the instrument panel, thinking that the gauge might be merely stuck. The red needle quivered, but did not move beyond the empty mark.

"She's empty, Jerry. And there's nothing we can do about it. And—look!"

Across the hangar, from a door, a line of blue-clad priests was emerging at a trot.

"The mop-up squad," Henred said. "They'll pry us out of here like sardines out of a can."

"Can you hide us somewhere?" Utah spoke to Nerissa.

"For a little while, maybe, I can hide you someplace."

"Then come on, before those priests get here."

SHOVING open the door of the ship, the three leaped out. They had fought like fools to reach this ship, now they were being forced to leave it. Fierce shouts sounded from the priests as they were sighted.

As fast as they could run, they fled across the cavern and into the nearest tunnel. The priests charged after them. Ulruk had disappeared.

"They'll find us if all they have left to hunt for are our bones," Henred panted. "There won't be a cockroach with an undisturbed nest on this whole moon, before they get through hunting for us."

"I've got one more idea," Utah answered. He spoke to the girl. "Can you take us to the heart of the moon?"

"I think so. But—why?"

He told them why. They listened, the girl wonderingly, Henred with doubt and apprehension and despair mingling on his face. "My God, Jerry, what an idea!" the engineer blurted out.

"Can you think of a better one?"

"My idea-tank ran dry long ago."

"Then we'll try my idea. If it works, fine. If it fails—what have we got to lose?"

"But you may pull the whole moon to pieces," the engineer protested.

"As I said before—what have we got to lose?" Utah answered. He didn't think his idea would work. He didn't think anything would work any more. But what did they have to lose, except their lives, and those were already lost.

They moved forward again. Behind them, they could hear the priests searching. The Martians were having trouble in the maze of dark tunnels but they were like a pack of hounds hot on the scent of prey. Every priest on the whole moon would soon be hunting for them.

Nerissa, leading the way, stopped abruptly. Ahead of them was a wall torch. Grouped under it were six armed priests.

"Road block," Henred whispered. "End of the trail, end of the line, everybody out."

"Is there a way around them?" Utah spoke to Nerissa.

She shook her head. "We'll have to go back. They haven't seen us yet." Turning, she stopped. The sounds coming along the tunnel told them that the priests were close behind them, too near for them to turn back.

"I said this was the end of the line," Henred spoke. He laughed again, at some secret joke that he alone knew.

"I guess you're right," Utah answered. Down the tunnel, he caught a glimpse of light where a torch was held aloft. The priests searching for them. He tried to estimate their numbers. At least eight or ten Martians were there.

The priests were coming along the tunnel but they were being cautious about it.

"Do we want to tackle six Martians or do we want to tackle ten?" Utah said softly.

"Eh?" Henred questioned. Then he understood what Utah meant. He laughed. "Six, of course. Better odds that way."

OUT OF the darkness, the three humans came upon the six priests huddled under the torch like three small but very violent tornadoes erupting out of a fog. Their hope—it was a small hope—was to cut the enemy down to their size in the first charge, then to drive on through them.

Two priests went down when the humans hit them, one dropped his sword and ran. But three stood firm. Steel clashed on steel, a sword leaped out, the point was deflected downward by a shield or by another blade. Henred grumbled something. Out of the corner of his eyes, Utah caught a glimpse of the engineer. A sword point had caught Henred's forehead and his face was a mass of blood. The engineer's lips moved to form words. *"Morituri—"*

The ancient salute of the gladiators!

"To hell with that *morituri* stuff!" Utah grunted. Yet he knew the engineer was right. They, who were about to die— This was a fight that could not last long, he tried to estimate how long he could endure physically, then had no time to wonder about such things. Two of the priests had ganged up on him. They ignored Nerissa. While one fiercely attacked the pilot from the front, the second began a circling motion.

Nerissa darted toward the one who was circling—and slipped and fell on the bloody floor. The priest kicked at her contemptuously. Utah lunged at the one in front of him, lunging with the point of the sword like it was a lance held in a rest. Perhaps this was not the way to fight with swords, perhaps this violated Martian custom, he neither knew nor cared. He had no time to find a better way.

The hard-driven sword point went into the belly of the priest, was rammed home there. As the priest fell, he struck at the sword, then reached out, grabbed Utah and took the human down with him.

Utah was vaguely aware that the priest who had circled him was lunging at his back. He caught a quick glimpse of what happened. From the floor, Nerissa extended a slim foot—and tripped the lunging priest.

The Martian hit the floor flat on his face, all the fight knocked out of him. Utah got quickly to his feet. Henred had pinned his priest against the wall.

The fight here was over.

"Thanks, Nerissa. He would have run that sword all the way through me if you hadn't tripped him."

She scrambled to her feet. All three were desperately winded. Pursuit was coming along the tunnel. Tired and winded or not, they had to move on. They stumbled past the spot where the priests had set up a roadblock and moved on into the darkness.

Ahead of them, under another torch, another Martian stood, on guard.

"Only one? Hell, we can take him," Utah grunted. In his heart, he knew he was lying. He could barely stand. Henred's labored breathing told him the engineer was in little better shape. Nerissa, panting, was near exhaustion. The three of them were no match for even one Martian.

But they had to take him.

They moved slowly forward.

"That fellow looks familiar to me," Henred whispered.

Utah strained his eyes to see what Henred had distinguished. "Hell on wheels!" he muttered.

The Martian was Kavish. He had escaped from the arena too, and somehow he had managed to follow them here.

"Still trying to win, I suppose." Henred spoke. "He couldn't have picked a better time."

"All we can do is to go in on him!" Utah said.

THEY WENT forward slowly, two very tired men and one very tired woman, the men clad like gladiators and bloodier than any gladiators had ever been in the Coliseum of Imperial Rome.

Kavish heard them coming. "Who comes?" he called. His voice was tight with strong overtones of emotion in it.

"We come!" Utah answered.

The single sword point and the single shield menaced them as they advanced.

They came into the circle of light case downward from the torch.

As they advanced, Kavish very slowly lowered his sword point so that it rested on the rocky floor in front of him. He stood leaning on it, silently regarding them. He had been standing in this same position when last they had seen him in the arena.

Kavish stood there staring at them. He made no move to lift his sword.

"What's the answer?" Utah spoke, in Martian. He felt a gulp form in his throat. Deep in his heart he suspected he knew the answer, and if his suspicion was true, here was taking place a greater miracle than had ever happened on the whole Red Planet.

Kavish did not answer. His face moved as he swallowed. His face was the face of a wolf that has seen a dog and is wondering what it is like to be tame.

"I followed you from the arena," his words came slowly. "When you slipped through the hole, I came after you."

They said nothing.

"I was watching when Ulruk used what we Martians call the *dragnal druth* on you, the god-striker that stops movement. All our lives we have been taught that this *dragnal druth* is a power of the gods that is given to the high priest to use. I saw you crush the golden ball that is the symbol of the *dragnal druth*. Pah!" He spat out the exclamation.

Disgust and bitterness, showed on the face of this wild wolf who was trying to become at least partly tame. "I say again—pah! The *dragnal druth* is no god-power, it is a trick, and we Martians have been lied to, we have been held in slavery, in worse than slavery, by our beliefs!"

His voice faltered. This was sacrilege, from his viewpoint, this was the rankest of heresy. But he was working hard to become something he had not been, he was wrestling with an idea, a big idea. His voice came again, stronger now.

"And this whole moon, which we have been taught is a sacred place, our holy of holies, is nothing but a fake and a fraud, and a stench in the nostrils of honest Martians!"

Again his voice went into silence. Something moved on his face. Very subtly his features changed. Little by little, the look of the wolf began to go away.

"I have been looking for you." His voice rose harsh and hard and bitter in the narrow tunnel but full of resolution. "From now on, humans, I fight on your side."

The point of his weapon came away from the floor—and swept upward in the Martian sword salute.

They answered it in kind.

Noise came from behind them.

"Blundering fools follow you down this tunnel," Kavish spoke. "I will lead them astray. Do you find a haven somewhere—I will soon join you again."

He moved around them and past them. Soon they heard his voice behind them. He was talking to the Martian priests, searching for them, telling them loudly that no humans were in this tunnel, urging them to hurry in the either direction. A palaver followed. The footsteps of the priests could be heard—dying away into the distance.

Then single soft footsteps came toward them. It was Kavish returning after he had sent the priests away.

"You once said something about bread—" Henred spoke. Then he could go no farther. His voice choked into silence.

"Sometimes it doesn't come back." Utah said huskily. "Sometimes it does. This time it came back. When it comes back, the result is worth all the failures."

Kavish was there with them, grinning, asking them where they went next, what was to be done. They told him. Then the four of them, three humans and one Martian, slid away into the dark maze of tunnels that wound their way through the interior of Phobos, the inner moon of Mars.

CHAPTER NINE

ULRUK, high priest of all Mars, fleeing hastily from the hangars on foot—which was the first time any of the priesthood had ever seen him travel in any way except in his ornate sedan chair—went first to his own quarters. There, hidden away, was another of the golden balls that hid the equipment of the dragnal druth, the powerful radiation that paralyzed those against whom it was directed. Not until he had this golden ball in his hands did the high priest really feel safe. Then he began to summon his temple hierarchy and his slaves, to hear his orders.

Time was needed to get the hierarchy and the slaves together. There was vast confusion on this moon. Rumors were flying thick and fast. Each priest had some new tale of something that had happened or was about to happen. And every priest was scared. Something new had happened here, custom had been broken, heresy walked abroad. So the gathering was slow and even the lash of the high priest's anger could not drive his underlings faster.

Ulruk was frightened. He could not remember when he had been so badly frightened, certainly not in the arena, when he had entered the lists and had competed for the prize so long ago. He hadn't been scared then, not really scared, for he had had the dragnal druth with him even then, with the result that it had been easy to slay his opponents.

When your enemy can neither flee nor resist you, slaying him is not difficult. But if he hadn't been scared then, Ulruk was scared now. And with fear came hate. What he would do to these human vermin when he caught them, what he would do to Nerissa, that traitorous girl who had dared to help them! Never again would a human being be allowed on this moon, not even as a child. Even when you took them as children, they seemed to retain some lingering memory of their own kind, some strange loyalty to their own race. Nerissa had never seen a man until men had been brought here, but the instant she had seen a man, she had betrayed the kind priests who had raised her from a child. At the thought of that betrayal, savage bitterness rose in Ulruk. You couldn't trust a human! You just couldn't do it.

More than two zonars had passed before Ulruk got everything in order, his sedan chair recovered, and his singing slaves reassembled.

The humans, he knew, were hiding somewhere in the tunnels of this moon. He would find them! The hangars were heavily guarded, they could not steal a sky-ship and escape. Though they might run like rats from hiding place to hiding place for many zonars, the end result was inevitable.

WITH GREAT pomp and dignity, Ulruk took his seat in the sedan chair. The slaves knelt, the spearmen likewise. This was decreed by tradition and by custom.

"Slaves, shoulder chair!" Ulruk ordered. It struck him at the moment that his voice did not sound quite as loud and as clear as ordinary. He dismissed it as of no importance, in fact, he scarcely noticed this odd little effect.

But he did notice that the slaves seemed to have trouble in lifting the chair.

"Weaklings! Get this chair on your shoulders and move along."

Under the lash of his voice, they hastily lifted the chair.

"Begin chant," he ordered.

Their voices lifted but again came that strange effect. The chorus seemed thin and somehow distant. A sudden thought struck Ulruk. No, this could not be true! He dismissed the idea from his mind.

"Move faster, you!"

The slaves tried. He could see they were trying. But they were having trouble in carrying the chair. He tried to compose himself to use the *uni projection* to locate the hidden humans. The projection would not help much, he knew, since he did not know where the rats were hiding.

The slaves sang. Their voices were thin and distant, not easily heard. And they were sweating. Ulruk stared at them. Inside his mind consternation was growing. It was appearing on his face in the form of horror. The slaves had never sweated before; this chair was not a heavy burden. Why should they sweat now?

One slave stumbled.

Seeing the slave stumble, a spearman moved instantly. Custom decreed what should happen now. It happened. The spearman drove his weapon straight through the slave's body.

The slaves who carried the sedan chair of the high priest were not supposed to stumble. This was considered to be sacrilege. Ulruk motioned to the spearman to take the place of the writhing slave who lay dying.

The spear bearer slid his shoulder under the lifting rail of the sedan chair.

And three slaves stumbled. Where the floor was perfectly smooth, they stumbled and went down, dragging the others with them. The chair crunched heavily to the floor. Ulruk was thrown from it.

The spearman stared aghast at the luckless slaves who had committed this act. They started forward, to carry out what custom decreed. Ulruk, with a gesture, stopped them. Now for the first time, Ulruk was beginning to realize how much actual difficulty he was having in breathing. His chest was laboring. He could feel sweat gathering on his body. It didn't seem he could get enough air into his lungs to breathe.

"What—what's happening—to air?" he mumbled.

The spearmen were showing signs of distress. Ulruk could see their chests rising and falling, could hear the sounds of their labored breathing. One spearman had let the point of his weapon sink to the floor and he was leaning on it as if he did not have the strength to stand alone.

Inside Ulruk's mind consternation was growing again. The suspicion that he had forced down inside him was rising, like a monster, to the surface.

A yellow-hooded priest came stumbling into the room. He was panting as if his laboring lungs were about to collapse. His gait was a shambling run as if his legs could not hold him erect.

It was no trouble for this priest to prostrate himself before Ulruk. He sprawled forward on the stone floor.

"Great One—" His gasped whisper was a thin sound in the shocked and silent room. "The humans are in the rooms—where the air and gravity machines—are located—" The priest gasped out the words, then ceased gasping. Yellow sweat that matched the color of his hood appeared in globules on his face, his eyes took on a fixed stare, he tried to lift himself on his hands—and fell. Inside of him something had run out of energy.

In this moment Ulruk knew the truth. He knew now what had happened, why the chant of the slaves had seemed thin and distant, why his own voice had sounded strange.

Grasping the golden ball of the *dragnal druth,* Ulruk pulled himself erect.

The slaves helped him. Or tried to. But they were in trouble too. One of them went down, then another. Finally Ulruk himself went down.

There was no one left to help him. He was alone, alone with all that he had been but was no longer. He began to crawl. All-powerful high-priest of Mars, he had been, now he was a crawling skeleton trying to find the strength to drag himself to the core of the moon.

He clutched the *dragnal druth.* If he could only reach the core of the moon with it!

His chest heaved, he panted for breath, saliva drooled from his lips, he looked like a cornered cur gone rabid from hydrophobia. Only the hate in his eyes was still alive.

Even after he could no longer move his body, the hate was still alive in his eyes, like a glittering yellow flame. Then, little by little, like twin yellow candles burning themselves out in their own juice, the lights went out in his eyes.

Thus died Ulruk, high priest of all Mars. The golden ball rolled from his fingers and came to rest against the wall.

THE LITTLE moon groaned as it turned slowly on its axis. Vast forces, greater than the forces of tidal waves, seethed through it. As the force of the artificial gravity generated the heart of the moon began to lessen, pressures that had been built up against it began to collapse. Here and there roofs fell and walls collapsed. The moon was being tortured and it wailed and groaned like an animal in pain.

In the core of the moon, in the big power room located there, Jerry Utah listened to the groaning and the grumbling in the roof above him. "Like Samson, we may pull down the walls of the temple," he muttered.

"To hell with 'em, let 'em come down," Henred answered. Over and over again he was repeating: "I can run any power plant that has a wheel to turn or a jet to thrust. I can even run this damned perversion of a power plant." He was not at all sure of the way this power plant functioned, or of what was happening to the energy derived from it, but he knew for certain that the plant was running down, that it was generating less energy, by the simple fact that he was getting lighter on his feet all the time as the pull of gravity lessened.

Air was moving out of the interior of the moon as the artificial gravity field began to collapse upon it. Air moved slowly through the maze of tunnels and passages, seeking outlets. Here and there projections formed vibrating surfaces, becoming in effect, vast organ reeds, so that the whole moon vibrated with various loud howling noises, like a tremendous organ badly out of tune.

"Don't let the air pressure get down too low or we'll be cooked too," Utah warned.

"Don't you worry, I'm making this monster eat right out of my hand," Henred answered.

The air would linger longest here, and as long as they kept the artificial gravity on even part way, they would have oxygen. Perhaps it would be thin air but it would sustain life. Utah wouldn't think of what was happening elsewhere on Phobos, as air and life left the moon. Near him on the floor was the body of a dead priest, a member of the working crew who had not escaped when they charged this room.

Perhaps this priest had been lucky.

"Here they come!" Kavish, on watch at the door, yelled. The Martian stood at the peephole looking out.

The first charge of the priests, while hastily organized, had power in it. They charged the door—made of stout metal— and it resisted. The humans, entering, had not broken this door in getting in. Kavish had secured the opening of the door, by marching boldly up to it and demanding entrance.

When the first wave of priests charged the door and found it did not budge, they remained outside for a few minutes, yelling their rage and their hatred. They didn't yell long. Very soon they began to realize that the air was going away.

As the first attack subsided, and other priests put in an appearance, they gathered outside the door. First they were an angry, threatening mob who promised the humans inside what would happen when Ulruk arrived. As time passed and the high priest didn't arrive, they ceased being threatening. Their anger began to go away. Fear was replacing it.

"We'll die," a yellow-hooded priest cried. "We'll smother."

"Smother, you good-for-nothing rascals!" Kavish yelled. He did not call them rascals. The term he used was strictly Martian and it covered their ancestry in precise detail back for ten generations. "Where is Ulruk?"

There was no answer. No one knew where Ulruk was. And no one cared, now. Every priest out there knew it was too late for the high priest to help them.

Mingled with the creaks and grumbles from the moon itself, and with the shrill screams of the out-of-tune organ pipes, were the wails of the priests. They were begging now, for air, for mercy, for life itself.

"Let 'em learn what it feels like," Utah said. "When they do, we'll give them air—and more gravity to hold it. And when we leave this moon—Kavish, would you like to stay?"

"Stay behind?" The Martian was startled. "They would cut my throat!"

"Not if the situation was handled right. And before we leave you we will make certain that it is handled right. I imagine Ulruk is certainly dead by now and—" He hesitated.

"And what?" Kavish said.

"If you could take Ulruk's place, if you could become high priest of all Mars, what would you do?"

Kavish's eyes glowed. "If I were high priest, brother, there would be some changes made on Mars." The tone of his voice indicated he meant exactly what he said. The glint in his eyes showed what the changes would be. "I would wipe out this whole priesthood and start all over again—"

Utah sighed. "Turn up the juice," he called to Henred. "We've got a new world here in the making."

MANY ZONARS later, a little scene took place in the main hangar of the moon. The ship that had been on the ramp was still there, but it was fueled now, by hustling priests who looked as if they had risen from the dead—and were greatly surprised to find themselves alive again. They were taking orders from a new high priest who was backing up his orders with the holy religious symbol, the *dragnal druth* which had been found near Ulruk's body and brought to the new high priest, as a symbol of his authority.

In essence, the whole situation meant a new deal here on Phobos, a great many changes made and to be made, by an exceedingly angry and disgusted new high priest, one Kavish. And because of the changes made here, there would be a new deal on all Mars. Which would be all to the good.

The ship's motors were warm, Utah was at the controls. Henred, like an old, wary hawk, was watching the instrument, panel and muttering with satisfaction at the position of the meters and at the sound of the warming motors.

Outside the ship, well away from the zone of blast, Kavish was waving and grinning at them.

"Come back soon," he was yelling. "Come back soon—and be always welcome here."

Utah grinned. He waved his hand in the ancient gesture of parting and pressed home the throttle. The motors roared. The ship went up the runway, gathered speed, and hurled itself into the clear sky.

Below lay Mars, a mighty red balloon in the sky. Utah turned to the girl sitting beside him. "There is Mars. And off there—" he pointed to a stellar body barely visible, "—is Earth. Home."

The girl was smiling, he saw. Her eyes were shining with bright and eager lights. Earth—home—where she had never been. Earth was calling her home just as it was calling Jerry Utah and Harry Henred.

Earth—Earth—the green planet across space. Earth—Home—

On Jerry Utah's face a grin appeared, a reflection of the vast feeling moving inside of him. "Earth and home." The whispered words were a paen of victory in his heart.

THE END

IT WAS AN EIGHT-SIDED TRIANGLE!

Don't try to figure out what this means without reading the story. You'll understand it (maybe) by the time you get to the last chapter. "The Man with Five Lives" may well be one of the strangest science fiction novels ever written. It deals with the evil that lies within the souls of all men and man's attempt to expel this evil (albeit accidentally) through scientific means. This tale was the brainchild of David V. Reed (David Levine) one of editor Raymond A. Palmer's best writers for his pulp magazine, Fantastic Adventures. *In many ways this tale is a precursor to the Richard Shaver stories that Palmer championed so fiercely in the mid-to-late 1940s. Reed and Palmer present this tale as being essentially "true." The lead character is a fellow named Clyde Woodruff. The author of the story (as first published) was also Clyde Woodruff—a pseudonym Dave Reed would use more than once. Palmer himself is one of the central characters and actually wrote one of the later chapters. This tale is filled with scientific speculation and enough mystery and intrigue to fill a dozen whodunits. In its own weird way, "The Man with Five Lives" is a very engaging and entertaining opus, and certainly one of the most bizarre tales Armchair Fiction has ever published.*

TO THE READER:

Unusual as it may appear for a story to begin with an explanation, there is a reason for it. The reason, however, is so complicated that the author has little hope of it being understood at this point. He offers instead, temporarily, a simpler reason: this explanation was actually written after most of this story. But why, you may well ask, is it placed here? For one, as you will later discover, there seems to be no other suitable place for such a note. More important, it is meant to serve as a warning. For the following pages are not, in a strict sense, a work of fiction. Nor are they, truthfully, the truth. The best I can offer now is to say that my story is entirely true when viewed whole. But only upon that condition! As a matter of fact, it is only because so much of it is untrue (though all of it is true) that it is here in print at all. I might add that it has been printed over my protests, a contention which, however much you may scoff at now, will become increasingly clear as you read. Be warned.

*–The Author**

---

*Pay no attention to the author's foreword. —Raymond A. Palmer, Editor, "Fantastic Adventures" magazine

THE MAN
WITH FIVE
LIVES

By
DAVID V. REED
(Originally writing as Clyde Woodruff)

ARMCHAIR FICTION
PO Box 4369, Medford, Oregon 97504

For more information about Armchair Books and products, visit our website at…

www.armchairfiction.com

Or email us at…

armchairfiction@yahoo.com

CHAPTER ONE
The Mystery Begins

IT BEGAN on the most memorable Friday evening of my life, though it seemed innocent enough at the time. I was at the Astor bar when a waiter said that Jenks wanted me on the phone. It burbled around in my head, making no sense, and I said to Mahoney, "How does Jenks know where I am? Invite him down here to have dinner with us."

A minute later, Mahoney shuffled back to the bar. He said to the bartender, "I'll have another Coca-Cola with an egg in it." There are few men who can ask for a thing like that and get away with it, but Mahoney is six feet of muscle, with a head like a buffalo.

"Is Jenks coming?" I asked.

"Wasn't nobody on the phone," Mahoney grunted.

I thought about it. As I said, this was a Friday, and generally when I'm entertaining over the weekend, I get to a bar early Friday afternoon and get into condition. I'd been at the bar since three and it was now six-thirty, and the world had assumed very fuzzy outlines. I thought about Mahoney's answer and I tried to remember what it was I had to remember about Jenks, but I got nowhere.

"Hey, Mahoney," I said, "doesn't it seem a bit strange—"

"No, boss. Nothing your jerk friends do seems strange."

It was a good answer, generally speaking, but it didn't really apply to Jenks. David Jenks was one of the few worthwhile guys I knew.

"Mahoney, how do you know there was no one on the phone?"

"Listen, boss, anytime I get on the phone and I say hello five—six times and nobody answers, I start thinking maybe nobody's there."

I had another drink. I tried to think about all the things I had to think about, and there were plenty, but I couldn't place it.

I am a guy with enough troubles, "Mahoney," I said, "maybe there's a clue on this list of appointments. Would you mind reading it for me?"

Mahoney scowled at the memo pad I held out to him. "I told you a hundred times I can't read the butler's handwriting," he said. "He writes too damn fancy for me."

I said, "The valet wrote this."

"I'm crazy about him, too," Mahoney said, taking the pad. He read the list. *"Nine A.M.: canter through park.* Haw!" Mahoney sneered, "You fell outa bed at eleven. *Eleven A.M.: see Reverend Jasper for final arrangements."*

"What arrangements?"

Mahoney regarded me with distaste, "Boss, if that's why you're drinking, there ain't enough Scotch in the world to make you forget it. You're getting married at four o'clock, Sunday— remember? *Noon: lunch with Ray Vanness at the Algonquin.* You was an hour late," Mahoney said. "Vanness had had his lunch and left you the check. *One P.M.: see Riley, Riley and Shapiro about estate settlements.* You did that. *Two P.M.: see photographer from picture magazine—"*

"What picture magazine?"

"How do I know? I heard the butler telling the rest of your menagerie that some picture magazine wanted to photograph your wedding. So you missed the appointment. Still two P.M. *See editor of Daily Mirror, protest about item in Winchell.* Ain't that the one about you and a certain strip-teaser going steady?"

"Shut up," I sighed. "Anything there about Jenks?"

"There's a special note here under three o'clock, *No drinking, as per solemn oath to Miss Dykstra.* So you're drinking the joint dry."

"Stick your nose back into that egg," I said abruptly. "What's with—"

"Yeah, Jenks. It says here to be sure to read his telegram."

"Ah-h-h-h," I breathed, and something in my head went click! I heard it. "I'm beginning to remember. He said something about a great discovery he had made. And he couldn't come to the wedding." From there it grew fuzzy again. "I called the laboratory a while back—"

"You didn't call nobody," Mahoney said. "You can't even move."

"Shut up," I said. "You were in the men's room. I called, but I can't remember who spoke to me. It was something about notes..."

SUDDENLY everything began dancing before me. I grabbed hold of the bar and steadied myself. You know how things are sometimes when you've got something on your mind? Somebody says something and it doesn't begin to register until a long while later? That was what was happening to me—it was beginning to register!

"Mahoney!" I said. "Jenks' notes are missing!"

"Like for a breach of promise?"

"He said they were a military secret!"

Mahoney told me later that this last remark, hurled at the bartender, caused quite a stir. I ran out of the place with Mahoney behind me and grabbed a taxi. The laboratory was only half a mile away, but bucking midtown Manhattan traffic at seven o'clock, it took us twenty minutes to get to the East Thirties, and by then I remembered a lot.

You see, David Jenks was a sort of protégé of mine. I mean, he had the brains and I had the money. We'd gone to college together, and in those days I had been interested in things. Things like psychological research, for instance; I majored in Psych with Jenks. He was serious, talented, brilliant, and after school—that was five years ago—when I had taken over my inheritance, which Riley, Riley and Shapiro are still estimating, though it seems to be somewhere between fourteen and fifteen million, Dave Jenks had gone on with his work. But we'd met again last year at the Christmas reunion and had a hell of a time, and he told me what he was doing. The upshot of it was that I got him to take a leave of absence, outfitted a lab for him, and let him work. I'd seen him maybe half a dozen times in the six months that had followed.

Then, the day before, I phoned and left word for him that I was really marrying Dorothy Dykstra and I wanted him to come to my wedding. I wanted the society notes to say that a real Professor, a useful member of society, was there, in addition to the kind of people I knew.

And this morning the telegram had come. Had it really been so strangely worded, or was it the hangover? I might as well admit it: I'd been drinking on other days besides Fridays since the day Dorothy asked me to marry her and I said yes. Not that I mean I didn't do the actual proposing. Don't get me wrong. Dorothy was a fine girl, too good for me; only for a guy like me...anyway, I suppose the idea of getting married frightened me, and to hell with what the gossip columns say.

But I'll tell you this: I had the craziest feeling something was wrong with Dave Jenks. Miss my wedding? Dave? I tried to remember the phone conversation, and I decided I had spoken to him. He had sounded terribly upset. And I had gotten so stinko it had slipped my mind the minute I left the phone booth and saw the bar again. But would you believe it—the whole thing didn't sober me up even then!

We pulled into East Thirty-eighth in a hurry. It was a dead-end street, fronting on the river, and at this hour it was quiet and empty. The lab building itself was an old redbrick affair, two stories high. There were lights on upstairs.

Before we had a chance to ring the bell, the downstairs door swung open, and there stood two men, almost as big as Mahoney. One of them jerked his head at us in a silent invitation to come in. In the darkness I barely made out the black automatic in his hand.

"Jeez!" Mahoney roared. "Another minute and I'd have laid the both of you out colder than an Eskimo's donkey!"

"It's Mahoney," said the man with the gun. "It's nobody but old blow-hard Mahoney. What the hell are you doing here?"

"What am *I* doing here?" Mahoney demanded, "What are you doing here? Why ain't you G-men out chasing spies like in the comics?"

"You should talk!" the man retorted. "I hear that bunch of ambulance chasers you work for got you playing nurse-maid to a rich—"

"PARDON me," I said, edging past them, or trying to, when the door at the top of the stairwell opened and two more men came out, one of them—their chief, as it turned out—shouting down to inquire what the rumpus was about. So Mahoney introduced me. It was one of the few times his connections came in handy. Did I mention that he was a bodyguard wished on me by Riley, Riley and Shapiro? And a good one, too.

The chief's name was Bancroft—a bony, red-faced man. He said something about Jenks having tried to get me all over town and led me through the lab. Meanwhile he was muttering something to himself, but I hardly listened because I was busy trying to see what was going on there. Jenks' four assistants were standing around near one of the long lab benches. They were quiet, sober-faced men in stained lab coats, and one of them, the blonde Yarovitch, nodded politely to me. Everything seemed to be in order. The myriad bottles and vials and retorts and complicated mechanisms gleamed brightly, and the eye was everywhere attracted by the colorful dabs of liquids in pots and test-tubes that bubbled and smoked like they do in the Boris Karloff pictures. But it was the rational, meticulous laboratory I'd known...

When Bancroft opened the door to Jenks' private workroom, I saw that Jenks had been waiting for us, as if he had been afraid to leave the room—as indeed he might have been, if only to avoid facing his staff in his present condition. He ran across the room, seizing my hand. "Woody!" he cried, his features working, "I've been trying to get you all day. Thank God you've come!"

I'd never seen him so overwrought, nor suspected his capacity for such distress. He had always been as unemotional as a scientific experiment. When I stole a glance at Bancroft, I saw that he too was waiting for Jenks to speak, though, as I subsequently learned, he had already heard the story once. And what a story it was, when Jenks did speak…what an incredible story…

Put briefly, though none the less stunningly for it, the total result was this: that he and his staff, working together, had accidentally discovered the formula for a new explosive of tremendous power, and that this formula had either been stolen already, or was about to be stolen. And the thief was one, possibly more than one, of the members of Jenks' staff.

Naturally, there were numerous details to be explained in this brief account, and though I was hardly in a condition where I welcomed asking questions, I did ask a few.

What did Jenks mean, first of all, by saying that the discovery was accidental? Perhaps more to the point, how was it that a man engaged in psychological research had wandered so far afield?

He shook off my questions impatiently. I was neglecting one of the most important aspects of his work. He was not only an experimenter in symptoms, an investigator of superficial behavior. He was as much a physiologist, a physicist, a chemist, as anything else. He was, he told us, speaking, as always when he spoke of his work, in florid, almost archaic language, a scientist of the human mind. I agreed that his work had taken him along strange paths before, and in this case, he said, one of the by-products of his work had been this chemical formula.

"My staff and I shared the work," he told us. "Our tasks were minutely broken up and inter-related. One part was meaningless without the rest. Only I knew the specific direction of our work—I was looking for a new drug, to produce a new pattern of behavior it doesn't matter now what it was… But somewhere along the course of these separate experiments, the paths crossed—and that crossroad was this new explosive!

"Do you see what I mean?" he asked anxiously. "Of course, when the time came for checking our work (I generally correlated our experiments every few weeks) I would have seen this crossroad myself. Or at least I think so. But what happened was that someone on my staff, in some way, saw it for himself. This person, or persons, understood the nature of this by-product immediately!"

HE PAUSED for a few moments, collecting himself.

"I first suspected it three nights ago," he went on. "I had come back to the lab Tuesday night, and I came in here to finish a test. I set the test up, and then, having an hour to wait for a precipitation, I set my alarm clock, turned off the lights, and took a nap. Something wakened me during that hour. I thought I heard a voice from the outer lab, and listening at the door, hearing numerous pauses in what seemed to be a conversation—though only one voice spoke—I realized that whoever it was out there was speaking on the phone.

"The outer lab phone has an extension in here. I lifted the receiver and listened. I couldn't tell who it was out there, but the conversation concerned the experiments we've been carrying on here—I heard just enough to convince me of that. But mainly, what these two spoke of was some urgent business that was to be consummated this week. This Sunday, the voice at the other end repeated several times, with emphatic insistence.

"The laboratory voice said that not all the notes had been taken down yet, that it might take more time, especially to avoid asking for notes not yet due this experimenter. Sunday, said the voice at the other end, adding that no attempt was to be made to get in touch with him until then. He would contact the experimenter himself in his own way and take the notes.

"When the laboratory voice asked how he would know this other person (and this was the first indication I had that neither man knew the other personally) the answer was that he would approach shortly after four o'clock and ask what time it was, and upon being told, he would then say: 'But that is impossible.' His final word was for this experimenter, naturally, to keep himself available during that hour, preferably outdoors.

"The moment the conversation ended, I started for the door, hoping to surprise whoever it was. Unfortunately, in the darkness I fell across a stool, and made enough noise to warn the person in the next room. I ran out then and turned on all the lights. There was no one there. I searched the entire lab systematically, and at the door I found this…"

Jenks held out a section of moving picture film. It was rolled up, perhaps six inches in length, and designed for an 8mm camera. I offered it to Bancroft, who said he had already seen it. I held it up to the light and saw that each frame held a view of a sheet of paper, each sheet covered with writing and chemical symbols.

"These are photographs of five pages of notes," said Jenks. "Two of them are my own, two others are Miller's, and the last is Forman's. Mr. Bancroft says they may be compact copies of pictures taken by another camera. It seems to be a section of a longer length of film."

Jenks stopped speaking for a moment, and his attitude resembled that of a man listening intently, but all I heard was the constant ringing in my ears. I was sick. I had troubles of my own, and here I was mixed up in something with G-men. Not that I wasn't concerned: David Jenks meant too much to me for that. I tried to meet his eyes then, but their gray depths had turned cold and opaque. When he spoke again, it was with a great weariness.

"I began checking over all our notes. That was Tuesday night, and I've been here ever since. Early this morning I found what I was looking for…the accidental juncture of our experiments. A tiny pinch of powder…" He held up a thumb and forefinger, "…no more than three milligrams, forming the residue of this fantastic compound, exerted enough force to smash a large steel cylinder to bits."

BANCROFT whistled. "Where'd you try it?"

"In the yard behind this building, early this morning. But after that I didn't know what to do. When my staff arrived this morning, I realized how helpless I was. That was when I wired you, Woody. I had remembered your phoning and inviting me to the wedding. I thought if I said something about a discovery, and the fact that it would prevent me from attending, that it would bring you immediately."

"I had a hangover," I said, feeling like a damned fool.

"And when you did call this afternoon, I couldn't get a coherent word out of you. You said you were at the Astor bar, so I understood." He said it without reproach, stating a melancholy fact as only an old friend like he could have done. "So I gave up and called in the F.B.I. It seemed to me that, in times like these, such a dangerous—"

"But you called me back," I said, "then you hung up before I had—"

"What's the difference?" Bancroft moaned, impatiently. "I been here long enough to hear the story twice now and I still don't know a lot of things. Listen, Professor, does your staff know why we're here?"

"I told them nothing. But surely one of them knows only too well."

"Assuming it's only one of them. Tell me this, has this person had a chance to get at the rest of the notes since then?"

"Perhaps. I couldn't very well tell my staff to stop working before I knew what, if anything, had happened. They needed the notes."

Bancroft scratched his head. "The hell with it," he said. "It don't make any difference. The important thing—and I'll be damned if I understand it—is the fact that our culprit has a definite appointment this Sunday at four o'clock. If we keep him in sight—"

"Keep which one in sight?" I mumbled.

"All four of them. Even if the culprit thinks he's suspected, we know he has no way of changing the appointment. All we have to do is keep shadowing the four of them, and the best way is to keep a twenty-four hour watch on them. Offhand it sounds tough, but we're in luck. I got it all figured out, and you have to help us, Mr. Woodruff."

"Sure," I said, "You want me to adopt one?"

"Amounts to the same thing," he said. "I want you to invite the whole staff to your wedding."

"Huh?"

"Why not? How many people you honestly expecting there?"

"Millions," I said. "The way it looks now, half the town plans to weekend at Seaside."

Seaside was the estate my paternal grandfather had built in the days when millionaires lived like feudal barons. It was an enormous place, to which my father had added greenhouses and swimming pools. It occupied an island all its own, twenty miles from the city and a hundred yards off the South Shore of Long Island, to which it was connected by a covered, rustic bridge.

"Millions," said Bancroft, happily, "is what I read by the papers. So you invite the staff for the weekend. Sort of a vacation for them. And I station my men all around the place. The beautiful part—"

"It stinks," I said. "My wedding's scheduled for four o'clock."

"I'm amazed at you, Mr. Woodruff, I hope you don't think we'd allow the slightest disturbance. No, sir! And the beautiful part of it is the fact that whoever is going to meet our culprit— why, he'll have no trouble at all crashing your wedding."

"Sure," I said. "Every deadbeat in town'll be there."

"Fine, fine…" Bancroft enthused, rubbing his hands. "Here's the dope, I take my gang away, and you, Professor Jenks, tell your staff anything you can think of, then say Mr. Woodruff invited them for the weekend."

"What if they don't want to go?" I asked.

"Impossible! I heard you're going to serve breast of pheasant. Champagne, roast suckling—" He stopped himself and took a deep breath. "But just in case, Professor, you tell them that they have to go—they can't afford to offend Mr. Woodruff. He pays the bills and so on."

"Boy, are you building up my character," I groaned.

"Why not? You're a great guy, Mr. Woodruff, a great guy. And now, Professor, you come in there with me and tell them."

HE HALF shook my arm out of its socket and led Jenks out, leaving me alone in the smaller lab. I closed my eyes and let my head go for a swim. What an incredible business it was. And there I was, mixed up in it. I thought of Dorothy and I half remembered a dinner date I'd had. It was now eight o'clock. If Dorothy had had the slightest inkling of the new mess I was in... She had no use for Jenks. The one or two times she'd come with me to the lab, she had reminded me how much it was costing me to keep it going...

Lord, I thought, if I had a drink. A good, stiff shot. Jenks was no teetotaler, either. He used to drink rum in a water glass; one slice of lemon and one pint of rum—drinking time: five minutes. I took the keys that were in the door and began hunting through the large desk, and damn it—there it was! Just where he had kept it in school, bottom drawer, rear. Not very much, just a shot or so, but that bit of good Jamaica rum looked like quiescent fire through the pale amber of the slender bottle. Did I say fire? Maybe you won't believe it—but when I uncorked it, the damned stuff actually let out a tiny whiff of smoke! Smoke, you understand, like wood smoke, like the smell of wet logs smoldering, like the smell of fog in the fall. A wonderful smell.

So I put it down without further ado, shook my head, stuck out my tongue and said, "Ah-h-h-h," and felt fine...if I felt anything...

Because I had the strangest feeling, I felt as if I had left the place, as if I was then at home—my city home, I mean. But I was also leaving a place far uptown, and I was driving a car furiously, trying to get home. And I was also getting into a cab and asking to go home. In short, everywhere I thought I was, I wanted to go home.

And sitting there on Dave's desk, I really wanted to go home. It was the rum, I knew, on top of the Astor bar. I felt as sick as a dog, and I wanted to go home. Know what I mean?

Then Jenks came in. "It's all right, Woody," he said. "They're all going home for some clothes and they'll meet in half an hour to go out to Seaside together." I could hear the sound of taxi horns outside very plainly, "Bancroft said they'd be followed all the time until they get together again—he got the cabs himself."

I said, "I want to go home, too."

There was silence, and it continued.

After a while I opened my eyes and looked at Jenks. I took one look at him and almost fainted. It was the way he was standing there, looking at me and at the empty bottle I had put down on his chair. His face was absolutely frozen. The blood had run out of it. He stood immobile, horror and fear etched in his lean features, and his eyes glistening but unseeing.

"Woody...Woody..." he whispered, *did you drink that?"*

I nodded.

"Woody..." He couldn't say anything else. He lurched across the room and picked the empty bottle up in his hands. Then, slowly, he sank into the chair, staring at the bottle, then raising his eyes and looking at me. I wanted to say something bright, something like, "The hell with it. I'll get you another bottle." But this crazy fear had somehow gotten hold of me. I didn't remember when I first felt afraid, but it was there, a powerful, oppressive fear.

"Stop looking at me that way!" I cried out suddenly. "What's the matter with the bottle? Say something, damn you!"

Presently he said, "Woody, that story I told Bancroft isn't true." He barely whispered the words. He was holding the bottle so tightly that the tips of his fingers were white.

"What isn't true?" I said. "What are you talking about?"

"The part about the explosive isn't true. Woody, do you remember what I told once about...about...isolating evil?" He looked at me in that terrible way. "Woody..." he gasped. "I did it! I found a compound that does it. Do you understand me?"

MY HEAD was reeling. "Woody, we were in school then. You remember the talks we used to have, about personality, about character, about what made men what they are. They were experimenting with things like the truth serum in those days—they were opening all the twisted, crazy worlds hidden in man's subconscious—they were drugging him, studying his brain, searching parts of his soul that they had never been able to expose before...

"That's what I've been doing here these months, Woody. I've been compounding drugs, hoping to find one that might unlock the door to the evil in man—*to find a drug that would isolate the essential evils in a man,* that would magnify them so they could be examined minutely, so that motivation might be understood, so that greed and cowardice, lust and treachery might be examined..."

"I remember," I said. "What are you trying to tell me?"

"Woody, the formula this person was stealing from me was the formula for this drug! Don't you see? I found the drug—and it's a thousand times more dangerous than any explosive! The man who knew how to make that drug could hold the key to chaos..." He stared at me mutely. "I couldn't tell Bancroft that. I made up the story about the explosive. But if an enemy of our country were to get hold of the formula...a few gallons in a reservoir...in a lake, a river..."

"What does the drug do?" I heard my voice as if in a dream.

"It releases everything evil in him. It unchains the beast in a man, frees his passions, his desires."

"And that's the formula—" I stopped short. He was staring at the bottle, and for the first time I began to understand what he had tried to tell me, without finding the courage. A little shiver ran through me. I closed my eyes and I felt I was home,

"Dave," I said, "you mean that you had that compound in this rum bottle."

"Yes. God help us."

"What's going to happen to me?"

"I don't know...I don't know..." he half-whispered. "A hundred c.c.'s of it is enough. You drank it all, a thousand times the dose I know anything about! What made you do it, you insane..." And then he cracked. He couldn't go on. He just sat there helplessly, tears running down his face, looking at the amber bottle.

A long time passed. Outside a horn sounded once, twice. Then the bell rang. I heard Mahoney's voice bellowing from outside, saying he was waiting for us.

"I feel all right," I said; but when I tried to stand up, I was wobbly, as usual. "I don't feel evil at all," I said, steadying myself. "Except maybe I think I need a drink. And I want to go home. Boy, do I want to go home."

"I'll go with you," Jenks said. "I've got to go with you."

"You've got to get some clothes yourself," I said. "We'll stop by at your place." So we went down to the cab Mahoney had, and Mahoney shot me a sharp look that told me he was dying to know what was up. He took a second look at Jenks, and it seemed to convince him not to ask. We got to Jenks' place at Gramercy, and when Jenks showed his reluctance to leave me alone even for a few minutes, the mystified expression on Mahoney's face made me burst out laughing.

"I feel great," I laughed. "Hurry down, Dave."

And in that moment, as he left, I had that same absurd sensation of being in several other places, I closed my eyes, and I saw myself entering my apartment. It was an amazing vision. Every little object in the foyer was distinctly clear, not the way things are in one's imagination, but in reality. The next instant, as I had somehow expected, Robert, the butler, having heard my key in the door, carne hurrying into the foyer.

"MR. WOODY! Please!" he cried, astonished and perplexed. "I don't understand what you're doing, sir, really I don't!" And I knew why he was saying it—because I had already let myself in twice—no, three times—and each time I had gone into my study, only to appear at the door again. He thought I kept going out the back way.

"Driver," I said suddenly, "take us to 800 Central Park South."

"Hey, boss!" Mahoney protested. "You're supposed to wait for the professor. What's the big idea?"

I didn't know myself. All I knew was that I had to get home.

"And drive like mad!" I yelled at the driver. I had closed my eyes again and seen a girl sitting in the living room, a dark, lovely girl, with two suitcases on the floor near her.

Mahoney bounced off the seat as the startled driver suddenly let his clutch out. "Ah-hah! I get it!" Mahoney cried. "You and the professor have been auld-lang-syneing again with a bottle of rum. What the hell does he do—brew the stuff up there?"

The cab was racing up Fifth Avenue. I sat there, looking out of the window, and this time I hardly had to let my eyes close...I saw myself entering the apartment for a fourth time...I shook my head.

"Mahoney," I said, dizzily, "what does it mean?"

"It means you're past even your quota," Mahoney said moodily.

We were home soon afterward. Mahoney held my arm as inconspicuously as he could going through the lobby, and the elevator man said his good evening without batting an eye. We got off at my floor and I got out my key.

"The menagerie must be out at Seaside already," Mahoney said.

"No," I said. "Robert's waiting for me here." I knew, you see.

I opened the door and went into the foyer. I closed the door quietly; and instantly I heard Robert approaching. He would have been noiseless on the carpet if his shoes hadn't squeaked.

He hurried his two hundred and fifty pounds into the foyer and stopped dead.

"Mr. Woody, you've got to stop it," he moaned. He sat down on a fragile Chippendale chair and mopped his forehead. He was breathing heavily, "I don't understand it," he said, wearily. "Have you been trying to meet Mr. Mahoney in the hall? Is that it, sir?"

Mahoney swallowed loudly. "Do you mind telling me what you're talking about?" he exclaimed, baffled, "Don't tell me that Robert, the perfect butler, has finally taken to imbibing of the crushed grape?"

"I'll thank you to keep out of this, Mr. Mahoney," Robert said.

"With pleasure! With alacrity, too, whatever that is! One of these days the asylum is going to discover a branch outfit here…"

I threw Robert my coat, and walking into the living room, I saw her. That girl I had seen before, when I closed my eyes. There she was, sitting on one of the couches, legs crossed, smoking a cigarette, and her two suitcases nearby.

She hardly raised her eyes when I walked up to her.

"Hello, you," I said.

"Not again, Mr. Woodruff," she said, reprovingly. "Please, not again. I'm beginning to feel the way your butler does."

What a beautiful girl she was. She had black, lustrous hair and eyes so blue that the contrast was startling. She was wearing an evening gown of gold cloth, and a little ermine jacket covered one shoulder.

"You know," I said, "I hardly know how to tell you this, but—"

"You saw me in a dream, Mr. Woodruff," she said, pleasantly, but I could see she was the least bit annoyed. "In a sort of vision," she said. "That makes five times you've said it. Believe me, Mr. Woodruff, I accept it as an imperishable truth. I don't know what you're trying to prove, but I'll accept that, too. Yes, I'll wait here while you hurry into dinner clothes. Yes, I know you have some urgent business in the library."

THE absolutely crazy part of it was that I had been about to say the very things she said for me. I don't know why. I knew that I had to get into the study—the library, she called it—without knowing exactly why. The way I knew I had to get home.

"But who are you?" I blurted.

She smiled. "Very well, we'll do it again," she said. "Only this time promise me that if you like the way I introduce myself, we'll call it quits." She stood up and extended a hand. She was slender, and her figure...I was getting married in two days, I remembered. "I'm Ann Hunter. You had an appointment with me this afternoon, remember? I'm the photographer who's going to take the pictures of your wedding. Oh, it's perfectly all right. No excuses necessary, I assure you. If you'd had the slightest idea of how interesting a photographer was being sent, you'd have torn yourself away. Yes, of course I'll wait." And she smiled again, with that beautiful, impersonal smile.

"I'll be out as soon as I can," I said. "Mahoney, you wrestle yourself into that soup and fish I rented for you."

It was only then, when I looked at Mahoney, that I realized how I felt. He moved his big shoulders slowly, like a man struggling feebly with some unseen assailant, and his face was a hopeless blank. "Yeah," he said, shuffling away. "Yeah, I gotta get dressed."

I nodded politely and went upstairs to the study. The apartment was a duplex, with an upstairs bedroom and adjoining study. The door was locked. I fumbled around for a key and opened it.

I don't know how long I stood there with the door open. It seemed an eternity before I could think that perhaps I had better shut it. I remember how I felt when I saw what was in the study, but there's no way of describing the sensation. It was like...like knowing, suddenly, that you've gone insane, and knowing that this is the last coherent thought you will ever have...like stopping to exist, but feeling somehow that your mind is still slowly functioning...something terrifying and unbelievable and meaningless and, yes...and funny too, in a way... I stood there, my back pressed against the door, and I looked slowly from one to the other, trying to think, but somehow knowing what it meant all at once, and in one blinding flash—say, of intuition—but even more than that, of *knowing* actually, I understood it...

For there, sitting in my study, were four men. The four men were all me. I know what it sounds like, but that's the only way to put it. One sat carelessly on a corner of my desk. A second was at the window that faced the park. A third leaned back in my favorite chair and drew on a cigarette. The fourth was stretched out on the small leather couch. They were all wearing gray tweeds identical with my own suit, and their shoes, shirts, ties were duplicates of mine. They seemed to have been waiting for me, for as I entered, the one on the couch sat up expectantly and turned to look at the others, as if to say here I was.

They might have been my doubles, but they weren't. They were me, beyond all similarity of clothes. They sat like me, they smoked the way I did. Every movement, every gesture, was mine. Every line of their faces was mine. Standing there, looking at them, meeting their gaze. I thought that anyone of them might be me, and somehow...that I couldn't be sure I wasn't...one...of...them. The instant the thought occurred I knew it was because they wanted it—that to a large extent they knew what I thought, just as I knew what they were thinking about. Not entirely, of course, but I knew.

CHAPTER TWO
Who's Who

I DON'T know how long tile silence lasted...that cold, electric, clairvoyant silence. It was the man who sat in my chair who finally put it into words. He crushed his cigarette deliberately, and he said in a quiet voice, "There's no sense sitting here this way. There must be a solution to this deadlock and we've got to find it."

Suddenly I laughed out loud, I understood what he meant. There was something terrifying in the idea, that, and something more, a sort of fascination that held me in a relentless grip, I had to laugh to find a release.

"But I'm the real Woodruff," I said. "You know I am."

The man at the window said, without turning around, "Are you?"

The man on the couch smiled lazily and held his hands out in a palms-up gesture of inquiry. "But if you're the real Woodruff, who am I? There's really no meaning in what you say. Who is the real Clyde Woodruff? Is he you, or is he…" and he smiled again, because we all knew what he meant.

There was a knock on the door and Robert's voice came through it.

"Professor Jenks is here, Mr. Woody. He wants to come in."

I didn't know what to do. Before I could think, the man who had been sitting in my chair got up and crossed rapidly to the door. He called, "Coming, Robert!" and he opened the door just enough for Robert to see him, "I've been waiting for you, Dave," he said, and he started to open the door.

I didn't want Jenks to come in. I was afraid of what might happen to him if he saw what was in the room. I watched the door open a bit farther, and then the man said, "I'm sorry I ran off, Dave. I felt sick for a moment, but I'm all right now. Be with you as soon as I'm dressed. You use one of the guest rooms." And he closed the door before Jenks had had a chance to come in.

Or, rather, I closed that door. I closed it without moving, without raising a hand, I did it because I *willed* it—as I had willed the words the man at the door had said. And I knew, as we all did, that I had not been alone in wanting the door shut, in not wanting Jenks to come in. At least two others—though which two neither I nor anyone else knew—had shared my thoughts and impulse I

I knew this as I knew everything else. Somehow I had only to seek deep inside myself, or inside the common mind I seemed to share with these four men, to find the answers. I knew then that we were inextricably bound together. When we were alone, each of us shared this common mind, and yet each of us retained a mind that was private. So long as we were alone, and our thoughts and actions concerned none but ourselves, freedom of will and thought and action existed.

But it did not exist when it concerned anyone else!

The moment it became necessary to speak to anyone else (to anyone of the outer world, I found myself thinking) or to show ourselves, or *one* of ourselves—in short, any positive *action* of any kind that involved anyone but us five—from that instant it became necessary to obtain the acquiescence, at least, of a majority of the five of us!

I knew, standing there, that from the moment I had entered this room, I had become the prisoner of these four men. It was their combined will that had so irresistibly driven me home. And I knew also that each of the others was as much a prisoner of the other four as I was. Or, to bring it to its final end, the five of us were, at any time, the captives of three of us who thought and willed alike.

And the most bitter part of this monstrous pact was the knowledge that none of us could predict how our diverse wills might act. For we were basically antagonists, locked in a mortal struggle.

But perhaps you don't understand what I'm trying to say.

THINK of a man, one man. Was he, in reality, one man? Was he not the synthesis of many men? He could think what he liked, desire all he dared. His mind might be the battleground of conflicting desires, he might be tortured by yearnings and lust— but the wounds of these battles and the scars of these lusts, could remain his secret forever. He would be known by what he had done, by the sum of his actions.

Then, suppose there was a way of unlocking these secrets?

Suppose the synthesis of men that was every man—suppose that synthesis was broken down to its dominant components? Suppose the conflicting qualities of his character were released from influence by each other, were allowed to go free, to do with the man as they liked?

Suppose the battle that had always been an inner one became a battle visible to the outer world? Suppose the battleground of the mind was transferred to the battleground of the real world...

For that was what had happened to me.

I knew who these four men were. I knew what they represented in me. I knew what one of them meant when he said: "Who is the *real* Clyde Woodruff?" I knew I was the real Clyde Woodruff, but looking around the room, recognizing the other Woodruffs, the men who were part of me, I understood what he meant.

For David Jenks, seeking to isolate the essential evils in a man, had found his drug. Perhaps it was the overdose, the dose he knew nothing about, that had done it, but his experiment had gone beyond his wildest dreams. The evils in Clyde Woodruff had been released—all of them—but they had now taken their independence in tangible form!

I said it before, and I say it again—I know what it sounds like. It was impossible. It was insane, meaningless, it couldn't have happened. Call it anything you like. *But it had happened...* That was what I meant when I said we were inextricably bound together, that we were the prisoners of each other. We were like that one man who held the many men within him as captives. We had our own minds, but we shared a mind in common. We had our own will, our own ability to act, but it was subject to the combined will, as the actions of every man are, in the final analysis, the decision of the whole man. Here the whole man had become five men.

And that was what I meant when I said we were basically antagonists. For the five men were locked in a struggle for survival, each determined that he alone would survive. Yet, understanding the limitations that bound him, each was ready for expedient alliances, for temporary compromise.

Each of the five was determined that he alone would be the real Clyde Woodruff. Looking at them was like introspecting. Most men can identify the evil in themselves and in that way I could identify the men who were in the room with me...not as individuals, but collectively, I looked at them and knew them, as they must have known me, and some of the terror I had felt was gone.

I wasn't afraid of them anymore. I was Woodruff. I had kept them prisoner before, and I could win again. It was the way of winning that worried me now. There were so many other things happening now. I was mixed up with Dave Jenks problem, my wedding—

"*My* wedding," smiled the man on the couch.

"Mine," said the man at the window.

"Or mine," said the man at the desk. "No one of us will be at the wedding unless all of us—or most of us—agree on it. So it may be any one of us who finally goes to the wedding. Why not me?"

You see, they knew what I was thinking. All these thoughts that I have written down here were theirs, too. All the thoughts that bound us were ours in common. Even the identifications. As I thought of them, it was like thinking out loud, for each of them spoke up.

THE man at the window said, "One of us is a fool."

"One of us is a liar," said the man on the couch.

"One of us is a coward," said the man at the desk.

The man near me, the one who had gone to the door, said, "And one of us is a killer. Which leaves the fifth one here unaccounted for, so we may safely assume that he is the real Woodruff all of us claim to be. The Woodruff who is master of these evils." He added, reflectively, "What a peculiar man this Woodruff is. For all his good nature and such minor failings as lying—"

"He lies magnificently," interrupted the man on the couch. "Only that talent saves him. The man's troubles are legendary."

"Which may explain the fool in the room. And possibly the coward. What an unpleasant thought it is for a man to realize he is a coward. But who could have suspected that Clyde Woodruff could also be a killer? How strange."

"Nonsense!" I snapped. "I've a temper, but it's a rare occasion when I lose it. As for being a coward—"

Jenks was knocking on the door again. "Woody!" he called. "What's keeping you in there? Who's in there with you?"

So he could hear us. It must have sounded as if I was talking to myself. "There's no one in here," I called back.

"But I can hear you talking. Is anything wrong?"

"I'm talking to myself. Will you please sit down and wait for me to get dressed? Entertain Miss Hunter. Give her a drink or something."

He went away. "What was I saying?" I said, irritably. "It doesn't matter now. The main thing is that none of us wants Jenks to come in here and see us, and it's a sure thing that he'll come in if I don't go out. So if you gentlemen will wait here until—"

"You're not going anywhere," said the man at the window.

"But I've got to go. I'm due at Seaside this minute…"

It was a mistake to have spoken as I did. I saw it then. Each of them had referred to Woodruff in the third person, but I had somehow violated the unexpressed agreement. And there was no sense saying I had to go, when my going was for them to decide.

"Precisely," said the man at the window. "You're behaving like a fool. It seems a fair clue to your identity."

"Or like a clever liar," said the man beside me, smiling coldly.

There was nothing I could do, and knowing it, I still went to the door and tried to open it. I couldn't move the doorknob.

My hand wouldn't respond. I stood there, shaking with anger that was past concealing; my mind a furious, bewildered haze, scarcely able to function.

The man on the couch looked at me with a great show of interest. "The temper, I see," he said, flexing his hands. "One could hardly suspect such capacity for anger. But if we're going to take guesses at each other's identity..." and he looked at all of us.

That was the way it began, in unspoken agreement among them. In that, and in all of the ensuing conversation, I took no part. I listened to them with the sensation of a man in a dream, alive only by virtue of a feverish, futile rage that burned within me, but for all of it, I knew I was bound by everything they decided.

FOR WE had silently entered upon a new compact, understanding immediately what the man on the couch had left unfinished. *"... if we're going to take guesses at each other's identity—why not guess with stakes in the balance? Do we all claim to be Clyde Woodruff? Then we'll end the deadlock. We'll make the stakes the only ones that mean anything to us: survival. We'll let each of us have a chance at action, at being Clyde Woodruff..."*

"And the penalty?"

"Instant dissolution! We all understand what we mean by that. We bind ourselves here irrevocably, to surrender our independent existence as the penalty for failure to protect the secret of our identity."

"How will it operate?"

"We'll draw straws to determine an order. The first to go will leave this room as Clyde Woodruff. We four here will, naturally, know everything he does, everything he says and sees and hears. Thus scrutinized, he will remain Clyde Woodruff until one of us ventures a guess as to his identity. If the guess is correct, he surrenders existence—and instantly his place is taken. The next to go becomes Woodruff in whatever circumstance the previous Woodruff was left—no matter where he was, or what he was doing, so that the actions of one affects all."

"And if the guess is wrong?"

"Whoever makes a wrong guess pays the penalty himself."

"How will we determine whether the guess is right or wrong?"

"When one of us makes a guess, the other three here must venture their own guesses too. Whenever three of the four agree, the judgment of the majority will be correct—and the other, wrong."

"What if the guesses vary, and no majority can agree?"

"Then whoever was Woodruff at the time will go to the end of the line. By this action, he will measurably improve his own chances for survival, while at the same time we will be commensurately penalized."

"Ah, but suppose the first to go is identified by three of us as, say, the coward—when in reality he is someone else?"

"The question is meaningless. You might compare it to a man who believed he had acted like a coward. Could anyone but he ever really know the truth? The world may judge a man to have been brave, when he knows the opposite is true. Only a man who knows what he is capable of doing—thus, a man who understands himself—can correctly judge his actions. Only he can weigh the alternatives that faced him as an individual. And as we here are the several components of a man who now understands himself, our decision will be as final as it must be right."

"But what of this: suppose the one whom we judged the coward was the real Woodruff—the fifth one here?"

"Understand this: there is no real Woodruff, in the sense you mean it. We are all the real Woodruff now, but only one of us will survive this, and that survivor will be the real Woodruff. If the one you call real is identified as the coward—he is the coward. And he pays the penalty."

"Very well. But what happens to the majority rule when there are only four left, then three, and finally…two?"

"The one who is Woodruff at any given time will never vote. Excepting him now, four of us will remain, and three will be a majority. When the next one leaves, three will remain here, and two will be a majority. After that, when two are left here in this room, they will have to agree to be able to render a binding decision."

"But, finally, two will be left—one of them here in this room, the other acting as Woodruff. Who will decide between them?"

"Either one may then take his guess. To make it binding, he will have to offer the other incontrovertible evidence."

"Such as?"

"The testimony of a third person, perhaps. Why not? The problem becomes intriguing. Incontrovertible evidence will consist of the testimony of a third person, identifying him in agreement with the guesser."

"But how can such testimony be gotten?"

"We leave that to the devices of the last two survivors."

AND now that the terms of the pact were settled, it remained only to seal them. There was no clasping of hands, no outward sign, and not a word was said, but the bargain was made. I thought then that it might have been different if one of us had been treacherous and untrustworthy, but there wasn't. Whatever evil was in this room, whether cowardice or stupidity, murder or falsehood, the word of all of us was sufficient, I was bound by the decision whether I wanted it or not.

But other things had gone through my mind. I had seen them almost at once, though I hadn't allowed myself to think about them. I had kept telling myself that this fantastic game would work out somehow. But I had not lost sight of the enormously dangerous situation in which Jenks, and to a large extent, in which I was involved. Because of what I now knew, it loomed in the background as something infinitely more fraught with disaster than whatever faced me personally. Insidiously, a subconscious, recurrent fear had grown in me—a fear that Jenks had not told me everything. Was it because he dared tell no one? What was to happen before this had ended...if end it would...this insane web that had trapped me and left me powerless to interfere with the pattern in which it was presently to unravel itself?

I saw only one hope—to draw the first chance, to regain my freedom of action and instantly tell Jenks everything!

One of the four had taken a package of pipe cleaners from my desk. He cut five graduated lengths, hiding the uneven ends in his palm. The shortest was to go first, the others in order. In spite of my almost feverish anxiety, I was aware of the irony in the situation—that each of these four men who wanted to be *me* was still hoping to draw the last position, while I had banked my hope on going first.

Too much hope, for when it was over, I saw that I had drawn the third position...

The man who had been at the window was first. Without a word to us, he went through the connecting door into my bedroom and began to change into the evening clothes my valet had laid out. When he shut the door, he had severed all primary contact with us.

We heard him call Robert (though we knew it without hearing him) and instruct him to close both doors leading to the study. Under no circumstances, he said, were the doors to be opened, or anyone let in.

I went to my desk and took a sheaf of paper and a pen. The others watched me curiously, for since this was a private action and concerned none but me, they had no way of knowing what I intended to do.

I was going to write an account of everything that had happened, and of everything that was going to happen. Since I would know only of actions, my account would be written in third person—but precisely because of this, they were powerless to stop me!

So long as they were with me I could not communicate with the outer world, but I could plan such communication behind the barrier of my own private thoughts, secure in my private world. For whatever good it might somehow accomplish, to whatever use I might put it, I had determined to preserve a record.

You have been reading this record.

The rest of it follows from the time *Clyde Woodruff* left his bedroom. From that moment on, the rest of us in the study were intent upon everything that happened, watching for the slightest clue to the real identity of *Clyde Woodruff,* the clue that would enable us to prove him either a coward, a liar, a killer or a fool—the clue that would mean his end...

CHAPTER THREE
And Then There Were Four

AS Woodruff came out of his room, the first thing that forced itself upon his notice was the strained, miserable look that seemed indelibly imprinted on David Jenks' face. It appeared that Jenks was about to say something, or commit some action that he had already decided, for he got up, unsteady from the effects of several drinks, his manner tense, and began to say, "Woody, I must—"

He got no further, Woodruff cheerfully interrupted by saying, "No, you mustn't. No one must say anything now," and abruptly breaking the trend of conversation, he went on, "Miss Hunter, I see you're drinking them straight, and I congratulate you, Robert, tell William to bring the car around downstairs. And you, Mahoney—"

"Beg pardon, Mr. Woody," Robert broke in, unhappily. "William drove Miss Dykstra to Seaside an hour ago. I tried to tell you, sir, but you kept running in and out of the hall." Confronted by the blank look on Woodruff's face, he blurted, "But you had a dinner engagement at the Dykstras' tonight! Didn't Alonzo list it on your memorandum?"

Woodruff looked at Mahoney and Mahoney grimly shook his head. A groan escaped Robert, but with sudden vehemence he turned on Mahoney. "I trust you'll stop interfering with the way this household is run after this, Mr. Mahoney..."

"Nuts," said Mahoney. "Learn to write English."

"Learn to read it," Robert retorted, acidly, "and nuts in larger quantities to you!" Mopping his forehead, Robert said, "The Dykstras waited until seven, sir, then Miss Dykstra came here and waited and finally went herself. I ordered the convertible."

"Thank you, Robert," Woodruff sighed. "You see how it is, Miss Hunter? Will you pour me a stiff one, please?"

Ann Hunter smiled and poured two drinks, and when Jenks nodded, poured another for him. She raised her glass. "Here's to the complicated life of Mr. Woodruff," she said, "and to Robert, William, Alonzo and Mahoney, the men who keep it that way. And to good pictures of the new complication-to-be in the life of said Mr. Woodruff."

The three touched glasses and drank. "Gee, boss," said Mahoney reflectively, "what a fresh dame, huh?"

"Yep," Woodruff smiled. "Let's get going now." He helped the girl on with her wrap. "Robert, remember the dim-out regulations and turn off the lights." He added, "I'll take care of the study."

He returned to the study and unlocked it. He crossed the room without saying a word to any of the four men there. After he had securely drawn the shades and blackout curtains, he winked solemnly at the man who sat on the couch and went out without turning off the lights.

In the hall, waiting for the elevator, Jenks touched Woodruff's arm, "Woody," he said, softly, "I've got to talk to you. Is everything all right?"

"Sensational," Woodruff grinned. "Couldn't be better..."

It was a beautiful night. Speeding across the Triborough bridge, they saw Manhattan in its strange, newly found darkness, and somehow as lovely in spite of it. Once a plane droned overhead and suddenly glistened like a tiny moth as two searchlight batteries caught it with white, brilliant fingers. Woodruff switched on the radio to end a brief, hot argument that sprang up between Mahoney and Robert, and after that there was little talking. Once, when Woodruff had difficulty lighting a cigarette, Ann Hunter lit one for him. He yelled something about the lipstick on it, grinned at her dismay and took it anyway.

Forty-five minutes after they had started, they left South Shore Drive and became part of a caravan on the winding, private road that led to Seaside. They heard the house before they came to it—a general, diffuse blanket of sound, loud and gay. The gatekeeper called to them as they went by, and Mahoney sprang up to shout something and sat down quickly as they reached the covered bridge.

SUDDENLY, out of the soft gloom, the columned main house of Seaside loomed before them, and Ann Hunter sighed at the sight. Like all shore houses, Seaside had been blacked out, but accidental splashes of light fell from its careless, festive interior to the terraces and gardens. Inside a band was jamming *Blues In The Night,* the saxophones barely audible over the laughter and confusion.

Woodruff put his fingers in his ears and said, "Home again," and that was the last he saw of any of them for a while. For his car had been spotted immediately, and the band began swinging the wedding march, and people poured down from the veranda to carry Woodruff back there amid cheering. After that he was lost in a mass of people, shaking hands and taking his turn as glass-filled trays slid by endlessly. He kept laughingly insistent on finding Dorothy, and though dozens of people left to find her for him, nothing came of these excursions.

He was on the dance floor, almost an hour later, when Robert tugged at his arm and whispered something to him. He left the Conga line and followed Robert to the back of the house. Dorothy Dykstra was waiting there, and a strange man with her.

"Hello, Dorothy," Woodruff mumbled. "I've been looking for—"

"We'll go into that later, Woody," said Dorothy, her voice soft but incisive. "Right now you're expected in the garage." She turned to follow the man with her. They went out the back way, Woodruff hurrying along to keep in sight of the flashlight the man carried.

"They've arrested Mr. Mahoney!" Robert breathed, running along.

"Who?"

"They," Robert panted, mysteriously. "The military police."

In the garage they found Mahoney handcuffed to a banister, his mouth covered with a handkerchief. Vague, furious noises came from the handkerchief and he kept kicking out, trying to reach Bancroft and the other two men with him.

"What's going on here?" cried Woodruff in amazement.

Bancroft, his red face more flushed than ever, looking very little like a detective in his evening clothes, said, "Sorry to trouble you, Mr. Woodruff. We've been having quite a time with this ape, Mahoney. I warned him to stop nosing around, but he wouldn't. He keeps talking to my men and identifying them. About ten minutes ago we found him crawling on all fours along the beach, following Miss Dykstra. I'm going to send him back to the city and clap him into the can."

Mahoney suddenly lunged forward and kicked at Bancroft, missing him by inches, while muffled roars issued from the handkerchief.

"Shut up, Mahoney," said Woodruff, going up to him and taking off the gag. "Now what's going on here?"

"What's going on here, huh?" Mahoney roared, feeling his jaw tenderly. "That's what *I* want to know! There's an army of these guys in here! They got all the roads blocked off—I seen one of them at the gates when we drove in, wearing a uniform like the staff. Everywhere I went I found these guys snooping around!"

"Why were you following Miss Dykstra?"

"I was *not* following Miss Dykstra!" Mahoney shouted. "Anyway, I didn't start out to follow her—I must've gotten mixed up. I see a guy following a guy named Miller—the Miller who works in the laboratory—so I follow him. After awhile he spots me and flashes a G-man badge on me and asks me what I want. I tell him who I am and then I come back and keep following him, and pretty soon he goes up to Miller and I hear him call him something like Mulheimer. Then along comes a woman and she calls him Mulheimer too. Then the G-man ducks and the other two go out to the beach, so I follow them.

The next thing I know, two more of these crazy G-men jump me and it turns out I'm following Miss Dykstra and the professor by mistake. But I started out fol—"

"The whole story's imaginary," Bancroft interposed. "I've already interviewed my men and none of them spoke to any woman or any—"

"You couldn't interview that army in two days!" Mahoney stormed. "I couldn't make a move without some guy stepping up to me and flashing a badge. I must've run into ten guys in half an hour!"

"So help me, Mahoney," said Bancroft, angrily, "I'm going to keep you in the can until I find out what you're up to." To Woodruff he said, "Aside from the men on road detail, I've no more than five here on the grounds."

"Then where's Miller?" Mahoney demanded, "Why don't you look?"

AT THIS point David Jenks came into the garage, and seeing Woodruff, he said, "I've been hunting you everywhere, Woody. Mahoney half frightened the life out of Dorothy. What do you make of it?"

"Be damned if I know," said Woodruff vaguely. He regarded Mahoney with puzzled eyes, then said, "Turn him loose, Mr. Bancroft. I'll be responsible for his behavior."

"Are you sure you—"

"Yes," said Woodruff, impatiently. "I know what I'm doing. I've known Mahoney longer than a day. Turn him loose."

Reluctantly, Bancroft had the handcuffs removed. Mahoney glared after him as he and his men left. "I got to see you alone for a minute, boss," he said. "There's a couple of things—"

"Get out of here immediately," said Dorothy Dykstra. "Get off the grounds. I'm sick of looking at that stupid face of yours."

Mahoney's face flushed but he stood there. "I take orders from the boss," he said, quietly. "Can I see you for a minute?"

"Not now," said Woodruff. "I know all about it; but it's none of your business, Mahoney, just the same. Take the night off. Go get a good drunk for once in your life. I'll see you later."

Mahoney walked out of the garage without a word, and Robert discreetly went after him. Woodruff turned to Dorothy. "I'm sorry about Mahoney, dear. He takes his job very seriously. You shouldn't have said what you did to him."

"Is that all you have to say to me?" Standing there, her eyes were cool even now and anger made her quite beautiful, emphasizing the imperious tilt of her chin. Tall, her carriage erect, her blonde hair impeccably arranged, her feelings showed only in her voice.

"What else do you want me to say, dear?"

"Nothing," she said, and turning to Jenks, "Will you please take me back to the house?"

Woodruff took her arm. "Please, Dorothy, let's not quarrel. Not tonight. I said I'm sorry. I'm sorry about everything, about being late, about missing my appointment. It just couldn't be helped. Didn't Dave tell you what happened at the laboratory?"

"I didn't," said Jenks, embarrassed. "Bancroft said to keep it quiet." To Dorothy he said, "It was really my fault, Miss Dykstra."

In spite of her control, her eyes were clearly filled with tears. "I know it was, Dr. Jenks," she said, softly. "It's never Woody's fault, no matter what it was. If Robert isn't around to take the blame, he finds someone else who will."

"But darling, you might give me a chance to explain…"

"It's a little late for explanations. My parents were so upset tonight they wouldn't come here with me. You know I don't mind your occasional lapses, but we're getting married Sunday. You might have had the decency to remember that. Instead the house is filed with hordes of people I detest, gamblers and louts and Wall Street speculators—"

"But I'm a speculator myself, dear."

"You're also Clyde Woodruff, the third. You might spare my friends the necessity of mingling with these people!" She was pronouncing each word incisively now, her anger released, "Instead I find the place full of detectives and a mysterious scandal apparently under way. Your bodyguard—and you wouldn't need one if you stopped drinking—follows me around and when I order him off the place, you subject me to the humiliation of allowing him to remain!"

Jenks, his embarrassment more acute than before, had slowly gone out of the garage, leaving them alone. Woodruff said nothing for a full minute. His lips were tense, and a little ball of muscle showed in his jaw. "If you're quite through," he said, "I'll take you back, now."

"You haven't answered me!"

"I'm not going to. The only kind of answer I'd give you now would get me slapped."

SHE hesitated for a fraction of an instant, then deliberately raised her hand and slapped Woodruff across the face—and simultaneously there was a brilliant blue-white flash of light!

Woodruff spun around. Standing on the stairway that led to the upper story of the garage was Ann Hunter, camera in hand. She started back up the stairs when Dorothy cried, "Come down here, you!"

Ann hesitated. Woodruff said, "Please come here, Miss Hunter." She started down the stairs slowly, folding her camera and removing the used flash bulb, her expression non-committal.

"Who are you?" Dorothy demanded, "What were you doing there?"

Woodruff said, "Dorothy, this is Miss Hunter. Miss Hunter, Miss Dykstra, my fiancée. Miss Hunter's here to take pictures of our wedding for a magazine, *Life,* or *Look,* I think. I arranged for her to—"

"*You* arranged?" Dorothy said acidly. "Really, Woody, this is too much. You might have had the common decency to ask *me* about it. As for you, Miss whatever your name is, I suppose decency is too much to expect from one of your kind—"

"Please, Dorothy, Miss Hunter is a guest here."

"Indeed! Are you defending her too? Are you telling me that I must allow your guests to pry into my personal affairs—to come sneaking around and taking pictures of…of…"

"Of you slapping Mr. Woodruff?" Ann supplied. "Yes, I did get a shot of it. Should be a beauty. But you're mistaken about my prying, Miss whatever your name is. Robert said I could keep my equipment over the garage. Your voices were so loud I couldn't help overhearing."

"I suppose you couldn't help taking that picture, either?"

"Not if I want to get a really good set of pictures."

"Really, this is too much! Clyde, I demand that you destroy that picture and have this woman escorted off the premises!"

After an awkward moment of silence, Woodruff said, "Of course I'll attend to the picture, Dorothy, but I can't ask Miss Hunter to—"

"I've said all I'm going to say about it!" With this, Dorothy Dykstra turned and walked rapidly out of the garage.

"Dorothy! Wait a moment!" Woodruff called. He took a step after her, but she had already disappeared into the darkness. Woodruff stood there gloomily. He scratched his head and sighed.

"I'm sorry I caused you so much trouble, Mr. Woodruff."

"Well, there's no help for it now." He surveyed her with absent eyes. "I suppose I'd have done the same thing myself, in your place. But I'm afraid I'll have to ask you to destroy the picture."

"And leave the premises?"

"I…I'm afraid so."

"Funny," the girl said, thoughtfully.

"What is?"

"The way you keep using the word *afraid*. You're afraid this and afraid that. Yet all the time I keep thinking you're probably not the least bit afraid of anything. Or are you? I wonder…"

"It's just a speaking habit, I guess."

"Maybe. Still, the psychologists say our speech habits reveal a great deal about us. Ever go to a psychologist, Mr. Woodruff? You'd be a wonderful subject, I think."

"Why do you say that?"

"Oh, I don't know. Just a feeling. You seem so—so different from the man I thought you were when I first met you. Not that the change has been radical, but it's there. I feel it without quite knowing what it is, exactly, that I feel. But you've changed somehow."

Woodruff said, quietly, "There's an excellent reason for what you feel, Miss Hunter. You're very perceptive—almost intuitive. How do you think I've changed?"

She smiled. "You like to talk about yourself, don't you? Shows you're egocentric or something. Well, I suppose I'd better get my things together. Would you give me a hand?"

THEY both went upstairs. The blinds had been drawn and a light was burning. A table was piled high with cartons of flash bulbs and there were several packages of differently sized film. Two more cameras lay on the table, ready for use. Close by were several shallow pans filled with clear liquid like water, but with a slight acidic odor. A red, shaded bulb had been screwed into one of the hanging sockets.

"Looks like you prepared a darkroom up here," said Woodruff.

"Sort of. I wanted to develop a few test shots to see where I was going. An assignment like this has to be hit right the first time—a Woodruff wedding generally comes along once a generation."

She began opening the camera she had used. "Well, here goes a shot that might have made photographic history:

Dorothy Dykstra Slaps Woody Woodruff Forty Hours Before Their Fashionable Wedding...I don't often get a chance to expose a film like this. Hold this, please."

"Wait a second," said Woodruff. He smiled to himself, then said, "Do you suppose you could develop the picture before you exposed it? I mean, I'd like to have it. Sort of a memento." He put the camera down. "I don't often get slapped, you know."

"Of course," Ann said, returning his smile. She busied herself a moment, then turned off the light and snapped on the red one. "May fog a little, but I need some light. The hell of it is I could have taken the shot without either of you knowing. I've a camera here that shoots with the new infrared film—doesn't need a flash bulb or any light at all hardly."

"I almost wish you had."

"Used the infrared, you mean? It needs preparation. I was up here when they brought your man Mahoney in. I had no idea it was going to develop into a rough and tumble, or I'd have gotten ready."

He watched her take out the film pack and drop the negative into one of the pans. She played it with a pair of tongs. "Would you mind letting the water run, Mr. Woodruff? I've a hose feeding from the faucet. There now, it's coming along." After a moment she said, "Why did you say you almost wished I had used the infrared film?"

"I don't know, really. I don't like to get people into trouble with their bosses. This may be trouble for you, Miss Hunter?"

"More water, please. Trouble? My managing editor'll probably get to the bottom of it, and if Miss Dykstra writes him a letter—"

"What makes you say that?"

"Just a hunch—the way I size her up. She'll probably write an insulting letter to *Look* and *Life* both. Right? You needn't answer. And then I suppose I'll run a good chance of getting fired. Stories like these are hard enough to arrange without silly female photographers spoiling them. Look out—this thing drips. Here we are…"

"Miss Hunter—"

"Yes?" She lifted the wet negative and turned on the light. "It is a beauty," she said, holding it up. Woodruff stood behind her and looked at it quizzically. "I don't suppose you can read a negative," she said. "Takes practice. If you've some time now, I'll be glad to give you a contact print with this crude apparatus I brought along."

"Sure," said Woodruff. "I've got plenty of time. You go to work and I'll come back with a couple of drinks. What'll it be?"

"Straight Scotch. We've got water here."

Woodruff went back to the main house. He went into the pantry and ran into Alonzo, who was sitting on a high stool, a bottle in his hand. "Mista Woody!" he cried out, his pleasant Filipino face tragic, "I look every place for you. Robert, he say I forget—"

Woodruff smiled. "It's all right, Lonz. You stay with that bottle and forget the rest of it." The pantry staff kept getting in his way trying to help. The noise was louder than ever; the party was in full swing. Doors kept opening and closing and half a dozen guests were puttering around the refrigerator while the cooks kept yelling about the food that was to be found at the buffet tables.

As Woodruff was about to leave, Robert came running in ponderously, "Mr. Woody, Professor Jenks wants you! He's been searching for you since you left the garage. I'll take you to him."

"No, you won't," said Woodruff, "Don't tell him you saw me."

WHEN he returned to the upper story of the garage, Ann said, "I think your friend the Professor is looking for you. I heard him come in downstairs and call your name."

"You didn't answer?"

"No. I was afraid you might not get back. With the drink, I mean," she added. "Curious thing about the picture. There's someone in the background. I imagined I saw it in the negative, but it's quite plain here. What do you think of it?"

Woodruff looked at the small, wet sheet of paper. "It's a wow of a shot," he said, wryly. There he was, his back arching a little as the blow caught him flush across the face. Dorothy's face was half-hidden by the angle, but what showed of it was alive with anger. By contrast, his own expression seemed quite calm, his eyes fixed on her. "Did I really look like that?" he asked.

"At that moment, anyway. You had a distinctly different look on you before and after; I didn't like it. But what about the silent observer here in the background? Does it look like two men to you?" She added, as Woodruff studied the print, "Pity the red light fogged a bit. It looks to me like a peeper or two; that white spot looks like a huge, glaring eye."

Woodruff handed Ann the drink he had poured. He filled a glass with water and both drank. "Feels good," he said. "About this—one of them looks somewhat like Jenks. He went out just about then, I think. Embarrassed him, especially since this whole mess was his doing."

"You mean he wasn't really covering up for you?"

Woodruff hesitated, pouring another round. "I shouldn't have said that. Things are going on around here, as you may have guessed if you heard Mahoney and those F.B.I. men." He touched glasses with her. "But if it isn't Jenks, my guess is that it's a couple of Miss Dykstra's blue-blooded friends feasting on a juicy bit of gossip. Would you care to know what I think of them, Miss Hunter?"

Ann smiled pleasantly. "Not that I don't enjoy your company, Mr. Woodruff, but I'd rather not. It really isn't any of my business." She began gathering up her things. "It strikes me I've been a little, too personal already. You've been very kind."

"I suppose you're right. My fault. See here!" he said suddenly. "What are you doing?"

"I'm packing, Mr. Woodruff. Remember?"

"Nothing of the sort. You've already given me the negative, and that's enough. I'm not going to get you fired. You stay here."

She stopped packing her camera and let her hands fall to her side. "You're letting yourself in for more trouble than it's worth," she said.

"I'm afraid I am—dammit—I'm not afraid I am! Anyway, I want you to stay. You're a good photographer. I like your pictures. I may be a little high but I know what I'm doing. You just go on about your business."

"I don't know how to thank you, Mr. Woodruff."

"By having the next dance with me, Miss Hunter."

"Thank you, but no. I'm here to work. And besides..."

"Besides what?"

"It wouldn't be wise, would it?"

"I'm afraid you're right." He put his glass down. "I said it again, didn't I?" he laughed. "Well, so long for now. Stay out of trouble, Miss Hunter. And out of Miss Dykstra's way, if you can."

She laughed with him and her blue eyes sparkled. "I can and I intend to, Mr. Woodruff. And thanks, again."

WOODRUFF wandered back to the house again. He pushed his way through crowds wherever he went, watching them have a good time. He seemed to be preoccupied. Finally he ended by returning to the veranda, where he ran into Ray Vanness and a gang that had decided to practice choir singing; they were doing a solemn version of *Home On The Range*. Vanness disengaged himself from the singing long enough to say something about Woodruff's lateness for their lunch appointment.

"Thanks for taking the check, old boy," he mumbled affectionately. "And thanks for the swell party. Swell party—did I tell you? And thanks for taking that check. Got to have lunch again with you soon."

"Sure," said Woodruff, going away. He wasn't walking any too steadily—there were too many drinks in him for that, but he kept on wandering about aimlessly. Once he was invited by a group to drink a toast to the host, and he drank. It was immediately after that that he returned to the pantry. Alonzo was sitting on the floor, in a corner. His face brightened as he saw Woodruff. "Lonz, have you seen Mahoney?" Woodruff asked. "Or Robert? I want to see a familiar face."

"I am familiar face, Mista Woody," Alonzo beamed, waving his almost empty bottle. "Sit here with me. Wait for more faces to come."

Woodruff broke open a new bottle and sat down with Alonzo behind a barricade of empty soda boxes. The bottle was half gone and the Bataan peninsula battle thoroughly discussed before Robert appeared in the pantry again. Ann Hunter was with him. She waved, raised her camera and took a shot of Woodruff and Alonzo in the barricaded corner.

"Hey!" Woodruff shouted after her retreating form. "Come back!"

"Work to be done!" she laughed.

"Mr. Woody," said Robert, anxiously, "have you seen Professor Jenks yet?"

"No. Where's Mahoney? Got to see Mahoney." He regarded Robert carefully, then pronounced, "You been drinking, Robert. Shame on you! Faultless butler caught stinko. Sit down and wait for Mahoney."

"The guests keep forcing liquor on me, sir. And Mr. Mahoney was with Professor Jenks, the last I saw of him. May I take you there? Or will you wait here until I bring the professor?"

"Both," said Woodruff. "I'll do both, and I'm the man can do it. I got friends can help me be in two places at once. More. Five places." He laughed, then stopped speaking abruptly. "Okay. I wait."

"Hurry, fat Robert!" Alonzo cried cheerfully. "I wait, too!"

When Robert returned a few minutes later, bringing Jenks with him. Woodruff was busy helping Alonzo blow his nose. Alonzo was wailing, his face tear-stained, "So sorry I forget to write in memorandum. Sorry…"

Jenks shoved the boxes to one side.

He grasped Woodruff's hands and hauled him to his feet. "Woody," he said, sharply, "You've got to pull yourself together. I must talk to you. Robert, brew some black coffee and bring it to the private library. Knock before you come in."

Still holding him, Jenks guided Woodruff to the library. Woodruff sank into a chair, blinking at Jenks affectionately. How strange Jenks looked. The paleness of his face was accentuated by a large blue vein that pulsated visibly on his forehead.

"Woody, I've got to tell you this because you've a right to know. I've thought about telling you ever since I found out." His voice had quieted to a whisper. "I told you I didn't know what so large an amount of the compound might do to you. When I went home, I looked through our earlier notes, because I had remembered. I prayed I was wrong...but I wasn't. Woody, you've got to tell me what's been happening to you— what you feel—what you think about..."

Woodruff stirred in his chair. "What I think about?" he repeated. "The same things, I guess. Nothing more or less. And nothing's been happening to me. What makes you think anything has?"

"Because something must...because the truth is the amount you took is going to kill you!"

WOODRUFF stared at him. Presently, he said, "You're sure?"

Jenks covered his face with his hands for a moment. "Yes," he said, brokenly. "If nothing's happened to you—if you've felt nothing strange, then the only answer is that the concentrate was too strong to accomplish its initial purpose. It hasn't changed you. If it had, we would have a chance. We could combat its manifestations while we hoped to find an antidote. But as it is, the drug in you is slowly eating you, sapping your will and strength. Instead of weakening parts of you, it is weakening your body entirely..."

Jenks stopped speaking and looked carefully at Woodruff. Then he said, deliberately, "You're lying to me, Woody! You *have* changed!"

Woodruff said nothing while he lit a cigarette. He drew a long drag. "That's a strange thing to say, Dave," he said, frowning. "Do I seem different to you? Am I a different Woody from the one you've always known? What makes you say I've changed?"

"I can't place it," Jenks said slowly, "I don't know *how* you've changed, but it's there. I know it. I sense it..."

Woodruff's frown deepened. He was about to say something when there was a knock on the door and Robert came in with a tray. "Never mind the coffee, Robert," Woodruff said. "I'm quite sober now." He waited until the door had closed before he said, "You know, Dave, I've never heard you speak like this. You're the kind of scientist who never uses words like *sensing* anything. You're—"

"Stop it!" Jenks said, hoarsely. "Don't you understand that I'm trying to tell you your life is hanging in the balance?"

"But what if it has changed me?"

"Then you must tell me. It's our one hope now."

"If I've changed then I won't die, after all?"

Jenks just stood there, looking at him. Finally he turned away and said, very quietly, "I don't know what's going to happen to you now. I can't understand you..."

Woodruff got up and went to him. He took Jenks' arm. "I'm sorry, Dave. It's just that what you've told me is such a...a shock to me that I don't know how to react. What does a man say when he's told he's going to die? I don't know what to say. I've never thought of dying. I'm...I'm rather young for a thing like that." He was standing at the fireplace now, and he said, quite calmly. "How long do you think it'll be?"

"I don't know. Not long."

"Then there's—"

Suddenly the door had burst open and Mahoney rushed in, Robert at his feet, trying to stop him. "Boss, they're at it again!"

Mahoney cried. "I tell you there's something screwy going on here. I just saw that Miller with the dame again and she keeps calling him Mulheimer."

"Listen. Mahoney," Woodruff began. "I haven't the—"

"I know what you think but if you'll just come with me I'll prove it. That guy of Bancroft's is in on it! You've got to come with me..." He stood there, breathing heavily, tortured by Woodruff's indecision. "Dammit!" he cried. "Have I ever tipped you wrong?"

A moment later, Woodruff had followed him out of the room.

Mahoney led the way around the back of the house and across one of the lawns. He knew his way like a cat. He ran along a gravel path toward one of the bathhouses, leaving it when they were a hundred yards short. In the moonless night the sky was a dusty velvet robe. The sounds that echoed from the house, from many corners of the grounds, seemed unreal here in the stillness. The surf roared against the rocks near them with a sound like someone hushing them.

Then the ornate spire of a small covered pavilion, set on a high point overlooking the beach, rose before them, faintly silhouetted against the stars. Mahoney and Woodruff crept along toward it. They could hear three voices in hushed conversation.

"...you like to have them know you're Hans Mulheimer, Mr. Miller?"

"No," said a man's voice carefully. "But you're asking something—"

"Something you can deliver," said a woman's voice, "Something you've got on you, no doubt, or hidden away within easy reach."

"I haven't, I tell you!"

"All right, then," said the first voice. "We'll meet your price. I tell you we can't wait for the Sunday appointment."

"I don't know what you're—"

"Shhh!" Silence. Then, "There's someone hiding there!"

SUDDENLY a light! It stabbed out from the pavilion and caught Woodruff full in its beam. The next instant there was a heavy sound, the sound of flesh meeting flesh. Someone groaned and the light fell crashing to the wooden floor and began rolling. A woman screamed and her voice was suddenly muffled. A hand reached down for the light and snapped it off.

Then Mahoney's voice. "Shut up, the both of you, or you'll go out like that light." And the least bit louder: "Okay, boss, I got it under control."

But Woodruff, overcoming a first moment of bewilderment, had already started for the pavilion. He clambered up, half groping in the darkness. Mahoney struck a match. The flickering light revealed Jenks' assistant, Miller, and a young woman. Near Mahoney's feet, a man lay on the floor, "Sneaked up nice and quiet-like, huh, boss?" Mahoney said. "I'd—"

"Look out!" Even as he cried the warning, Woodruff sprang. The last split instant of light, as the match went out, had revealed the prone man's movement and the dull gleam of a revolver as he slid it out of a pocket, and then the man had started rising from the floor.

Woodruff's shoulders smashed into the man's middle and hurled him back to the floor. His arms encircled Woodruff and both fell together, crashing into a pair of benches, rolling over while Woodruff pounded his fists into the man's face. Mahoney came in with a rush. The man lashed out a foot and caught Mahoney in the belly. Mahoney went down with a choking gasp. But as the man had kicked, Woodruff swung his body about and fell on the man's out-stretched hand. He caught the revolver firmly between his knees. He brought his hands up...

* * *

"STOP it," I said. "I call for identification."

I looked about me at the three men in the room with me. Two of them had been elsewhere in the house, but they had returned to this room when *Woodruff* had gone out with Mahoney. Had they, as I had, also felt that some climactic point was near? The struggle in which we had been silent accomplices as well as witnesses had affected each of us greatly. It emphasized how closely bound together we were.

But had I called a halt too late? Or too quickly? The elimination of the first *Woodruff* was a thing to be desired for its own sake, but it was just as important to eliminate these others. If I had been late with my call—but that was impossible; I had, after all, been the one to make the call. At worst, even if these men had arrived at the same conclusion, I had beaten them to it by a moment or two.

But what if I had called too soon? What if the things that were apparent to me were still mysteries to them? What if my analysis was too premature for them? For there was no such thing as objective correctness among us: it was the majority opinion that would be correct. And perhaps I had not given that majority opinion time enough to reach my conclusion...

I realized then how dangerous a course I had taken, and I resolved not to risk it again. It hardly occurred to me that I might have been voted wrong, for if they did not agree with me, they could hardly have pieced together enough evidence to substantiate any other view. If they did not agree with me, the odds greatly favored a split opinion. And if that happened I had lost time, for the first *Woodruff* would then go to the end of the line.

Because I had called, I wrote my identification first. I scribbled it on a bridge score-pad and tossed sheets of paper to the others.

He had been clever, that first *Woodruff.* There had been no clues in his actions to the very last. My identification of him had been the result of careful reasoning from the *lack* of clues. At no time had he done anything I might not have done. Indeed, watching him, hearing him talk, had frightened me, so perfectly was he Woodruff, the real.

But it was more than that. It was not only that he, living and breathing and being Woodruff to even those who had known him for years, had seemed so terribly real—but that we in the room had seemed, to ourselves and to each other, so horribly unreal. For, in that strange way that we knew things, we knew that so long as our compact held, we were like shadows. We were nothings, waiting for a chance to exist. We had no need of food or drink. We could not tire. We needed no sleep. Here in this room we would exist like substanceless beings, as divorced from the world of the living as if we had long been buried.

And now even our meager view of that world had ceased, shut off from the moment I made the call to identify. The very meaning of time had changed where it concerned us. However long it would now take us to reach some decision, between the time we had last seen *Woodruff* and the time our decision would affect, to the outer world that time would be an infinitesimal fraction of a second. The continuity of *Woodruff's* existence and his actions would be unbroken.

It was useless even to think of science in a matter like this. Perhaps that was what lay behind Jenks' questions. Had he really *sensed* the difference, as he had said? The word must have been repugnant to him, for he was a scientist even in his thoughts, but perhaps even he had felt there was no other word for what he felt. But why had *Woodruff* so steadfastly refused to tell Jenks what had happened to him? It had been a strange conversation from the beginning. *Woodruff's* fear had vanished the moment Jenks told him that only some evidence of change would indicate there was no fear of death—for *Woodruff* himself was at that moment the most complete evidence that the change had occurred. And evidently, for his own reasons, with the fear gone, Woodruff had decided to keep the story to himself, and his reason seemed clear enough.

I would have told Jenks. I had reason to tell him. The others could only lose by it. Still, it had been strange. Or did it only seem that way because I had seen it through the eyes of a Woodruff who was not, after all, the real me?

THE identifications had all been written. One of the three opened them. He laid them down on the desk.

"We all agree," he said.

I nodded. It was over for the first *Woodruff.* We had all understood the lack of clues. He had lied, but so did every man—so would the real Woodruff lie, and I damn well knew it. It proved nothing; it revealed nothing of the essential character of the man. The first *Woodruff* had not been a man whose life was built on falsehood. And though he had said foolish things and behaved foolishly, he had not been essentially a fool. Cowardly? He accepted the consequences of his actions with deadly calm. Even the first mention of death, when Jenks had spoken to him, had not shaken the structure of his character. And few men morally or intellectually cowards would have shown such unthinking, instantaneous physical courage as he had, hurling himself at the man Mahoney had knocked down.

The four identifications agreed: *Killer.*

The ability to kill was a thing a man carried within him. It was a thing hidden from the world, often from himself. Even those closest to him might never know until the fatal moment came. To the world such a man might be anything, liar, coward, and fool included, but that he was potentially a killer—that they could never know until he had shown it.

The killer was not a man. He was a deadly potential.

It was a realization to make any man shudder. I make no bones about its effect on me. I had always had a temper, but seldom shown it. The world was my oyster. It went smoothly enough. But what, I thought, if I hadn't been born into money—money that oiled the machinery of life until even a bad temper was a strange luxury? I had my horrible answer.

When I broke my musing and looked about the room again, I saw that there were only two men left with me.

The second *Clyde Woodruff* had gone.

CHAPTER FOUR
Three Agree

HE BROUGHT his hands up to the man's throat. He dug his fingers in deep, crushing the man's windpipe, feeling the flesh quiver under the pressure of his hands. Again and again the woman screamed. Woodruff relentlessly held his grip while the man thrashed about, his breathing a harsh, rattling sound.

Mahoney crawled back, the breath still knocked out of him, and he tried to unseat Woodruff. "Boss," he groaned, "let go—you're killing him!" Woodruff shook him off, his hands constricted around the man's throat. Mahoney swung himself back, butting savagely with his head.

That was when three dark figures came running into the pavilion. A flashlight told the story at a glance. One of the men grabbed Woodruff and toppled him. The second clamped a hand over the screaming woman's mouth. The third, in answer to Mahoney's cry, took after Miller, who had vaulted the wall and disappeared.

Swiftly, the entire group was hustled down to the bathhouse along the dark shores of the beach. Behind drawn shades the lights were turned up. "Here's the gun he pulled," said Mahoney. He was standing with Woodruff, both of them disheveled and battered. The woman was sobbing hysterically. The man Woodruff had fought was slumped in a cloth chair in a corner, holding his throat and trying to catch his breath.

Bancroft took the gun from Mahoney and went to the man who owned it. He ran his hands through the man's pockets. He took out a wallet, flipped it open. There was an F.B.I. badge pinned to it. Bancroft's face clouded.

The door swung open and the other of Bancroft's men came in, his gun stuck in Miller's back. "Miller..." Bancroft said, softly, then, to Mahoney, he said, "Tell me what happened out there."

Mahoney told the story quickly, passing over the fight. The woman cried, "Tell him he tried to kill him! Tell him, why don't you!"

Woodruff said, "She means me. I guess I did try to kill him. I must have been out of my mind."

"It doesn't matter," said Bancroft shortly. "You don't know who you're dealing with. They'd just as soon have killed you." He broke open the gun Mahoney had given him. "These shells..." he began to say, but he stopped in confusion. He looked up, frowning, and indicating Miller, said to one of his men, "Frisk him."

The F.B.I. man went through Miller's clothes swiftly. From one of his pockets he took out a flat packet of papers, wrapped in oilskin.

Suddenly Miller, who until now had been silent with fear, found his voice, "You can't do this to me!" he cried. "You can't make a case against me by planting papers on me! Those papers aren't mine! They were never in my pocket!"

"What are you talking about?" said Bancroft. He stood before the trembling man. "Who put these papers in your pocket?" But Miller, now that he had spoken, fell silent again, his eyes traveling from one to the other, his breath coming short and uneven. Bancroft opened the packet and went through the papers, and after a few moments, he motioned Woodruff to him. "Take a look at these, Mr. Woodruff," he said. "They look like the stuff, all right."

Woodruff examined the papers. They were covered with figures and chemical symbols, thin sheets completely covered with fine writing. At the bottom of the third page there was a short note. It said: *"...care must be taken with the fourth distillate, and above all with the residue of the compound—high volatility. When preparing explosive..."* He read no further.

"Mr. Bancroft," he said, "I don't think these are the notes."

"What makes you think so?" said Bancroft, his amazement growing.

"I can't go into it now, but if you'll send for Professor Jenks, I'm sure he'll bear me out. I think there's evidence here to show that someone wanted us to *think* Miller had the notes."

BANCROFT nodded. "Joe," he said to one of his men. "Bring Professor Jenks here." He stood there silently a few moments, lost in thought, absently playing with his fingers as if he were counting something on them. Finally he turned to Miller and said, civilly, "Your real name is Hans Mulheimer, isn't it? You needn't be afraid to answer. This man here was impersonating the F.B.I. Mr. Woodruff will tell you we're the real thing. I think I understand what you've been through, Mr. Miller, but you've got to tell us exactly what happened. If you can help us, we'll help you."

Miller said, "You don't think I'm a Nazi spy?"

"We have no reason to think so."

"But he...he said so." Miller pointed to the man whom Woodruff had fought. He seemed slow in understanding what Bancroft had told him. "He said the F.B.I. knew my name was Mulheimer, that he was going to arrest me as a Nazi spy unless I...I..."

"Unless what? Begin at the beginning and give us the details."

"I couldn't understand him..." Miller said, slowly. "I was dancing with this lady when it began. She called me Hans Mulheimer. I was frightened. I had changed my name a long time ago. I have a mother and two brothers in Germany—I didn't want the German agents here to bother me. It happened to friends of mine...they were forced to give money...they were threatened...I was afraid if I were known as a German I couldn't get work. I'm a chemical engineer..."

"I understand. What about this woman?"

"I went outside with her. She took me to this man. He showed me his badge. He said the F.B.I. knew all about me. He said that if I wanted to stay out of prison to do everything this woman told me. She took me to the beach. She said she knew I had stolen Professor Jenks' notes and that I would have to return them."

"Yes?"

"But I hadn't stolen the notes. I hadn't stolen anything! And when I told her that, she seemed satisfied. She said she would stay with me for the rest of the evening, and we went back to the house."

Bancroft said, "Tell me, Mr. Miller—while you were on the beach with her, did you hear any commotion—any sounds that might have been, say, fighting? Try to remember very carefully."

"Yes, I remember it distinctly. It happened shortly after we got to the beach. It was a few hundred feet behind us. It sounded like a serious fight, but this man with the badge came to us and said that some drunks were brawling. He told us to go back to the house, and that he would want to see me later."

Bancroft said, somewhat absently, "Those drunks must have been you, Mahoney."

"Sure," Mahoney said, sarcastically, "me getting drunk—a guy that never monkeys with anything stronger than orange juice. What they heard was those jerk men of yours grabbing me from behind."

"Anyway, it ties together," said Bancroft. "You followed Miller and this woman to the beach and then accidentally got your trails crossed and followed Miss Dykstra and the professor instead." He turned to Miller and asked, "Then what happened?"

"We were at the house together until half an hour ago, then this lady took me out to the pavilion. She started calling me Mulheimer again and saying I was in serious trouble. I couldn't understand it. Then this man with the badge came back and they stopped. About ten minutes later they started in all over again, saying all kinds of things—"

"You mean," said Bancroft, "things like they would meet your price? And the Sunday appointment? Did you understand that?"

"No," said Miller, bewildered. "They hadn't mentioned those things before. I hadn't heard a word about money or a Sunday appointment until that moment. That's what Mr. Mahoney overheard."

"Thank you, Mr. Miller," said Bancroft. "You've cleared things up very handsomely."

HE WENT over to where the man sat in the cloth chair. The man kept looking at the floor. Bancroft took hold of his hair and yanked his head up. "Where's Harrison?" he said. The man said nothing. Bancroft slapped him hard across the face. "What did you do to Harrison?" he demanded.

The man said, "You've got nothing on me." He looked into Bancroft's hard eyes. "You can beat my brains out," he said. "I won't talk."

Bancroft stepped away from him. He motioned Mahoney and Woodruff to follow him. The three men went into an adjoining room, keeping the door between the two rooms open. Bancroft held out his hand, showing them the shells he had taken from the man's gun. Mahoney picked one up, then another, until he had examined them all.

"Blank cartridges!" said Mahoney, puzzled.

"Phonies," Bancroft nodded. "Fake—like the rest of this business. Like the notes you said were fakes, Mr. Woodruff. Someone wanted us to think they were the real notes. This whole affair has been a blind alley, carefully planned and executed."

"I don't see it," said Woodruff, "How could they possibly hope to make us believe they were the real notes? It would take Jenks half a minute to decide the truth. And what about the rest of it?"

"The notes are the only wrong thing in it...but maybe they were playing for time. Maybe they hoped the notes would confuse us long enough for them to carry out some plan. Maybe we're too late already." His face was grim as he added,

"We're too late about one thing—one of my men, Harrison, is missing."

"Tom Harrison?" asked Mahoney.

"Yes," said Bancroft. "He was assigned to follow Miller. When you first came up with the story about Mulheimer, I checked. I've got Greeley at the main gate and the men call in every half hour to him to report; it keeps us from being seen together too often. Well, Greeley said Harrison had called in and hadn't said a word about Miller and any woman. But the man who called wasn't Harrison—that's obvious now. They got rid of Harrison somewhere and got one of their own men to call in, keeping us from finding out.

"The rest of it follows from there. They planned to have you, Mahoney, overhear enough of the conversation between the woman and Miller to follow them."

"What?" said Mahoney, astonished. "Where do you get that?"

"Because the woman called him Mulheimer only on the two occasions when she knew that you were following. First, the time they led you to the beach—as soon as you were stopped from following, they called it off. Then they laid low as long as you, evidently, didn't follow Miller again—"

"I got a terrific calling down," said Mahoney. "I was practically fired. No, that was okay with me, boss. I didn't mind—you were in a fix yourself with Miss Dykstra. But after awhile I couldn't help following them again. I didn't like the way it looked."

"It was designed that way," said Bancroft. "They wanted you to follow again, and you did. They obligingly led you to the pavilion and stayed there long enough for you to bring someone back with you, and the instant they spotted you, they went into that song and dance with poor Miller. Naturally, he didn't understand what they meant by offering him a price and a Sunday appointment—that was meant for your ears.

"All they had on Miller was some harmless information that he had once changed his name. He was frightened by it, especially when a badge was flashed on him, the same badge that was used on you, Mahoney. And that was enough to hook Miller into serving their plan. The notes were obviously planted on him while he was in the pavilion."

Bancroft nodded sullenly. "Even the gun was kept harmless. They wanted no trouble. I don't suppose they reckoned on being caught so soon. They underestimated Mahoney...and your temper, Mr. Woodruff."

"But where does it all lead?" said Woodruff.

"I don't know...yet. So far we've played the game according, to their schedule. We've been fooled according to plan and done everything they wanted us to do. But maybe—"

THE door to the other room opened and the man Bancroft had sent for Jenks came in. He ran into the adjoining room, out of breath. "We can't find Jenks anywhere!" he said. "Nobody's seen him for half an hour or more. And there's hell to pay all over the place: Ryerson picked up three men who were carrying counterfeit F.B.I. badges, and the way it looks there may be plenty more around here!"

Bancroft snapped, "This is it, but we're one step ahead of them! They've gotten Professor Jenks out of the way to keep us from finding out the notes are fakes!" He faced Woodruff. "You're sure they *are* fakes, Mr. Woodruff?"

"Positive."

"All right then, we'll play their game. We'll act as if we still thought we had the real notes—we'll close the case! We'll hustle Miller and the others to the can and give them enough leeway to tip us—"

"But what about Jenks?"

Bancroft said grimly, "I don't know, Mr. Woodruff, but we're in this for higher stakes than a man's life, than any—"

"I don't give a damn about any man's life!" Woodruff cried. "My friend Jenks isn't a professional hunter like your men are! You got him mixed up in this game of yours—you're supposed to protect him, not use him as bait! Game my foot! If you want to play games, play them with your men's lives, not with…"

The outer door had opened as Woodruff spoke, and David Jenks came in, pushing past the man Bancroft had left outside. He walked in quickly, surveying the rooms and the people there, his face puzzled as he saw the way his entrance was received.

"What's the matter?" he said. "What's going on here? Robert said some of Mr. Bancroft's men wanted me."

"Dave!" Woodruff cried in relief. "Where have you been?"

"Where? Surely there's no mystery about that? I've been with Dorothy. The poor girl's crying her heart out. Really, Woody, don't you think you ought to try to explain things to her? Instead of that, you keep flitting about… What's going on here anyway?"

"Mr. Bancroft, give me those notes, please," said Woodruff. He took the packet and gave it to Jenks.

Jenks took the packet and unfolded it. He steadied his hands as he slowly scanned the pages, then he looked up and said, "Where did you get these?"

Bancroft said, "They've discovered we're following your assistants and they tried to get us on a false trail, probably so's they could get at the man they really want. They planted these fake notes—"

"Fake notes?" said Jenks, looking from Bancroft to Woodruff, his face pale. "But they're not faked at all! These are the real notes!"

"But Mr. Woodruff said—"

"Dave," said Woodruff, anxiously, "are you sure? Have you seen this note here?" He fumbled through the pages and pointed. "They've got to be fakes, Dave—it doesn't make sense otherwise!"

JENKS looked at them curiously. "I don't understand," he said. "Woody, I know what you're trying to tell me, but these are the real notes. They're part of the last pages." He kept staring at them. "Why doesn't somebody say something?" he asked. "What's the matter?"

Bancroft said, quietly, "Are all the notes there, Professor?"

"I can't be sure offhand. I think so."

"All right," said Bancroft. "That ends it. If you don't know, nobody does. There's another answer to this somewhere, and it's got to be a better one than the one I figured out." He took the notes from Jenks and re-folded them carefully. "If you don't mind, Professor," he said, "I think they'll be safer with me."

But he stood there musing, and he laughed to himself. "That's one of the dangers of this business, Mr. Woodruff—you get so used to making hypotheses to keep you going that you can build a theory around any set of circumstances. You thought these notes were fakes and I found a theory—and all the time the truth was a much easier theory to work out. I could just as easily have decided that Mahoney had really stumbled on the main clue... Assuming that Miller really—"

"Miller!" said Jenks, turning involuntarily toward the other room. "Not Miller...it doesn't seem possible!"

Bancroft nodded. "Or Hans Mulheimer, if you prefer. He kept the notes where they'd least be looked for—on his person. Naturally he denied owning them, claiming they were planted on him. Unfortunately for him, he took no chances, not even after these agents had gone to the trouble of removing Harrison so's they could get to him. How could he be certain they were the agents he was expecting Sunday? And why should he believe the plans had been changed? He knew we were here—he might have suspected some sort of trap. So he played dumb, figuring he could wait a little, but Mahoney was nosing around."

There was chagrin in his laughter, "See how *this* theory fits the case? Perfectly. The other didn't—not after Professor Jenks showed up here, safe and sound. And now, gentlemen, if you'll excuse me, we still have a few details to clear up, for instance, the whereabouts of Tom Harrison. They couldn't have gotten him off the grounds."

Woodruff stood there dumbly. The turn of events seemed to have stunned him. "Mr. Bancroft," he said, "I don't mean to sound unfeeling, especially after what I said to you, but I must ask you to remember—"

Bancroft waved a hand. "I understand, Mr. Woodruff," he said, ironically. "You don't want any fuss. Well, there won't be any if we can help it, but a man's life may be at stake. We've a little interviewing to do with some men who like to carry badges. Be seeing you."

He returned to the other room, leaving Jenks with Woodruff and Mahoney. Woodruff stood there, shaking his head. "Funny the way it worked out, Dave," he said.

"I still don't know much more than when I came in," said Jenks. "Tell me what happened here, but I think you'd better go over and see Dorothy before she packs up and leaves." He looked at Woodruff earnestly. "Woody, what's the matter with you? Aren't you feeling well?"

Woodruff took Jenks by the arm and led him out of the bathhouse without so much as a sidewise glance at what was going on with Bancroft and the others. They started back to the house.

"Dave," Woodruff said, presently, "I've got something to tell you. I should have told you before, but somehow I couldn't. Now that this whole horrible mess is finished..."

"What is it?" said Jenks, quietly. "Tell me, Woody."

Woodruff seemed to be searching for words. "I don't know where to begin." He held Jenks arm tightly and both men stopped walking. In the darkness, Woodruff could hear his own breath coming more swiftly. "You remember you asked me what had happened to me? You wanted to know if I had changed. I said no then, Dave...but the truth is..."

* * *

I WASN'T sure which of the three of us had first called the halt; it happened so close together that it was possible it was simultaneous. But however it happened, one thing seemed certain—the second one who had been *Clyde Woodruff* was finished. Our unanimity was proof of that. The case seemed cut and dried.

In spite of myself, however, I felt a tiny thrill of fear as we each wrote our opinions. One could never be sure. We had stopped *Woodruff* at a dangerous juncture.

One by one we turned up our sheets. They agreed: *Fool.*

For he was a fool, to be thinking of telling David Jenks the truth of the predicament that was personal to him. Not because he wasn't the real—real in the sense that I knew I was the only real one—Woodruff; the others in the room with me would hardly have agreed with me in identifying him as a fool for that. In their minds they were each determined to be the *real,* in the sense of *final,* Clyde Woodruff.

No, it wasn't that. Actually, from his limited point of view, *Clyde Woodruff* had acted cleverly. He had almost beaten me to the punch. I had determined long before to tell Jenks the truth the first chance I got. If it had been a wise decision for me, why not for him? He could have told Jenks everything I would have told him—begged Jenks to help him. And who knows what would have happened? We in the room were not alive, but *Woodruff* was...and what if Jenks had been able to do something to give *Woodruff* final and irrevocable life?

It was a clever move, as I say, and I had decided to make that move myself—*but I would not have done it then!* It was the time he chose to speak that branded him as the Fool! But for that we might never have been able to identify him until it was too late, until the sudden move had beaten us for good.

But too much had happened for any but a fool to have tried telling Jenks the truth then. I don't think I have to explain. You see what I mean, don't you?

It was my turn now...

CHAPTER FIVE
From the Sea

"WHAT'S the matter with you, Woody? What were you saying?"

"I have changed, Dave," I said.

"In what way?"

"In many ways. I feel different."

Impatiently, Jenks said, "But how, Woody? You started to tell me something but you're not saying a thing. You've got to give me details, even the most minute ones…"

"I—I don't think you quite understood me," I said. "It isn't what you think, Dave. I don't feel—well, the kind of evil you said I'd feel. And I haven't changed in the way you implied when we spoke in the library a while ago."

"Then what do you mean?"

"I'm sorry, Dave. I wish I could put it better, but I can't. I just feel a sort of newness, as if I were seeing things for the first time. It's a sort of release, somehow. Maybe it's because this whole mess with Miller and the others has been hanging over me. Now I suddenly feel as if I had stepped newborn into the world."

"Is that all you have to tell me?" he said, despairingly.

"Yes," I said.

We started walking to the house again. I could understand how he felt. For a moment it had seemed to him that his fears had come true, and that they were to be admitted. Now he was back to that miserable state where he could only guess, where fear was greater precisely because he didn't know whether there was any reason for it. Though there was reason enough from what he had said. I fought the impulse to tell him everything, to break down and…

No, that wasn't the way. Trusted friend though he was. I had to keep silent now that I had determined my course. I wondered, in an oddly detached way, whether his suffering was greater than mine. Sometimes a doctor suffered more than his patient; it might be an intellectual kind of pain, but it could be deeper if only that a doctor could understand what the pain meant, and where it might lead…and yet, I thought, was the word *suffer* the right one?

For I had told him the truth—I did feel a release. In spite of the urgency, in spite of everything, I felt almost happy. I felt alive again! Beside that simple fact, everything seemed relatively unimportant. It was with difficulty that I remembered the invisible ties that bound me to a world of shadows. It seemed to me that now I was…*alive* again…that nothing could possibly happen to change the world again, to thrust me back to the shadows…

The world had changed. Everything I saw was different somehow. This was no longer the world I had seen through another's eyes, felt through another's senses. This was my world, my personal world. When I looked at David Jenks, catching a glimpse of his worn, haggard face in the darkness, he seemed like a different person to me. Even my memories seemed different. I thought of what had happened at the pavilion and it seemed remote, and the people like figures in a book read long ago. Bancroft, for instance, seemed even to have *spoken* differently. There had been a joviality about him, a broad feeling for humor. It had disappeared. Was it because the disastrous turn of events had choked off the humor in him? And Mahoney too had changed, though he was a man who had seldom let the outside world affect the inner Mahoney.

Jenks broke into my thoughts abruptly. "You'll find Dorothy in her rooms," he said. "I'll be here if you want me."

He sat down on the veranda and I went into the house. The party had reached the first stages of stupor. One of the bands was resting, and in its place a string orchestra played soft dance music, but the floor was no longer crowded. Tired, aimless snatches of conversation flitted by; in one corner two men were arguing about Alsab's chances at the Preakness. Robert, weary but still efficient, presided over the bartenders, I made my way up the stairs through the couples who sat there.

THERE was no answer when I knocked on Dorothy's door. I pushed the door open and found her sitting in a chair near one of the windows. Her room was dark, and her figure softly outlined by the faint light of the late-rising quarter-moon. She turned her head slightly when she heard me come in, then she turned away again.

I sat down on a hassock beside her. In the moonlight she looked as cool and beautiful as if she had been carved out of marble. I thought back to the first time I had seen her; it was at a reception at my aunt's home, and I had counted the afternoon wasted until I saw her coming across the lawn, escorted by half a dozen men. It took me weeks to get her to spend an evening with me, and the gossip columns had spoiled it by conjecturing how much money this latest romance was going to cost me.

The gossip columns had played the dominant role in our relationship ever since. They had broken our engagement by revealing I had lent her father money for investments I chose for him; for she wore her pride like armor, and its one weakness was the mention of money; her father had lost almost everything when Wall Street laid its famous egg. How many times since then, for one reason or another, had our engagement been broken? Thinking so, and looking at her, I felt that she too had in an almost imperceptible way undergone a change.

"Dorothy," I said, "I'm sorry about tonight. I wanted to tell you the truth earlier, but I couldn't. I didn't want you to feel—"

"It's all right, Woody. Dr. Jenks told me everything."

"Then you do understand?"

"Perfectly." She turned to me and asked, "What was the answer you didn't want to give me—the one you said would get you slapped?"

"I don't remember," I said. "I was angry. I might have been thinking of saying anything. It doesn't matter."

Presently she said, "How many times have I heard you say 'it doesn't matter?' Sometimes I wonder if anything matters between us."

I knew what she wanted me to say. I had said that too, many times before. But somehow I didn't say it. There were too many things going on in my head. "You're tired, dear," I said. "I'll leave you now…"

I didn't finish what I was saying. There were tears glistening on her face. She sat there, crying, making no sound. I took her in my arms, "Woody," she sobbed, "you do love me, don't you? Tell me you do."

I brushed her tears away with a handkerchief. "That's a fine question to ask a groom two days before his wedding," I said. She put her arms around me and held me tightly to her. I felt her breath against my throat, and the perfume of her body was heady and sweet.

"Good night, Woody," she whispered.

When I went downstairs I didn't know what I wanted to do. Jenks was out on the veranda, but I was in no mood to talk to him. I felt exhausted, but my head was teeming with a thousand thoughts. If only I could solve the endless riddles that surrounded me…if I could sit down somewhere and think. But I couldn't. There was no beginning and no ending. All my life I had been surrounded. In the end I made the same decision I had made so many times before. I went for a drink.

AT THE bar, Robert said, "Miss Hunter has been asking for you, sir. She's dancing with Mr. Vanness over there."

How many drinks had I had that night? I had been drinking all day—I had been drunk several times already, but I was developing a magnificent tolerance for alcohol. I wondered whether one day I might wake up and find little red veins on my face. I said to Robert, "No, not the Scotch. It's stopped affecting me."

"I'm sorry, sir," said Robert. "That hasn't happened for two or three weeks at least. May I suggest champagne and brandy?"

"And fix me something to eat," I said, and I remembered what he had said about Miss Hunter. I looked out on the floor. She was there with Ray Vanness. They were the only couple on the floor at the moment. She looked wonderful, I thought. When the number ended, I waved to her and got her attention, and she and Vanness started towards me. They had looked very well dancing together, but they walked unsteadily, laughing with each other. "You've been drinking," I said to her.

"Not at all," she laughed. "Nothing but a few sips of something Robert—oh, look!—he's making you one, too. Robert, one for me, please, and Mr. Vanness." She added, "Makes one conspicuous not to drink around here, and I hate being conspic—conshpic—Isn't that the funniest thing? I just said it right and now I can't!" And she was off in another fit of laughter.

"What about your work?" I asked her.

"All work and no play makes Ann a dull girl."

"How is it coming? Did you get any good pictures?"

"You know what she does?" Vanness said loudly. "She's got a new kind of camera. Takes pictures in the dark. Imagine anything so—"

"Shush," said Ann. "It's a secret. Makes people self-conscious to know there's a camera watching them."

"I'll say it does!" Vanness laughed. "Almost started a riot on the lawn when..." He stopped sheepishly, putting his index finger over his mouth, "Forgot. That's another secret. Well, Woody, old friend, how about having lunch with me one of these days?"

Robert said gravely, as he brought up a tray, "I'll book you at the earliest opportunity, Mr. Vanness." We drank, toasting Timoshenko, and Vanness went off into a speech about it, and while he was speaking I signaled Ann. She nodded.

"Excuse me a moment, gentlemen," she said, holding up two fingers in the V sign. "V for victory, and other things."

"For Vanness," said Vanness, brightly.

And for veranda, I thought, as she left. "Robert," I said, "did you ever hear of mass production?" I took the champagne bottle and poured two tumblers of brandy into it. "For a sick friend," I said to Vanness. "You wait here for Miss Hunter."

I went out to the veranda and Mahoney was there, talking to Ann. He stopped when he saw me. Ann said, cheerfully, "Well, thank you so much, Mr. Mahoney. I'll be sure to send you a picture." Mahoney waved to me and started to leave.

"Come back here," I said to him. He stopped. "What's going on here? Who do you think you're kidding?" I looked at both of them and I said, "Something's cooking here. What is it, Mahoney?"

He looked at her. "I'm sure I don't know what you mean," she said to me. "Don't tell me you brought a bottle without glasses."

"Well, Mahoney?" I said.

"I'm sorry, Miss Hunter," Mahoney mumbled. "I think the boss ought to know regardless." He scowled. "Somebody went upstairs over the garage and wrecked Miss Hunter's stuff."

"What? Who wrecked what?" It didn't make sense to me.

"It's nothing," said Ann. "Someone must have stumbled up there by mistake and fallen on my things. It's so dark here, and well, it didn't amount to anything at all. Really it didn't."

"The hell it didn't," said Mahoney, fiercely. "If you ask me, they knew just what they were doing. It looked like somebody was looking for something. All the packages opened up, even the cases, and the trays spilled all over the floor. That was no accident, boss."

"Thanks, Mahoney," I said. I didn't know what to make of it. Why should anyone have wanted to search the storeroom? And what could they have been looking for? "Have you seen Bancroft around?" I asked.

"He's around, all right," said Mahoney. "He's laying low. Had a talk with his men. Seems the guys they found here with those phony badges were all wearing white carnations—sort of a private badge for themselves. He found two more that way. It's just like I told him. The place was crawling with guys with badges."

SOMETHING clicked in my mind. I put a hand in my pocket, half afraid that I wouldn't find it there. But is was there; it had to be. I waited until Mahoney had left, then I took out the print Ann had made earlier that evening. We stood near the door where there was some light and I held the picture up.

I was right. The figures in the background were two men. One of them had his back to the camera; that seemed fairly plain. But there was an unmistakable white spot over his shoulder. Ann was watching me and I showed her the picture. "Look at that spot," I said. "Could that be a white carnation?"

She studied it. "It might be. But if it is, there were two men out there because we can see the back of one of them, and the carnation wouldn't show unless there was another man facing him and the camera." She said, after a moment, "If it was Professor Jenks out there, he would know, wouldn't he?"

I nodded. Yes, I thought, Jenks would know. But where was he? He had said he would be on the veranda, but there was no sign of him.

"Is it important?" she asked.

"I think it is," I said. "I think it's the answer to who went through your things. There was someone outside the garage who was afraid you had gotten him in the picture."

"No," said Ann. "If this person wanted the picture destroyed, why did he wait so long? He could have come up while you were gone to get me a drink. I was alone, developing the negative. He could easily have spoiled it by pretending to turn on a light accidentally, if it didn't want more desperate measures."

"You're missing the point," I said, "The picture didn't mean a thing to him until Bancroft discovered that all these men were wearing white carnations! When he found that out, he remembered the picture and the possibility that he was in it. And that's when he decided to go after it!" But when I looked at her,

I saw that of course she didn't understand what I was talking about.

"This mysterious business of the white carnations doesn't make much sense to me," she said. "Not that I'm anxious to find out. Just the same, my feeling is that the explanation is much more simple."

"I think you know something," I said, slowly.

"Nothing at all," she said, seriously, then grabbing my hand, she added, "Except that here comes Mr. Vanness, looking for someone..."

We ran down the stairs to the lawn and lost ourselves in the garden. After a moment I said to her, "Robert said you were looking for me."

"That was when I first discovered what had happened up there," she said, "I was a bit excited about it, I guess, and then I decided you had too many troubles of your own without taking on mine."

"So you don't want to see me?"

"I didn't say that."

I said, "I wish I could see the expression on your face."

"I'll show it to you," she said, stepping out from under the tree into the pale moonlight. "I was smiling, as I recall it."

"Shall we go for a walk?" I said.

"It might do my head some good," she said. "It's spinning a bit."

So we walked, and we had been walking for five minutes when Ann said, "Walking in circles isn't helping my head in the least."

I looked about us and saw that we must have made a tour of the flowerbeds several times. "I brought some headache remedy with me," I said. "If you don't mind drinking from a bottle."

"But I've a glass..." she smiled, holding up a brandy glass. "Snatched it from the veranda railing on the dead run, what's more."

So we toasted MacArthur, and she said, "I don't want to make any speeches, but you seem terribly tired and overwrought. I'm not complaining, understand, but maybe you'd like to be alone with whatever thoughts were making you walk in circles."

"I'm not sure I want to be left alone with them. Is that what you meant by that remark about my troubles?"

"I'm talking out of turn again. I must be good and drunk."

WE WERE walking along the path that led to the beach. The paving blocks of the path shone with a dull lustre, and the moonlight caught droplets of dew on the grass. The night seemed very quiet then.

I said, "A few hours ago you wouldn't even dance with me, and how you're walking arm in arm with me in the moonlight." I mimicked her. "I'm not complaining, understand, but I'm glad you changed your mind."

"Maybe it's because you've changed, too."

"Have I? In what way?"

"There you go again!" she laughed. "You just can't be teased. The moment we mention you and your personality, off you fly. I don't remember the last time I met anyone so preoccupied with himself."

I said nothing, and she said, "Is that why you drink so much?"

"Is what why I drink so much?"

"Because you're all mixed up inside?"

"Maybe. I don't think about it as much as you imagine."

We walked on without speaking until we came to the beach. The surf was running along the shore in long, phosphorescent combers, and the sand was pleasant underfoot. The bathhouses stood huddled together as if from fear of the sea, and a pier, thin and exploratory, stretched from them until it was lost in the black waters. In the basin, boats rose gently with the swell.

We went on to where the shore formed a slight peninsula. There were rocks that rose from the hard-packed beach, outlined against the gray sand, and we sat down there and looked at the sea. A breeze had come in, moving the warm, moist atmosphere, running through Ann's hair. The moonlight that had turned the gold cloth of her gown to silver lay in her eyes like deep, molten pools.

"You're not happy, are you?" she said. "Not deep inside you."

It was strange, her talking to me that way. I remembered the definiteness with which she had discouraged my first attempts to become friendly with her. She had kept a cool balance, plainly telling me she had no interest in my personal affairs. And yet, for minutes past, she had spoken of little else. She had been drinking, but that alone could not possibly explain it. Something had happened that had broken down her reserve, but it was more than that; the interest she showed in me perplexed me.

"You haven't answered me," she said.

I answered her then. I didn't care why she was talking to me. I wanted to talk to someone—to her; and the words came pouring out of me. I hadn't thought I was unhappy; a few short hours before I had felt quite the opposite. But as I spoke to her, I said things that I hadn't realized I felt. I spoke about all kinds of things, irrelevant little stories. I told her that I hated Seaside. She looked at me oddly and she asked me why, and when I tried to tell her, I couldn't because the thought was so new, because I hadn't known, before that moment, that I felt that way about it.

"I'll tell you why," she said. "I know why, because I hate it, too. It's a lovely place, but it doesn't belong to anyone. It's a monument to everything that's wasteful and meaningless. Lives, for instance…your life, in particular. This place stands for everything you hate—for your fiancée's friends, whom you can't stomach, and for the people you call your own friends, whom you bring out here because you hate the others so much. But they don't help. You care for them as little as they care for you…

"But it isn't only this place—it's the same wherever you are. Your only friends are Mahoney and Robert, and you pay them just as you pay your other friends, one way or another. You're a lonely guy, Woody, and that's why you drink. And deep down inside, you're all mixed up, and I don't think you like Woody Woodruff when you catch sight of him. I don't think you like him at all..."

A LONG time passed. We sat there and once or twice we drank, but there was no talking. I suppose she felt she had said too much after all, and there was nothing I could have said, not then. It was so quiet I could hear my watch ticking. Thin drifts of clouds had blown in, hiding the moon for long intervals that were pitch dark.

"Woody!"

"Yes?"

"Do you see it? There—look! I thought I was imagining it."

I thought I saw it, but I waited for the moon to come out again. It was a long, low boat, coming in towards the beach. It was moving very slowly. When it was closer I saw that it was a cruiser, with a cabin so low-slung that I hadn't noticed it before. There was no sound of a motor.

"Is it one of your boats?" Ann whispered.

For an instant something gleamed. It had been a wet oar, raised a bit too far, catching the light. A cabin cruiser—being rowed in toward shore! Surely it took several men to row such a boat. But what was it doing here, and why was it so secretive? It had no running lights. I tried to remember the ruling the Coast Guard had made about pleasure craft in these waters. It was violating every peacetime maritime law as well as the war regulations.

"Get back against the rocks," I whispered. "Don't move."

When the boat was no more than thirty yards offshore, it stopped. A faint light flashed from it toward the shore. After a few minutes, the light winked again, twice in rapid succession.

"Can you see the basin and pier from here?"

"Yes," she breathed. "What are you going to do?"

"Never mind. Keep looking. Tell me if you see anything."

I kept my eyes glued to the boat while I stripped. That boat had come to keep a rendezvous and it wasn't difficult to guess with whom. The boat signaled again, riding just beyond the point where the waves gathered to break, and when the moon showed again, there were several figures standing in the bow.

Ann grabbed my arm. I turned in time to see a tiny blue light blinking at the foot of the pier. Someone was standing there. The boat started moving again, parallel to the shore, heading for the basin. I pressed Ann's hand. "No matter what, you stay put," I told her. When I looked into her eyes, there was bewilderment there, but no fear.

I waited for the moment when the first bathhouse would come between the boat and its view of the beach. Then, keeping low, I sprinted for the water. It was like ice. I held my breath and came up twenty yards out. I started swimming breaststroke, careful not to break water.

Just as the boat reached the pier, it swung about and came up along the outside edge of the pier. The maneuver had shielded it from sight of anyone between the pier and the main house, while its access to the sea remained unimpaired. At the same time, it had ruined my best chance of coming up to the pier unobserved.

Someone came walking quickly down the pier. It was now or never. I came a little closer, as much as I dared, and ducked under. I swam underwater until I felt my temples would burst, but before I came up, I rolled over and stuck my nose out. Before I came up, my forehead hit something and I went under again. I felt the side of the boat—I had bumped it coming up. If I had made much noise, they would be watching the water. I hadn't had time to catch a breath. I was beginning to lose my sense of direction. Still feeling the boat, I dove down as deep as I could. When I came up, I felt the starboard side of the boat. I was under the pier. There was no sound.

PRESENTLY a voice said, "Must have been the boat against the pier. Let's get on with our arrangements."

A throaty, guttural voice answered, "I tell you again I have no authority to make any arrangements. You were supposed to have him now."

"Can't you understand what I'm telling you? They've rounded up most of our people. They're guarding him very carefully."

There was a momentary hesitation, then the second voice said, "This I do not understand. Why they should be guarding *him?* How do they know we are after *him?*"

"They're watching everybody now. The only—"

"But you must make him understand that the plans must be changed! We cannot wait for Sunday now!" The voice grew angrier, "I have ten good men here. We make an attack on the house and we take him!"

"How far do you think you'll get with him?"

"Far enough, my friend. One of our submarines comes tonight for fuel. He could be making his way to the Fatherland in—"

"Impossible!" the first voice snapped. "We can't risk it. By the time you return tomorrow, we'll have him and the rest of the notes."

Again the hesitation. "Notes?"

"My last word to you is to return tomorrow at the same time. That's an order!"

"So?" the second voice growled. "An order, my friend? You'll hear about this. We'll see who gives the orders."

"Good night. Heil Hitler!"

"Heil Hitler."

I heard the man's retreating footsteps on the pier. I grabbed the piling and began pulling myself toward the beach. The boat was casting off. The guttural voice, in subdued anger, "An order, he said! For us the dirty work, the games with the Coast Guard on a moonlight night, to come here. An order! Pull away there. Careful, Paul..."

I was still several feet from the end of the pier when the man left it. I couldn't follow immediately without running the risk of being seen by the men in the boat. But I did get a look at the man who had been on the pier; he turned left and started back to the main house. He was a tall, heavily built man in evening clothes, blonde haired. I looked under the pier to see how far away the boat was. I had had to keep my mouth muscles taut to keep my teeth from chattering. The icy waters had penetrated my bones, it seemed to me.

In the end, coldness won out over caution. I left the water sooner than I should have and started running along the beach after him. I might have lost him entirely if he hadn't heard me coming; I was breathing like an engine, and he spun around. Maybe the sight of me, dripping wet and half-naked, startled him, for instead of running he just stood there a moment, and then he suddenly, belatedly, clutched his left shoulder under his jacket.

I hit him in that position. I dove in and grabbed his knees and we both went tumbling over in the sand. He whipped an arm free and smashed a fist into my face. The blow stunned me sufficiently for him to scramble to his feet. He pulled a gun out of a shoulder holster and stopped. "Mr. Woodruff!" he exclaimed. "What in the name of..." He pulled a badge out of a pocket. "You don't understand!" he said. "I'm here with Mr. Bancroft!"

I tried to look confused. I needed about thirty seconds more.

"I didn't know who you were," I gasped.

"You mean you were—you must have been under the pier. I—" He must have been warned by some false move of mine, for he spun around just before Ann got to him. She had circled around behind us and come up from the direction of the house. In her right hand she held the champagne bottle, ready to bring it down on his head. He swung his left arm up and smashed the bottle out of her hand, and in that instant, I grabbed his right arm, swung him back into position and brought my fist down between his nose and one of his eyes.

It was a magnificent punch. He went down as if he'd been hit by a sledgehammer, and he lay there on the beach without another movement. I bent over and picked up his gun. "We're a good team," I said to Ann, surprised at my own coolness. She mumbled something and I grabbed her. I thought she was going to faint. I picked up the champagne bottle and opened it. I was holding it to her lips when they came running.

BANCROFT was the first of the four to get to us. He stopped short and looked at me in sheer amazement, "Good lord!" he shouted. "What the hell have you done here, Woodruff?"

"Just take him to the house," I said, "Here's one you missed, and there's a nice story goes with it."

"Are you crazy?" Bancroft shouted. "This man is Steve Holmes! He's one of my best men. What the hell do you mean—"

"You're sure?"

"Am I sure? Of course I'm sure! You've gone out of your mind!"

"Then it's better than I bargained for," I said. "I overheard a little conversation that may interest you. I was under the pier when—"

"Under the pier?" Bancroft roared. For the first time he seemed to notice that I was soaked through and standing in a pair of pants, "So that's it, damn your hide! You were under the pier and you heard Holmes talking to those men in the boat!" He stood there, shivering with rage. "Well, listen to this, Mr. Woodruff—I sent him out on that pier!"

I looked down to where the other men were reviving Holmes. I tried to say something, but before I made a sound, Ann sighed, dropped the bottle, and passed out in my arms.

*　*　*

I WAS back in the study of my apartment. One of the two men I had left there was sitting in my chair. At the same time, I knew that at that moment there was a *Clyde Woodruff* on the beach at Seaside. I could see him trying to revive Ann Hunter. I could hear Bancroft still shouting furiously…

"One of you called for identification," I said, confused. "That's why I'm back here. But what happened?"

"Seems obvious, doesn't it? Even if it hasn't happened until now. The other fellow thought he had you figured out, and he made the call. I couldn't agree with his identification—so here you are again, and according to our compact, you've now inherited the last position. So you'll have your chance again, you see."

I didn't know what to make of it. It seemed only natural to me that they hadn't been able to agree. They had had only two choices: deciding I was either a liar or a coward. How in the name of heaven could they have decided I was either? Was this impasse the stumbling block I had prayed for? Was it possible that whatever happened, there could never be agreement between these two on my identity, precisely because I was the real Clyde Woodruff?

Or was I interpreting a fantastically fortunate twist of circumstance in my own way? What was to prevent them from agreeing? I looked at the man who sat opposite me and I saw no such realization on his face. He sat there, calm and confident, smoking a cigarette. I wondered what had prompted the one who had been with him into making the identification. By what action, or sum of actions, had he judged me? And what had he judged me to be?

When I tried to ask him about it, the man ignored me. He was intent on the flow of events from where the fourth *Clyde Woodruff* had plunged—the *Clyde Woodruff* who was either a liar or a coward. What would he do with the facts that now were his—with the swift-shaping events that were now for him to control?

CHAPTER SIX
Bancroft Sums It Up

"SHUT up!" Woodruff shouted at Bancroft. "Lend me a hand here." Still white hot and grinding out oaths, Bancroft took hold of Ann's face and slapped it smartly. After the second slap she flinched and opened her eyes. Bancroft bent down to Holmes, who had regained consciousness.

Holmes sat up dizzily, shaking his head.

"Did you get the name?" Bancroft said, tensely.

"Get somebody on a phone," Holmes groaned, "Name *Odalisque* on her starboard, ten men hidden her cabin, armed and—"

"To hell with the boat! Did they mention any name?"

Holmes cried, "Listen to me! She's rigged like a fishing boat, false masts, heavily armed, speedy, nets and lobster pots—but she's part of a submarine supply gang! They mustn't lose her."

"Holy smoke!" Bancroft exclaimed softly. One of the men broke away and swiftly ran down the beach toward the house. Bancroft said, "Holmes, what about the name?"

"He didn't mention any names at all. Maybe he was leery of me. When I saw the kind of boat it was, I tried to get him to come back tomorrow night, in case the Coast Guard hadn't made it. He wanted to come out and take whoever they were after by force. I bluffed him with an order to come back tomorrow, but it's an even money bet his boss'll smell something funny. If the Guard doesn't get him, it's muffed."

"Why didn't you let them try coming to the house?"

Holmes shook his head. "They had tommy guns hidden under their nets in the bow...and there are five hundred people around here yet."

Bancroft brushed his face. "You're right. Anything else—any word at all that might be some kind of a lead?"

As Holmes rose unsteadily, Woodruff pressed forward. "There were at least two things that might be clues," he said. "I heard—"

"Thank you, Mr. Woodruff," Bancroft snapped. "Holmes here probably heard at least as much as you did. I'll take his version."

Holmes said, "The whole thing was screwy. We weren't talking about the same things. He kept waiting for me to talk…" He stopped and said, "I need a drink. My head's buzzing from that wallop."

Bancroft muttered an oath as he and his men started back to the house. Woodruff, his teeth chattering, left behind with Ann, saw Mahoney come sprinting toward them. A few yards behind him, puffing valiantly and lugging a blanket, was Robert, calling, "Wait for me, Mr. Mahoney!"

Mahoney came to a dead stop and looked at Woodruff, amazed. "Then it's true what I heard about you being under the pier?" he exclaimed.

Woodruff took the blanket from the panting Robert and wrapped it around himself. "Ann, are you all right now?"

"Mr. Woody, you're wet all through! You've got to—"

"Shut up, will you…" said Mahoney.

"Boss, were you really under—"

"Shut up, the both of you!" said Woodruff. "Ann, are you okay?"

She nodded her head and smiled wryly. "I guess so."

"You were wonderful," Woodruff said. "That's a small word for it."

"Maybe if I'd been less wonderful," she said, "there'd have been less trouble. And you weren't so bad yourself."

"Mr. Woody, I must insist that you get out of those wet clothes without any further delay," said Robert quietly, "or I shall take the necessary measures, much as I enjoy such a display of mutual admiration."

"All right," Woodruff sighed. "Let's get back. Listen, Mahoney, do you know what all this is about? The pier business and all?"

"Sure I do. Bancroft called me in to help when he found out how many of them agents were hanging around. And anyway," he smiled broadly, "I kind of made myself useful. Seems they had trouble getting those babies to talk, and you know me, boss. I ain't a guy who likes to—"

"I know, I know," said Woodruff, wearily. "Get to the point."

"But that's the point! It started all over again, after they sent Miller or Mulheimer, whichever it is, back to the city under heavy guard. Bancroft is no dope, no matter what I thought previous. While he was trying to find his man Harrison, who is still missing, he kept on trying to find corroborating evidence against Miller. Well, since Bancroft got here tonight, every telephone wire in Seaside—incoming and outgoing—has been tapped.

"So what happened? Half an hour after he got his hands on Miller and the guy who had been in the pavilion with him, a call goes out of here to a drug store in the east eighties. A man says that the trick worked—"

"What trick?" said Woodruff, eagerly. "Do you mean that Miller was involved in a trick, after all—that he's really innocent?"

"Yeah," said Mahoney, surprised. "How did you know?"

THEY were at the house now, having come around to the back entrance. "Just a minute," said Woodruff, turning to Ann. He took her a few steps away. "You'd better go up and get some sleep," he said quietly. "It's been a tough day for you. I just wanted to tell you once more that I think you're a grand sport, and thanks a million."

She looked steadily into his eyes, then she murmured, "Good night, Mr. Woodruff," and turning quickly away, she ran into the house.

Woodruff stared after her. After a moment, he said to Mahoney, "Come up to my room with me while I change. No, Robert, you needn't bother—I know where everything is. And thanks for the blanket." He went through the kitchen up the back stairs. There was a weary group of some eight or ten people sprawled on the stairs, with a bottle on each alternating step. When Woodruff and Mahoney started up, they yelled that it was a private party, then, seeing Woodruff in his blanket, they began giving Indian calls until the pantry staff came running to see what new troubles were about to descend on them.

When they got to his room, Woodruff said, "Keep talking."

"Sure, boss…you mind if I ask how you knew it was Miller?"

"I had a hunch about it. How did Bancroft find out?"

"Well, when this guy says the trick worked, the one in the drug store asks why he is being called, seeing that everything must be fine now. So the guy calling from here says that the F.B.I is still all over the place hunting for Harrison, and it doesn't look as if they'll get a chance to contact their man on Sunday. At this point the guy in the drug store blows up and yells that they changed the Sunday plan the minute they found the F.B.I. was on to them, and that what he has to do is get the man they want to fork over the dope right away.

"So the first guy says that this man is still playing cagey and he refuses to change the plan. He won't give the stuff up before Sunday. Not only that, but he won't let Harrison out from where he's got him hidden away, so's the F.B.I. will pack up and get out. Then there's a long wait, and finally the guy in the drug store says. Get the man and have him ready for delivery at exactly 2:45 a.m. tonight. They are going to get into Seaside at the only place it ain't guarded—through the sea. He arranges how they will signal each other, and he hangs up."

Mahoney paused and said, "You going out again, boss?"

Woodruff put his shirt studs in. "Keep talking," he said.

"That's about all, I guess," said Mahoney. "Bancroft knew from that conversation that Miller couldn't have been the man they were talking about." He snapped his fingers. "And something else! Almost forgot to tell you the best part of it. When Bancroft hears what went on in that conversation, he goes to Professor Jenks and asks him to look at the notes again, to make sure they're really the real notes. And what do you supposed happened?"

"Professor Jenks changed his mind," said Woodruff, softly.

Mahoney looked at him with his mouth open. "I don't get it," he gulped. "That's exactly what happened! The professor went over the notes very carefully and he said he'd been wrong, and the notes were fakes. That put Bancroft back where he'd started, only worse off because he'd lost time." He scratched his head, adding, "Boss, it don't figure, you knowing everything Bancroft knows."

Woodruff nodded grimly, fixing his tie. "And maybe a couple of things Bancroft doesn't know," he said. "Tell me, Mahoney, when I met you on the veranda talking to Miss Hunter—about an hour and a half, maybe two, hours ago, and you told me her equipment had been wrecked—how much of this did you know then?"

"Just what I told you then. If I'd known more, I'd have told you the rest. All I knew was that Bancroft's men had rounded up a couple of the phony badge-carriers. While we were talking on the veranda, the professor was upstairs with Bancroft, going over the notes. I went in after you left and they invited me upstairs. Bancroft said they might need me, and would I agree to take orders? When I agreed, they told me everything I've just told you."

"You were there when they assigned Holmes to meet the boat?"

"Sure thing. That was a ticklish job they gave him. He was going out to meet that gang and try to get them to drop some kind of hint as to who they were expecting to take back with them. Meanwhile Bancroft had already notified the Coast Guard about the boat, but they weren't sure they could get there fast enough. There wasn't much time by then. All we can do now about that boat is hope the Coast Guard did pick them up later. And Holmes didn't get a thing…except a terrific black eye, from what I heard."

WOODRUFF had put on a fresh jacket. He paused at the light switch and said, "Do you know where Professor Jenks is now?"

"In his room, I suppose. He was feeling pretty sick before." He went out with Woodruff, saying, "I wanted to tell you the way I got one of those phonies to confide in me, but if you're in a hurry…"

Woodruff stopped in the hallway and smiled, "No, Mahoney," he said, "I'm in no hurry. And I really want to hear it."

"Thanks, boss!" Mahoney beamed. "You see, when these guys on the phone arranged their lights signals, the one in the drug store—they couldn't get anyone up there fast enough to grab him—anyway, he said that they would use the color they'd arranged. And Bancroft didn't know anything about a color, and he couldn't get the monkeys he'd rounded up to spill it. So I asked if I could have a chat with one of them, and I picked out a big, hefty son of a gun, cause the way I figure is like this: a little guy gets used to beatings, but a big guy who never has to take them is going to break down easier when he gets his lumps."

"So you gave him his lumps?"

"And he gave me the color," Mahoney admitted, with subdued pride. "It was blue. And the guy who gave it to me was the one who had been on the phone, so he should have known."

"Is that all?" Woodruff sighed.

"Ain't it enough?"

Woodruff sighed again and shook hands with Mahoney. "If you'll excuse me now, Mahoney, I'll tell you about the punch I landed on that poor fellow Holmes, sometime soon."

"Punch? I heard it was a bottle."

"That's what gave me the punch," said Woodruff, walking down the hallway to the adjoining wing.

There were lights showing under several of the doors in the wing, but except for subdued music from a few radios, the hall was quiet. Jenks was in a two-room suite at the end of the hall. Woodruff stopped before it and listened. There was no sound. He knocked softly and Jenks called, "Who is it?" Woodruff answered, and a moment later, Jenks opened the door. "Come in, Woody," he said.

He was in pajamas, but his bed was untouched. On a table beside an easy chair stood a bottle of rum and a half filled glass. An ashtray beside it was choked with butts. A flat cloud of smoke lay suspended in midair. Woodruff sat down on the bed. Jenks looked horribly tired as he sank back into his chair.

"What's the matter?" said Woodruff. "Mahoney said you weren't feeling well. You look like hell."

Jenks cut a slice of lemon and dropped it into the rum. "I feel like hell," he said. He raised the glass and emptied it slowly, closing his eyes as he drank. He kept his eyes still closed as he said, "And this isn't helping much. I don't know why I'm drinking. Maybe it's because everyone here does...the place stinks with the smell..."

"Would you rather I left?"

"Not at all. I can't sleep anyway. And you sort of looked as though you had something on your mind."

Woodruff smiled wryly. "I didn't think it showed. I wanted to ask you about the notes they found on Miller."

"You mean why I changed my mind about them?" He opened his eyes. They were very bloodshot, and the lids hung heavily. "You won't like my answer any more than Bancroft did. I told him I changed my mind because the notes *were* fakes, though I didn't think so at first. Why? Maybe because they were such excellent fakes. Even when I re-examined them, I was struck by their similarity to the figures in the genuine notes. Or maybe," he added, "because I couldn't think straight about anything anymore..."

Woodruff said nothing for a moment, then quietly, he observed, "That's no answer, Dave. Bancroft couldn't know the notes weren't genuine, because that little notation about explosives didn't mean anything to him. But I knew immediately as you must have known. Your answer about the figures can't explain what must have gone on in your mind when you saw that notation."

JENKS filled his glass again. "It isn't always possible to explain what goes on in one's mind," he said. When he finished filling the glass, he pushed it away. He lit a cigarette, watching the flame. "For instance," he said, "how would you explain your change of mind a few hours ago? When you refused to admit anything in the library, it might have been possible that there was nothing to admit. But later, when you started to speak—when you admitted you had changed, and in the next breath quickly turned the conversation aside, it was evident that you had changed your mind. Can you explain it?"

"What are you trying to say?"

"I've already said it: It isn't always possible to explain what is going on in one's mind."

Woodruff lit one of Jenks' cigarettes. He took a long, thoughtful drag. He said, "Do you want me to tell you now?"

"You have nothing to tell me now. I knew the answer from that moment on—the big answer, that is. I can't hope ever to know the details, and even if you told me, I could never be sure."

Woodruff seemed stunned by what Jenks said. Slowly he said, "You're trying to tell me something. What is it?"

Jenks let the question hang in silence.

Presently he said, "Listen to me carefully. I told you that the amount of that damned concentrate you had taken would kill you unless something happened to you—unless you changed. But you know, and you've known all along, that it will kill you unless you can overcome its power to change you, unless you can be the final victor in the compact in which you must have entered, or you could not be here at all."

"Then you lied to me before?"

"No."

"But before you gave me a different reason."

"I don't think I gave it *you.*"

Woodruff started so violently that the cigarette fell from his hand. He crushed it and lit another slowly, regaining his composure. "At any rate," he said, "you lied. You said then that it would kill me because it was sapping my will and strength. The truth is that it will kill me unless I am the final victor in the compact I entered. And you must have had a reason for lying then as you must have a reason for now acknowledging that lie, however backhandedly you've done it...

"And there are other questions I might ask. One: why should you tell me this now? Since you made a distinction in referring to my identity, why should you have chosen me? Why didn't you admit this an hour ago, or two hours ago, or at any time since I took the concentrate? Two: why should you give me so poor an explanation for your change of mind in identifying the notes Miller had planted on him? You must know that the explanation was worthless, yet you gave it without trying to hide its worthlessness..."

"You forget," said Jenks, "that while I am talking to you, I am also talking to Clyde Woodruff."

"You don't think I am Woodruff?"

"I have no way of knowing. If you are, I must hope that you understand. If you aren't, I still must hope that he understands."

"Understands what?"

"The answers to your questions."

Woodruff got up. "I am Woodruff," he said, "and I understand the answers to my questions. It's a simple answer. You're trying to confuse me. You're using what you know as an instrument against me." He smiled and said, softly, "But it won't work, Dave."

"It may," said Jenks, and he raised his glass to Woodruff as he left the room.

WOODRUFF went downstairs. Robert was supervising the cleaning. "I thought you were asleep, Mr. Woody," he said, yawning. "Mr. Bancroft wanted you a few minutes ago and I refused to wake you."

"Where is Bancroft?"

"In the private library. You wouldn't want me to fix you a bite to eat, would you, Mr. Woody? There's quite a mob in the kitchen."

"Nothing fancy; ham and eggs maybe. I'll be in in a little while."

Woodruff went to the back of the house. He knocked on the door of the library and went in. Bancroft was lying on a leather couch, his eyes half closed. He had his shoes off and only a small lamp was lit. He sat up as Woodruff came in. "Hello," he said, "I thought you were asleep. I wanted to have a word with you." He put his shoes on. "I trust you don't mind my using this room as a sort of emergency bedroom. The house is full up, your man Robert told me, and I have to be—"

"Perfectly all right," said Woodruff.

"What did you want?"

"It's about that pier business." He stopped, embarrassed. "I'm sorry I flew off the handle. You couldn't tell, Mahoney explained, because he'd told you about the phony badges. Anyway, I'm curious about those clues you thought you had. Holmes didn't seem to remember much of the conversation after that tussle."

"There were two things that struck me as odd," Woodruff replied, "First, the man on the boat seemed to assume that the man they're after wouldn't be watched. He said something like: 'Why should *he* be guarded?' That was in answer to Holmes saying that everyone was guarded."

"You're sure about that?"

Woodruff nodded. "Positive. He plainly felt that their man would not be guarded. Strange assumption, wasn't it?"

"I don't understand it, frankly."

"And the second clue," said Woodruff, "is stranger still. When Holmes said that he'd have both the man and the notes tomorrow night, this fellow on the boat questioned him. '*Notes?*' he said, as if that was something that took him rather by surprise."

"I'm glad you brought this up," said Bancroft. "Holmes mentioned this thing about the notes. I didn't know what to make of it; I thought maybe Holmes hadn't interpreted it correctly, but he said just what you say. Which makes matters even more confusing." He shook his head. "I confess, Mr. Woodruff, I've seldom come up against anything as muddled as this thing. I'll be damned if I know where I am."

Woodruff said, "I have some ideas, if you care to listen."

"By all means."

"Cigarette?" said Woodruff, opening a box. He lit both, then, leaning against a desk, he said, "I'll just ramble on for a few minutes, I think you'll get what I mean…"

"First, let's go back to the original clue. Professor Jenks gave you a strip of film with photographs of some of the notes on it, the assumption following that the notes were being photographed. That seems to me to have been an extremely troublesome procedure for someone who might easily have copied the notes. Or, assuming they were copied and then photographed, wasn't it a remarkable thing that the thief was carrying around copies of notes he already, had? To say nothing of his amazing carelessness in having dropped such a film? Are you following?"

BANCROFT nodded. "I've thought about these things myself, Mr. Woodruff," he said, "but you learn in this business that amazing things happen all the time. The amazing things must lead to a conclusion that is sound in spite of them."

"Fine," said Woodruff. "Another amazing thing about our thief: he received a business telephone call right in the laboratory. How could he dare take such a chance? What if he had seen Jenks in his private office—here would he have taken this urgent call? I would conclude from these circumstances that my friend, Professor Jenks, lied."

"Suppose he did lie? He lied about the notes we found on Miller. I showed them to Yarovitch, who's been Jenks' assistant longer than the rest, and he said they were good fakes and nothing more. I didn't say anything to the professor even then—not until we got more proof that Miller was innocent. Then, when I asked Jenks to look at the notes again, he changed his mind. Hell, *he* knew I understood he was lying, so now we all know. So where does it lead us?"

"Let's see," Bancroft pulled at his lip. "What if we assume that the man these spies were after tonight didn't need the notes at all? What if he knew the notes from memory? That would make a certain kind of sense. The spies had tried to get him to change the appointment. He was suspicious, or careful. The spies then decided to kidnap him—and we know that. Well, why should they kidnap him unless one of two things was true: either they thought he had the notes on his person, which is absurd; or they knew that he had the notes safely stowed in his mind."

"But Professor Jenks said the phone conversation he overheard definitely mentioned written notes to be delivered."

"Maybe he lied about that too."

"Then maybe he lied about the appointment altogether," said Bancroft. "We have to have something to go by to decide one way or another on any of these things."

Woodruff said, "If we assume that the man the spies intended to kidnap is Professor Jenks, the pier conversation adds up. He could have memorized five times as much, take my word for it; I've seen him memorize a textbook word for word. It also ties in with that other remark about having him guarded. You were guarding his four assistants, but Jenks himself was walking around free and easy. The spies wouldn't expect Jenks to be guarded."

Bancroft frowned. "And where would the Miller thing fit in?"

"It was staged to lead you up a blind alley, just as you said. Your first analysis of the thing was right, as I see it."

Bancroft got up and began pacing the floor. He rubbed his chin thoughtfully, glancing once or twice at Woodruff, then he said, "Tell me, Mr. Woodruff, how good are you at memorization?"

"Pretty fair. Why."

"Fair enough to memorize notes like those we're talking about?"

"Yes, I think so."

"Then why don't you fit every particular of the case you've just outlined against the professor? It is a case against him, isn't it?"

"You can't be serious."

"I'm giving you this straight, Mr. Woodruff. Matter of fact, I can give you a better case against you. Care to listen?"

"Sure."

"Okay. You've got a key to the laboratory. The man there that night was you. You were copying notes which you later had transferred on film. You know a girl who's here tonight who monkeys with cameras and things like film—"

"But I just met her tonight."

"I'm not contradicting you. So you had the notes put on film. Then it got hot, so you decided to destroy the films. I happen to know that this girl photographer was using your garage storeroom as a workshop, and that somebody ruined a lot of her stuff. It could have been you or her, or both of you. You got rid of the film and memorized the notes. That would make you a possible suspect in that conversation that Holmes had, because they might just as easily know that you carried the notes in your mind, as well as Professor Jenks. And just as it's true that we didn't have Jenks under guard—it's true that we didn't have you under guard."

WOODRUFF said, "Terrific, so far. Anything more?"

"Plenty. Suppose *you* and Mahoney, who is still your man, planted the fake notes on Miller. You could have gone into his background very easily and played that Mulheimer gag on him. Remember, it was your man Mahoney who first brought it up, who insisted the place was filled with phony F.B.I. badges. *You* could have hired all those men to gum up the works when you knew I would be here with my men. And it was *you* and Mahoney who actually caught Miller in the pavilion, which might also be classed as amazingly fortuitous."

"And why did I tell you the notes were fakes?"

"I'll get to that," said Bancroft. "Let's get on with this. When we tapped that call to Yorkville, and your men were caught, you went out to the beach, using the girl with you as a blind, making it look like a romantic interlude, if you'll excuse me for saying so. You went out there to warn the boat away. You swam out to head it off, but you missed it in the darkness, so you swam back under the pier, too late to warn them. Maybe you told them, after Holmes left, to watch out for the Coast Guard—they weren't caught. Then you went after Holmes, trying to get him out of the way before he could tell me the things that might incriminate you—the very clues you mentioned. And the girl helped you... Hold on, I'm not done...

"When we stopped you on the beach, you went back here with Mahoney and had a conference with him in your room. He told you that Professor Jenks had admitted the notes were fake, after first saying they were the real notes. So you went in to see Jenks, just a few minutes ago, and you found him half drunk, for very good reason. Maybe your talk with him convinced you that suspicion had finally come around to point at you, so down you came to talk to me.

"You told me things we already knew. Yes, Holmes told me both the things you did. You just wanted to check on it and then you saw how bad things were, so, to head me off, you tried to build up a case against your friend, Professor Jenks. This after Jenks had driven himself half crazy trying to protect you, after—"

"Me?" said Woodruff, quietly. "How do you figure that out?"

Bancroft smiled peculiarly. "It would explain some of the lies the professor told, when there seems to be no other explanation. You asked me why you branded the notes as fakes? Because you had drawn one trail with the Miller episode, and now you wanted to cross it, to throw everything into hopeless confusion. Did it occur to you that I might wonder how you could possibly know so quickly that they were fakes—or know anything about the notes? But if you had planted them, naturally you would know.

"Then Professor Jenks came in. He already suspected you; probably he had suspected you from the start. He saw the notes and he knew they were fakes, but he didn't know that you had counted on him to say so. He was so confused by then that he thought the best thing he could do was to lie—so he said they were genuine. That confounded you, and you undertook something fantastic: you pointed out something and insisted the notes were fakes, as if you knew more about them than he did, which was true in that instance. But what could poor Jenks do? Could he reverse himself on your obvious coaching and give the game away? He cut the argument short and stuck to his guns.

"It was only later, after you had had ample opportunity to let him, one way or another, that it didn't matter if he identified the notes as phonies, that he admitted it. It must have relieved him to know that his innocent assistant wouldn't suffer for your crime. And right now he is hoping against hope that you'll return the notes before it's too late, before he has to turn against you."

WOODRUFF said, "And what about your missing man, Harrison?"

"He was in the way when you planned to trick Miller, so you...well, I don't think you killed him. It wouldn't be necessary. You could always hide him—this is a big place."

Woodruff blew his breath out. "That's it, is it?" he asked. He opened a drawer in his desk as Bancroft nodded, saying, "I gather this is the point where I pull a gun out of my desk and shout that you'll never take me alive?" He took out a carton of cigarettes and broke open a fresh pack.

"Wouldn't do you much good it you did," Bancroft smiled. "I took the cartridges out of the gun in the bottom drawer."

"Picked the lock, eh?" Woodruff laughed. He was sober in a moment. "I must admit, Mr. Bancroft, that you've built up an astonishing case against me. I'm almost ready to begin believing in it myself, except for the fact that you neglected to mention what possible motive I might have."

"I'm glad you brought that up. It puzzles me too. It can't be that you'd be after the money involved in a thing like this, and I can't see anything else either. A thing like this takes a man without a conscience, without a heart. The Professor doesn't fit in there either, to resume your case against him, but—assuming for a moment that he was after the money involved—why in the name of heaven should he have called in the F.B.I. in the first place?" He let that peculiar smile come over his red face as he said, innocently enough, "Because when all is said and done, Mr. Woodruff, he *did* call us in. You might have considered this most amazing fact of all your...facts."

He pronounced the last word with a sharp little twist in it.

"A motive," Woodruff mused, ignoring him. "Where can we get a motive for something like this?"

"You think about it, Mr. Woodruff, and I'll think about it, and we'll confide in each other if we get any results. Because," he said, folding his hands together as he lay down on the couch, "when I get my motive, I'll get my man."

Woodruff paused at the door and turned back. "It just occurred to me to ask, Mr. Bancroft," he said, "how much of that hypothetical case against me you really believe in."

"You're not worried?"

"No, just interested."

"Well, then, suppose we say that I believe in nothing of the hypothetical case, but that I, too, am interested."

Woodruff said goodnight and went out. As he started for the kitchen, he saw someone turn down the hallway leading away from it. He called out and the man came back. Woodruff said, "You're one of Bancroft's men, aren't you?" He went on as the man hesitated, "Just a friendly word of warning. If, as I assume, you've been detailed to shadow me, stop right now. Because if I catch you, I'll beat your brains out, and not with a bottle either. Ask Holmes."

He continued on to the kitchen. Robert was sitting on a high stool before the stove, the skillet ready, the eggs waiting to be cracked. Perhaps ten people were milling about the kitchen, having a late snack, and Ann Hunter was among them. She was wearing flowered print pajamas and a robe, and she was devouring a plateful of dainty, crustless sandwiches and drinking milk out of a bottle.

"Hello," she said, her mouth full, and she reached out and prodded Robert, "Robert, crack the eggs. He's here."

Robert started. "Thank you; I must have dozed off. Ham and eggs, Mr. Woody, well done? Touch of Worcestershire? Coming up, sir…"

"What are you doing here in that get-up?" asked Woodruff.

"Can't sleep on an empty stomach, so down I came."

"Here, Robert," said Woodruff, pushing back his sleeves. "I'll help you. We can't allow Miss Hunter to eat that stuff." He snatched the plate of sandwiches away from her, "Ham and——on two!" he called.

WHILE he was frying the eggs, Ann lit a cigarette. He took it away from her, muttering something about women who smoked during meals. She broke out laughing at him. They gobbled the food down with only a minor incident to disturb them. One of the people in the kitchen opened a closet and Alonzo was inside, sitting on the floor. He shouted something in Spanish at the startled guest, then, catching sight of Woodruff, he suddenly burst into tears. "So sorry I forget," he blubbered. They could hear him still crying in the closet after Woodruff closed it again.

Ann kept laughing while she drank the milk. Woodruff gave her a straw and took another for himself, sharing the bottle. He looked at her and said, "Good girl. I was afraid you were going to say something about this not being the first bottle we've shared tonight."

"You wrong me. I knew you wouldn't," she said.

"I guess I've underestimated you in more ways than that."

"Thank you," she said, fluttering her eyelids with mock demureness. All the same, there had been something in her voice as she spoke.

Little by little the kitchen emptied.

Robert folded away his chef's cap and sleepily exchanged goodnights. Alonzo's crying stopped and was soon followed by soft, contented snoring. Occasional voices drifted in from other parts of the house, but slowly, silence was coming to Seaside. Between six and seven, between the late drinkers and the early tennis players, Seaside would enjoy its Saturday morning hour of rest.

When they had finished, Woodruff turned off the kitchen lights. They went out to the foyer. The front door was open, and the far horizon had the merest streak of pale blue across it. The house was quite dark now. Woodruff took Ann's hand. "Don't go up just yet," he said. "You can't sleep on a full stomach." He led her out to the veranda, and she said nothing and offered no resistance.

They sat down on a large wicker swing. For several minutes neither of them spoke. A cool morning breeze swept across the veranda, and Ann gathered her robe about her. "You're shivering," Woodruff said, putting an arm around her. Then he said, quietly, "You're still shivering. You're not cold?"

"No," she said.

He raised her face to him, and held her in his arms. He kissed her tenderly. She was close to him now, her breathing uneven, her body limp. She had pressed him against her, but now she pulled away. He took her back in his arms, kissing her again, her lips, her cheeks, her forehead. She trembled and was quiet, and minutes went by, then she got up.

She said, "It's been a wonderful night, but I must go now." But he held her hands, drawing her down again.

"No," she said, quietly.

"Why not?"

She looked down at him. "You shouldn't have kissed me."

"But I wanted to. I think I wanted to the first moment I saw you. What do you suppose it can be?"

"I don't know," she said, turning away. "It doesn't matter."

He stood beside her. But it does matter," he said. "It matters to me. I don't understand it."

Her eyes were dark bits of flame. "Woody, it isn't that I think we're doing something wrong. I'm not thinking of your wedding. I wouldn't let anything stop me...if I were sure we loved each other."

"Do you love me?"

"I couldn't sleep when I left you. I came downstairs again hoping I'd see you, hoping somehow that something like this would happen to me. I wanted you to kiss me, to hold me in your arms. And now that it's happened, I know it mustn't go any further. Because I love you, Woody, and I don't want to be hurt..."

He stood there, seeing the tears run down her face, and suddenly, irresistibly, he swept her into his arms again. "I love you, Ann," he whispered. "I don't know how or why. I don't know what will happen after tonight. My head's going round and round like a pinwheel and I can't think anymore. But I love you, Ann..."

*   *   *

I DON'T know why I didn't stop it sooner. We both had identified him a good deal earlier, but we let him continue—at least I did, for my own part—because he was so interesting. I wanted to see how his mind worked, and where it would lead him. I had wondered, seeing how Ann Hunter had acted with him earlier that evening, what *Clyde Woodruff* would do when he met her again in the kitchen, but I had hardly expected this. I had watched him, a little frightened, certainly fascinated. In the end, it was the man with me who made the call for identification.

He was the liar. It had been clear enough from the moment he had begun to plan against David Jenks. On the basis of a few flimsy arguments he had undertaken something that would not only have smashed every semblance of his friendship with Jenks, but he had placed himself in an almost intolerable position. I could not understand what had motivated him—for surely he must have been aware of the enormous flaws Bancroft had found in his story, but whatever had motivated him, only a liar could have pretended to believe something so patently untrue.

Was even that as vicious as the lie he had told Ann Hunter? For there was something about him that was utterly destructive. He had taken the life of Clyde Woodruff and dirtied it as badly as he could. He had not only placed himself under suspicion, but he had undertaken to break the heart of a girl who meant nothing to him. What kind of man would have done what he did?

And yet, was there not something of him in every liar? It was the liar who destroyed not only his life, but the lives of people around him. It was the liar who sullied everything he touched, eager only to satisfy himself, to provide new excitement for the dark workings of his mind. For I knew that I would never be able to understand him.

We had stopped him from hurting Ann, though it would be an almost impossible task to avoid it completely now. But what of Jenks and Bancroft? Bancroft had built an astonishing case against *Clyde Woodruff,* true, but it was still a completely untrue one. The questions that *Woodruff* had asked, however, must still have had some weight when viewed in that light. Why had Jenks lied? What had actually gone on in the lab? What was the answer to the ever-growing riddle of what had happened in the laboratory? Where would it end?

More than ever, it was important now for me to take over my own life, for now that we had eliminated three of us, I knew who the fourth man was. He was the coward, and Hat coward would now take over my life at the perilous juncture where it had stopped momentarily. And trembling at the thought of what might happen from now on, I saw the man with me had not yet left. He was still sitting near me, watching me...

Surely he realized that I now knew who he was. But the mere knowledge was useless to me. Under the terms of our compact final victory belonged to the one who could bring the testimony of a third person to support him. *"Incontrovertible evidence will consist of the testimony of a third person, identifying him in agreement with the guesser."* That was how it had been stated. But to fulfill those terms, I would have to find a third person whom I could bring into this completely unbelievable world—bring him, moreover, with understanding enough not only to accept what had happened, but to agree with me.

The solution of this predicament had been left to the devices of the last two survivors. It was the most bitter irony of all, as of the ones who had gone before us had left us this as their heritage. *But as I thought so; I realized that a new factor had come into existence...*

BOTH of us knew it, as we had known everything else that bound us. Now that we two alone survived—we had somehow regained an independence of each other! Where, before this, only the one who had been *Woodruff* at the time, had had life—

now both of us were equal. Within the bounds of our compact, I had regained my freedom of action I Where before I could not have left this room unless a majority had agreed, now I could do whatever I wanted.

But only within the terms of our compact. I could not, for example, take over my life again. That was his right; I was forced to obey that, I could not leave the building where others might see me at a time when *Clyde Woodruff* was known to be elsewhere, where he was being seen by others. That was interference with the life that belonged to him.

But if he, as *Woodruff,* were to return to this apartment and bring others with him—those others would be able to see me, to talk to me, to wonder, perhaps, which one of us was Woodruff and which was this amazing double he had found. And though I had thought this to be true when it had first happened, I knew now that if someone had come into this room before we two were left as sole survivors, that we would have been unable to communicate with those people—that we would not have been seen by them! Had Jenks come into this room when I had first entered and found the four men, he would have seen only me. But my actions and my words would have been dictated by them.

That was the essential difference, the new factor that had come into existence—the fact that there were only two of us had given me an independent existence, a freedom of action, within limits.

It had had to be that way. How else could either of us have fulfilled the terms of the compact? If I were to have a chance at identifying the other survivor, I needed that freedom of action, little—so terribly little—as it was.

I returned the gaze of the coward. Why hadn't he gone? What was he waiting for? And then I laughed, realizing the answer. He was afraid to go—afraid, now that his chance at life had come, to take it! He squirmed under my gaze. We understood each other perfectly.

"Why are you waiting?" I said.

"Nothing is lost," he answered. "There can be no confusion in time. Wherever he was, I will resume at precisely the point where we stopped him." He hadn't answered the question. He locked his fingers nervously and looked away from me. "You look worried," he said, hesitatingly. "You seem to be on edge, as if you begrudged me my turn."

"Begrudge you?" I repeated, bitterly. "I'd give anything if I had a chance to take your turn—to try to repair the monstrous things *he* did."

He looked up at me eagerly, trying to hide it. "Would you?" he said. "Does it really mean so much to you? Because I don't care one way or another—and if you want to go now, I agree."

"Your word on it?" I cried.

"Yes," he nodded.

And instantly, with that sudden electric swiftness that sometimes knifes through all uncertainty, through indecision, I realized that I had been given the instrument that would seal his doom! I understood why he had surrendered his turn. He was hanging on to the life that was still his, afraid to venture it lest I somehow find a way to destroy him. Remaining there, he thought, he was safe from me. However long this move might prolong his miserable life, he clutched at it, never considering the almost insuperable difficulties that would have faced me had he taken the turn. But now he was lost!

The plan I had conceived would see to that. I went to my desk, where most of this account, then unfinished, was lying, and I gathered up the sheets. He didn't understand what I was doing, but he watched me put the manuscript into an envelope. I was taking it with me, and he was powerless to stop me...

* * *

TWO hours have passed since the event I have just written about occurred. Two hours I returned to my life. I have done what I could for Ann Hunter. I have told her we will discuss our affairs tomorrow. And since then I have been writing this account, bringing it up to date.

For I am putting my hope of salvation in this manuscript. I am sending it to the one person who may understand it. That person is the editor of a magazine I frequently read for relaxation. I have never met him, but reading his editorial columns, I have come to understand his mind. Surely he will understand. Stories stranger than this are commonplace to him, because he deals with them every day.

His name is Raymond A. Palmer. In Chicago he edits a magazine called *Fantastic Adventures*. He signs his columns as Rap.

To that magazine, then, I am sending this fantastic adventure. It is now early Saturday morning, and I have had to charter a special plane. Reading this—*this very note*—he must understand that he is my only hope. I expect him here in New York tonight or early tomorrow morning, Sunday. I am paying all his expenses.

When he comes, I will carefully discuss the whole thing with him. Once he is convinced of my identity and there can be no doubt, for I will prove that all of it is true, the end will be in sight. He can verify anything in this manuscript by merely talking to the people involved. When he agrees that I am Clyde Woodruff, he will understand that the man in my apartment can only be the coward. We will go there together. Then, as expeditiously as possible, without further discussion or argument, Palmer will identify the coward, and by thus agreeing with me, fulfilling my compact. I will be free again.

CHAPTER SEVEN
A Note from R.A.P. to the Reader *

* This note, which I have called Chapter VII, actually was written by me. I have included it here not only at the author's insistence, but because it forms an integral part of this story. —Ed.

WHAT would you have done, in my place? The hazards of editing are little appreciated, but it is probably a statistical certainty that most sanitariums for nervous disorders are inhabited, to a great extent, by fiction editors. And the science-fiction editors are the cream of the crop. When most people are vacationing, they have a good time. I spend my two weeks in a big white building, talking to doctors, trying to get rid of the twitch I picked up from that last batch of fan mail. And, I might add, counting the little green Martians as they jump around on my bed.

When I received the strange manuscript, which you have just read, it was almost noon. I had a date with a fascinating blonde for lunch. In the evening I had a big bowling party arranged, and the night before I had dreamed of foaming steins of beer. I was leaving my house, fairly happy about things in general, when this special messenger drove up and caught me. "Mr. Palmer?" he said.

I gulped. I had seen the envelope he carried, and to me envelopes mean manuscripts, and manuscripts mean work, and this was Saturday and I wanted to see my blonde and go bowling and drink beer. But I admitted I was Palmer. "Mr. Raymond A. Palmer?" he asked me, suspiciously.

"Yes."

"This just arrived on a chartered plane from New York. I must ask you for identification. Sign here, please."

He scrutinized my driver's license, draft card, social security, and a telephone bill, and he dumped the envelope in my arms. Sure enough, it hadn't been mailed. It had been addressed to my office, with instructions to get my home address and forward it immediately. Well, a new writer will try anything to get into print, as I know from bitter experience, but he doesn't usually charter planes. I was pretty damn curious about it by the time I arrived at the restaurant where I was to meet my blonde.

As usual, however, she was late, I ripped open the envelope and began looking through the manuscript. By the time my woman arrived, I was deep in the story, and I kept reading all through lunch. You know how blondes are when they don't get enough attention—it wasn't what you might call a successful luncheon date. But the story had gripped me and I read until I finished it.

We went for a ride along the lakefront afterward. I couldn't get the story out of my mind. I passed a light and got a ticket, then I scraped fenders with a bus, and my conversation was something less than coherent. But, finally, I succeeded in driving it out of my by now rather skeptical mind and I tried to make up with Felicia. That's her name. It kills me, too.

When I got back home late that afternoon, the phone rang. It was the Chicago airport. They had been calling me all afternoon; they had a seat reserved for me on the six o'clock plane to New York. Paid for. I said I wasn't going. I had no sooner hung up when the phone went off again. It was Long Distance operator 91, and she had been calling me all afternoon from New York, and would I hold on, please, because a Mr. Clyde Woodruff wanted to talk to me.

He sounded sane. There was a quiet note of urgency in his voice. He had had the devil's own time finally locating me, out of all the Palmers in Chicago. Hadn't I read his manuscript? I had to come to New York. I had to, he kept saying.

I don't know what you would have done. I said no. Maybe he had money to burn on plane tickets, but I wasn't going to be roped into flying a thousand miles just to read the last chapter of a story. I said I liked the story immensely, and if the ending were good, I would buy it when he mailed the rest of it in to me. (I was thinking of another New York writer of mine who kept sending me stories without the last chapters; I couldn't let it become an editorial practice.)

It was at this point that his control cracked, but only for a moment. He ended by saying that he would keep a chartered plane waiting for me at the airport. He seemed pretty certain I would change my mind. And he said he would call me in an hour again.

MAYBE he called again. I wasn't home to receive it. I went out for a quiet hour of practice bowling. I bowled an 82, a 114 and a 97, and I gave it up. I went to a telephone and called the library and asked them to hunt something up in *Who's Who*. They had Clyde Woodruff III, all right, with information that bore out some of the details in the story. Then I called the *Chicago Sun* and spoke to the society editor. Yes, she knew the Woodruffs of Long Island, and Clyde Woodruff was engaged to be married the next day to Miss Dorothy Dykstra. I called the telephone company and asked for Operator 91. Where had the New York call to Raymond A. Palmer originated from? She said it had come from Seaside, Long Island. Was I Mr. Palmer? Mr. Woodruff had been trying to get in touch with me again. Would I take the call where I was?

I hung up. Nobody was going to rob me of my Saturday night bowling—not after I had dreamed of beer.

But it was no use, and I knew it. Half an hour later I took a taxi to the airport. There was a plane waiting for me, or, if I preferred, I could take the eight o'clock Mainliner—there was a seat reserved for me on every plane for New York. I took the Mainliner because I didn't like the thought of wasting so much gasoline just to get me to New York.

I read the manuscript again on the plane. I went over it very carefully. It really had me by then, and the more I read it, the more peculiar I felt. There were little details in it that puzzled me a good deal. Maybe some of them have occurred to you since you began reading this bizarre story. There were parts that didn't hang together, parts that lent themselves to a variety of interpretations. In short, there was a lot in the story that left me unsatisfied.

And that's why I decided to take the course of action I did. If I was going to go through with this business, at least I would do it my way. The thing that puzzled me most of all was the man who was supposedly at that very moment in Woodruff's New York apartment. That man was really the crux of the story. Unless I satisfied myself about him, I might never know what the devil had really happened. And, of course, there were other reasons, dictated by details of the story itself, that impelled me to go first to the apartment. Later I would go out to see Woodruff himself. An hour wouldn't make any difference.

So, when the plane landed at LaGuardia airport, I went back to the city, to 800 Central Park South, as the story said. And, as the story had said, New York was dimmed out. I hardly recognized it as the city where I had spent my Christmas vacation; it was so dark and quiet that I thought I was back in Chicago again. But they don't breed such snooty doormen in Chicago. He just wouldn't let me up. He said that Mr. Woodruff was at his home in Long Island.

I kept insisting until finally he called the apartment on the phone. Naturally, there was no answer. Still I insisted, though I was beginning to feel pretty silly. I wanted to go up in the elevator and ring the doorbell. "Five dollars just to ring a doorbell," I said.

The doorman's eyes lighted. "Ahhh," he said, nodding his head in new understanding. "You're one of them guys that gets a kick out of ringing doorbell, eh?"

"Yeah," I said, "I feel like it wuz Hallowe'en."

"For five bucks, it's Hallowe'en, buddy," he said, and he escorted me into the elevator and took me upstairs. He watched me as I rang the doorbell. No answer. It didn't mean anything—according to the story, if there was someone inside he couldn't show himself; he couldn't voluntarily interfere with Woodruff's life.

"Five more for another ring?" I said.

"Oh, mister…" smiled the doorman, taking the five.

I had a plan, naturally. I wasn't just wasting money.

I GAVE him five dollars for each time I rang the bell. I rang it with different rhythms, sometimes soft, sometimes loud. After it had cost me twenty-five dollars, I said, sounding disappointed, "I guess he didn't come yet. I must be early. Is it one-thirty yet?"

"It's 12:55," said the doorman.

"The hell it is!" I said, angry, and I took out my watch, shook it and glared at it. "This watch stinks!" I said, and I laid it on the rug and jumped on it. It came apart as only a cheap watch can. The doorman just stood there, taking it all in.

"Then I'll go inside and wait," I said, still mad. "Woody said he'd meet me here at one-thirty. We're cooking up something." I stood at the door and I said, "Open it up with your pass-key. I'm one of Mr. Woodruff's friends."

The doorman looked at the twenty-five dollars and my watch and he nodded soberly. "You didn't have to tell me that, mister," he said. "I know Mr. Woodruff's friends when I see them." And he opened the door and let me in.

The apartment was dark. I flipped on a switch, after nearly knocking over a vase finding it. It was a duplex, and it must have cost a tidy sum to furnish it. There hadn't been an accurate description of the place in the story, but this felt right. And there, across the living room, was the short flight of stairs that led to two adjoining rooms that should be a bedroom and a study.

There wasn't the slightest sound in the place. I went up the stairs and tried to look under the threshold of the doors to see if there was a light in either of the rooms, but the door fitted too well. At this point I began to feel like a damn fool. I knocked on the first door. There was no response. Nothing happened when I knocked on the other door. I thought to myself that I had paid the equivalent of twenty-nine dollars to ring one bell and knock on two doors. It would be difficult asking Woodruff to reimburse me such a sum. It was a hell of a thing to put down on an expense account.

Then I pushed open the first door—and there he was!

"Who are you?" he said. "What are you doing here?" He had been standing near the door, evidently hearing me in the living room, and certainly he had heard the doorbell and the knocking on his door. He was a tall young man, well built, with dark, puzzled eyes and close-cropped hair. He watched me as I walked into the room, putting my envelope down.

"My name's Palmer," I said. "The doorman let me in. I'm a friend of Clyde Woodruff's."

"I am Clyde Woodruff," he said. "What are you doing here?"

"I know all about you," I said. "Mr. Woodruff had me come a thousand miles to be sure about you. All I want to do now is look at you a few minutes, before I go out to Seaside."

"What are you talking about?" he said, bewildered. "What do you mean—you know all about me? And what is this about—"

"Never mind," I said. "I'm here to identify you." I took a hard swallow before I could get out the words. There was still a chance that this was a sensational, super-hoax of some sort. I said, with an effort to speak distinctly, "I'm the third person who is necessary to break the compact you made...if you know what I'm referring to."

I couldn't have hit him any harder if I had used an axe. He just stood there and he whispered, "Oh my lord." I thought he was going to fall and I took his arm. He shook me off. "It can't be," he said, shaking his head. "It's impossible. What can you possibly know about this? How can you..." He didn't finish. He was looking at me, one hand pressed against his face, staring at me.

"Is this a gag?" I said. He didn't answer. I said, "Well, it had to end sometime, and I guess you know that Woodruff would work out some way to beat you in the end."

His hands were at his sides, his fists tightly clenched, and his arms trembled as he tried to control himself. "But I am Woodruff!" he cried. "Don't you understand—*I am Woodruff!*"

I DIDN'T know what to say. There was no sense contradicting him. He came closer to me and he said, "Do you mean you understand everything that's happened here...all of it, from the beginning? Then you must know that I—"

"What's the use?" I said. I was beginning to feel sorry for him. He was really flesh and blood, though I was afraid to touch him. "I know the whole thing," I said. "You're the coward. Are you satisfied now?" I was waiting for him to break down. "I'm going to call Woodruff on the phone," I added. "He can save me a trip back here by coming out here right now himself."

"The *what?*" he said.

"The what what?"

"You called me…the *coward?*"

"Well, you are, aren't you? You've got to be. Process of elimination. You're the last one except for Woodruff himself."

"You mean you're identifying me as the *coward?*" he said. He had a peculiar quality in his voice. It did things to me, shook my insides somehow. It was the kind of voice you always imagine you'll hear from a condemned man, if you ever get in such a spot. It was the voice, more than anything else that first created the inkling of doubt. There had been doubt before, you may remember, but it had vanished the moment I laid eyes on him.

"But there never was a coward among us!" he said.

"No?"

"You don't understand."

"Was there a killer?" I interrupted. "And then a fool? And then Woodruff? And then a liar? That leaves you as the coward."

"No!" he cried. "There was no liar! And no coward! The liar—"

"Let's not waste any more time," I said. "Here's a little manuscript that will show you just how hopeless it is. You read it and I'll just relax a little from that ride I took."

I gave him the manuscript. His face was as pale as the sheets of paper. He sat down in a chair and began reading feverishly. Because I knew the effect it would have on him, I went out and sat in the living room, and I mixed myself a mild drink. I was satisfied that I had done the best I could. I had been fair to an extreme that might haunt me. But I would get this manuscript, and maybe it was worth it. The story would never be believed, but it was quite a story.

A little more than half an hour later, I went back. He had almost finished reading it, and he was at the last few pages. He read them with such care, such burning intensity that I marveled at it. When he finished, he stood up and surveyed me, as if he was seeing me for the first time. He seemed much calmer now. Resigned, I thought. He lit a cigarette, just as each Woodruff in the story had done so many times before.

"Mr. Palmer," he said, "from the start I felt that I would win out in this struggle, just as it says here. But I never dreamed I would run into such luck. I tell you honestly that I didn't know how to begin working out the last part of this compact."

"You're not admitting anything?" I asked, surprised.

He shook his head. "This manuscript is one of the shrewdest things ever concocted. I don't expect you to believe me—not yet. But if you'll just sit quietly and listen to me for five minutes, I'll give you the incontrovertible evidence that our compact called for."

I nodded for him to go ahead, wondering what he had thought up.

"WHILE I do not expect you to believe what I say, I want you, nevertheless, to pretend to yourself that you do believe it, to give my story the substance it cannot yet have.

"First," he continued, "though this manuscript was written by the supposedly real Clyde Woodruff, the truth is that I am the real Woodruff, and I did not write it. The story related in these pages is, nevertheless, true in the main. Its first lie is in the identification of the four other men who were in this room with me. *There never was a coward.* There was a killer, a fool, a liar and a fourth who was a crafty, ruthless person, shrewd and calculating. I can't define him in a single word as I could the others. I don't think any of us defined him in a single word; in a sense he was the most complex character of all.

"That is the first lie in this story. The episode, which describes the killer, is true. So is the one that deals with the fool. The chapter, which describes what happened to the real Woodruff when he went third, is likewise true. It happened, however, to me. I was brought back to this room, and I was then the last to go. The fourth to go was the man who accused Jenks of complicity in the missing notes. His story is true up to the end, with one serious defection.

"The fourth man was never identified as the liar. I and the man who was left here with me agreed that he was the—for the sake of convenience, I'll call him the crafty one. We ended the life of the crafty one by identifying him. Now, follow me carefully. When he had disposed of the killer, the fool, the crafty one—who was left? Only the liar and me.

'It was the liar who wrote this manuscript. I saw him writing it all the time I was here, without knowing what it was. He must have gotten the idea originally because he drew the fifth straw. He was to be the last to go, until I took over that place because they could not agree on my identification. He planned it with amazing cleverness.

"First, he assumed my identity in writing this story. Second, he created a category that never existed—by naming a coward instead of the crafty one. Third, he said that we had agreed that the fourth was the liar. *He did this because it eliminated the liar from the story altogether.* Suppose he had not done that. Suppose he had truthfully described the identification of the crafty one. He would then have come to the end of the story with two characters left—himself, supposedly the real Woodruff—and the liar.

"Now, if he told anyone this story, as he has told it here to you, admitting that the liar still existed, would there not be some faint possibility of doubt in your mind? If you knew that of the two who had survived, that one was a liar—might you not tread easily? Might you not be a bit more careful before you agreed with him? It was to avoid taking such a chance that he labeled the fourth the liar, thus completely removing that category from consideration…"

I interrupted. "Are you saying that the one who survived with you—assuming for a moment that you are the real Woodruff—was the liar?"

"Exactly."

"Then, if I follow you, you are saying that he built up a case from the beginning to assume your identity. But you are ascribing such foresight to him that it hardly seems credible."

"Not foresight," he said. "It was hindsight. He wrote only part of this story here in this room. He says he only finished the story this morning, but actually, he wrote a great deal of it then. He must have gone back through the beginning, doctoring it to fit the case he was building. Once things have happened, it is easier to re-interpret them according to a fixed plan. I intend to show you how that plan operated, and where it failed, for failed it has."

"Suppose you explain how you're here, if you're the real Woodruff, when this manuscript says the real Woodruff is at Seaside."

HE smiled. "Only a liar understands how strong a simple perversion of the truth is. Put yourself in his place. He had drawn the fifth chance. When I became last, I was to remain here after him. That is what happened. Now he wrote most of this story. He doctored is so that you would think he was the real Woodruff, and to substantiate that, he told a simple lie.

"He merely said *that the coward was afraid to go,* and offered him the chance. To make this plausible, he first had to have a coward. He didn't have one, so he *created* one. No matter what you might try to check in this story, you would find that the events described in it are all true—he saw to that. But how could you check up to find out if there had really been a coward? There was no way. The other three are gone. You would have to take his word for it. Since he could demonstrate the truth of the rest of the story, why should you doubt that?

And the way he told it, it does seem as if there was a coward, and that coward is me, the one who was afraid to go, and is therefore here.

"So he wrote in a minor change—a coward. The crafty one he never mentioned at all because he needed *his* place in the story for the liar—the liar he wanted to get rid of. Is it clear so far?"

"Yes," I said. "Very complicated, but clear. Go on."

"We come then to the conclusion of a seemingly perfect plan. The killer is eliminated, and so is the fool. He takes over the identity of the real Woodruff, describes what happened to *me* as having happened to *him,* and says he was now last. He then tells the story of the crafty one, labeling him the liar. That leaves only him, supposedly the real Woodruff, and the coward, whom he created: this as opposed to the real Woodruff, who I am, and the liar—which is he. He then neatly transposes the matter by saying that the coward offered him his chance, and he took it. And that, in your mind, fixes the location of the real Woodruff as being now at Seaside. All right?"

"Yes," I said, "though I think you're overdoing the repetition. You've said the same thing two or three times."

"I want to be sure it's perfectly clear."

"It is, so far."

"He then finished up the manuscript to agree with this plan. It wasn't difficult, for the most part. He sent it to you, expecting you to go to Seaside. I still don't know why you came here instead, but that is the turning point in this story. At any rate, once you were at Seaside, you could check up on his manuscript. You might talk to Bancroft, Jenks, Robert, Dorothy, Alonzo, Vanness, Holmes, Mahoney—to all of them, and you would see that this story was true.

"But you could not talk to Ann Hunter! He saw to that. When he took his turn, going fifth in regular order, he shrewdly told Ann early this morning that he had to reverse himself, that Dorothy insisted she leave the grounds, Ann packed up and left.

If you go to Seaside, you will find that Ann Hunter is no longer there.

"But why did he do that? He did it because he couldn't have Ann there! *Because the scene he described between Ann and Woodruff never happened!* It was a pure lie—a complete fabrication!"

That floored me. "I don't see that part of it," I said.

"It's a magnificent plan," he said sincerely. "I can almost detach myself from it and admire the brain that conceived it…

"Here's how it worked. He had to write that scene in because he needed it to label the fourth one a liar. If we go back through the chapter that describes the events in which the fourth Woodruff figured, we nowhere find any evidence to support the assumption that he was the liar. We find plenty of evidence to show that he was crafty, however. Did you see that?"

"Yes," I admitted. "I thought that part of it was weak, but the conclusion seemed sound enough. If he really lied to Ann that way—"

"BUT he didn't!" he interrupted. "That part of it never happened, as I've said. Now, examining those events, we see that the fourth Woodruff exhibited certain characteristics. He had an orderliness of mind. It showed, for instance, in the way he labeled his thoughts by numbers. He would say 'first' this and 'second' that—as I am well aware I am doing myself—but then, he was part of me.

"And he was the first of all four Woodruffs (including myself) to begin assembling the bits of evidence against Jenks. True, Bancroft built up a case against him that was wonderful, but we know that there is no truth to it. It is just one of those things. We do not, however, know that the case against Jenks is untrue. There are vital flaws in it, but I myself am still not convinced.

"Had I been there, I doubt that I would have gone about presenting the case to Bancroft in such a heartless fashion. The crafty one didn't care. The crafty part of Woodruff, the ruthless

Woodruff who gambles on the Stock Exchange, who destroys competitors, whose chief joy in life is outguessing the next fellow—that Woodruff wouldn't care much about Jenks. He would assemble the contradictions that pointed to a friend's guilt with no compunction. He would as soon outfox a friend as anyone else—the game was the thing for him.

"As it happened, he was stymied by Bancroft's objections. *But there was no evidence that he was a liar!* We know that everything he said about Jenks was true, if unexplained. How then could the liar, writing this story, re-interpret his actions so as to be able to call him a liar? There was no way, on the basis of what had happened. If he changed the details of the events, you might come across the discrepancy.

"So he made up a scene! Actually, Ann had gone up to bed. She did not come down. There never was any lovemaking between Woodruff and Ann. But when the liar wrote the scene in, that gave him his chance to call the fourth Woodruff a liar. He merely said that Woodruff had lied when he told Ann that he loved her. That accusation carried authority now. Now he could carry the stigma over. He could become indignant in his comment on that chapter as he spoke of the fourth Woodruff. He could call him a destroyer, and make that word synonymous with liar. He could say that Woodruff had lied when he accused his friend—and with that false scene between Ann and Woodruff, he could back it up!

"But there still remained one thing to be taken care of. If you, Mr. Palmer, came to Seaside to investigate, you might just possibly question Ann Hunter. It was easily avoided, in this way...

"The life of the fourth Woodruff actually ended when he left Bancroft in the library. We called for identification, and we agreed that the fourth Woodruff was the crafty one. That ended his life. Now the liar took his turn. The next morning, without much ado about it, as I've already told you, he told Ann she had better leave. When Ann left, the coast was clear. There was nothing more to fear. If you asked him about Ann, believing the scene was true, he could have told you anyone of a dozen stories—that she couldn't go through with it—that she hadn't the courage. Would you have suspected? You had no reason to.

"Then, once you had come to Seaside tonight, once he had convinced you, he would bring you here, and as he says—*without any further discussion or argument*—you would agree with him and end my life. Of course he wanted it without discussion. That might lead anywhere! It might even lead to the disclosure of the truth—as I have given it to you now!"

I DIDN'T say anything for a while after he had finished speaking. If I had thought the story bizarre before this, what could I think about it now? Even an editor, I was forced to admit to myself, seldom came across anything like this. It baffled me. It taunted and perplexed me. I was half dizzy from having read the story, with its hypotheses and counter-hypotheses, with one set of circumstances yielding first one story and then another. And here the story itself had become the basis for a completely different hypothesis!

"Of course," I said, at length, "the final test of your story depends on Ann Hunter. The fact that she can't be found is as bad for your version as you say it is for the version in be manuscript."

"But I know where you can find her!" he said, vehemently.

"Where?"

"When he told her that she had to leave, she smiled at him very sweetly. She said she didn't blame him a bit, she understood perfectly. And it hadn't been a wasted weekend, she said, because that morning Robert had told her where he had learned to mix the champagne cocktail she liked so much. She would spend the rest of the weekend at the Astor bar, she said, toasting the future happiness of the Woodruffs."

"Ironic?" I said.

"Why do you say that?"

"Oh, I don't know," I hedged. "But you heard her tell this to be...the fifth Woodruff? Seems funny."

"It wasn't funny to me. I didn't know why he had sent her away."

"You wouldn't have done it?" I said.

"No," he said, thoughtfully. "You know, now that you put it that way, there was something ironic about the way she said that..."

"Hmmm," I said, from the depths of my wisdom. Because as much as he had learned about himself, he still didn't really understand what Clyde Woodruff was all about. I got up and reached for my battered old hat. "You'd better give me a key," I said. "I can't afford to buy another door man when I come back."

"Where are you going?" he asked.

"To the Astor bar, to bring Miss Ann Hunter back here."

It bothered him. "Why don't you just talk to her—say you're my lawyer or something, and sound her out?"

"I like it my way," I said, flatly, without going into it. "And one more thing. I'm still an editor, you know, and I still want good stories. One of the conditions on which I offer my help is your promise that I can keep this manuscript, if we can find an ending, and publish it. And I've got some interesting ideas about ending it."

He didn't like it. He started to protest, so I took off my hat and sat down again. The argument ended abruptly. I'll be damned, I thought to myself, if I'll travel a thousand miles for a story and come back without it—especially one like this.

He gave me a key, and as I left, he said, "To get to the Astor—"

"Are you telling me?" I said. "I've been there, brother. I had enough champagne last Christmas to float a battle cruiser."

I took a taxi downtown. The doorman had asked me, "No luck?" and I told him I was going to bring me some company, to make the waiting easier. I wasn't half as confident as I sounded. In the first place, what made me assume she would be at the Astor bar? I had my own reasons for thinking she would, but that was neither here nor there. In the second place, assuming she was there, what made me think she would come back with me? And in the third place, though it should have been the first place—what made me believe *this* story more than the other one? I liked it better, maybe. But mainly it was because I am a sucker for the kind of twist I thought I saw coming up here.

THE minute I walked into the bar I knew it was she. Strangely, enough, he had forgotten to tell me what she looked like, but all I needed was the description in the story—and one look. A slender, beautiful, dark-haired girl with piercing blue eyes.

"Do I interest you so much?" she asked.

"I beg your pardon," I said. I had leaned over the bar and stared at her for perhaps half a minute before she made me aware of it. "I was trying to be sure you're the person I'm looking for," I explained. "I think you must be Miss Ann Hunter?"

"Yes, indeed," she said. "Have a drink with me. They make—"

"The best champagne cocktails I ever had," I finished, smiling at her. "Only they're not really cocktails. When you shoot brandy into champagne, you get a drink called a French .75—or didn't Robert tell you that? He makes one that's even better than the Astor's."

"Oh," she said, faintly. "How do you know—"

"Miss Hunter," I said, "right now I'm just about as omniscient as the Lord himself. Sometimes I think I know everything. I'm a friend of Clyde Woodruff's. To come right down to it, that's why I'm here. I'm acting as a sort of Mercury for him, wing-footing an urgent message. He wants to see you. Must see you, in fact."

"Really?" she said, dryly.

"I told you I was omniscient," I said. "It's my guess that you'd like to see him as much as he wants to see you. I know what you're thinking. Well, he couldn't come himself. It's a long, complicated, and thoroughly unbelievable story, but it's going to see print one of these days, and I'll mail you a copy. Now let's have a drink together and we'll run over there."

"Back to that foul, mob-ridden, haunted palace? Not me, mister!"

"Palmer's the name, and Woody's there at his apartment. He came all the way there just to see you. Tell me," I said, "don't you have a queer little tingling sensation inside when you mention his name?" I grinned at her and added, quietly, "Don't kid me, please."

She looked at her drink and swallowed it in one gulp. Then she gave me the same look and she said, "I'll be damned if I don't think you're something right out of a fairy tale. You're— you're supernatural! You've been dancing with elves in the light of the moon."

"Uh-huh," I agreed, slapping my hat back on and swallowing my drink. "And I've got a dancing date later tonight. Let's go."

You should have seen the look the doorman gave me when I popped out of the taxi with Ann in tow. "Got a five to lend me?" I whispered to Ann. She found one, and I sneaked it away and casually tossed it to him. "That's in case I accidentally ring the bell," I told him.

We went up, and I let us in with the passkey. I took her into the library. She walked in hesitantly. Woodruff stood there, looking across the room at her. You could hardly hear their voices when they exchanged hellos, but there was something in it, just the same, that got me. They might have stood that way, eating each other up with their eyes indefinitely, if I hadn't brought them back to life.

"Sit down, the both of you," I said. "I've got something here I want to read to you, Miss Hunter. This is something a clever young man wrote. I don't think it's true, but I want you to tell me whether it is or isn't—whether it happened, that is. Don't be shocked by it, and don't interrupt me. It isn't very long."

I FUMBLED through the manuscript, and I read them the story, beginning with Woodruff's return to the kitchen. My voice jumped a little when I got them out on the veranda, and I think I whispered the last part of it altogether. And when it was through, it was so quiet I could hear my heart thumping.

"Did it happen?" I asked.

"No," she said, very quietly, looking down at the floor. "Why did you bring me here?"

I waited, hoping Woodruff would give her the answer I had already phrased in my mind. But he sat like someone turned to stone. "I'll tell you why I brought you here," I said, disgusted. "Because—"

"Because it should have happened, Ann," said Woodruff. "Because with all my heart, I wanted it to happen."

After a moment, she said, "Then you found out?"

"Yes," he said. He could move, I discovered. He got off the chair and came to her and he took her in his arms, not the least bit ashamed before me. "I love you, Ann," he said, "Not the silly, stupid way it was written in that thing, but I love you. I'm not going to marry Dorothy. We'll go away tomorrow, the both of us. And I'll tell Dorothy tonight…"

He kissed her then, and maybe it was because his eyes were closed that he didn't see the effect his last words had had on her. But I hadn't missed a thing. I knew I should have silently stolen away, but I had to know what this thing I had perceived meant.

"Ann," I said, "if I may call you Ann—I've got to ask you something…" I waited until they melted apart, then I said, bluffing, because I didn't know the answer myself, "Suppose you tell Woody what you really meant when you asked him, a moment ago, whether he had found out?"

"He…he doesn't know?" she faltered.

"No," I said. "And I'd rather you told him than me."

In the moments that sped by while she debated the question within her, I must have run through a thousand conjectures. What was she going to tell him? Just before he had kissed her, when he had said, "I'll tell Dorothy tonight," she had been puzzled, as if she couldn't understand those simple few words.

Now, quietly, she went to her bag and took out a small photograph. I recalled having seen her holding it at the bar, but she had quickly put it away. She gave the photograph to Woodruff. He looked at it for a long time, then he gave it to me.

It had been taken in the garden. It was a picture of David Jenks and Dorothy Dykstra. They were locked in an embrace that could only have been classified as violent as they kissed in the darkness—for the photograph had evidently been taken without light.

"I thought you knew," she said, softly. "I took it last night while I was taking pictures around the grounds. I was using my infrared camera, and it was so dark I didn't know who the people were...until I developed the picture..."

"And you didn't tell me?" he asked.

She shook her head. "No, though I almost did when I found out someone had wrecked my things. I was so mad for awhile that..." She shrugged. "And then I thought that I had no right, that it was none of my business. If I had been her, and I thought I'd been discovered, I'd have wrecked a dozen places. I'd have had me kicked off the grounds..."

Wondering, Woodruff said, "And that's what you had in mind this morning when you left and you said you were going to toast my future happiness..." The implications behind that photograph were just beginning to become apparent to him. He shrugged involuntarily.

"But it's a thousand times better this way, darling," she said, gently. "I thought at first that I was getting you on the rebound, and I was happy to have you in any way. But you really do love me..."

I left them to each other for a few minutes, then I tapped Woodruff's shoulder. "There's still one or two details to be settled," I reminded him. "I'd better take Miss Hunter home now. You can go to her as soon as we've finished our business."

WELL, when she let go of him, she flung her arms around me and kissed me, and it was the kind of kiss I'd walk a thousand miles for, every day. She left us alone for a few minutes. I said to Woodruff, "Before I forget it, make a note of this—the workshop was wrecked not because of this photograph, but because Jenks was afraid it might show him talking to a man with a white carnation. Your first assumption was correct. He couldn't have known about this picture."

"What are you getting at?" he asked.

"Getting at?" I said, disgusted. "Why, you've got every damn bit of a clue you need by now, and now you're so doggone crazy in love that you can't see farther than your nose! You know what I'm going to do now? I'm going to find you that *motive* that your crafty friend was hunting for. But first I'm going out to fetch back our amazing liar."

"How will you do it?"

"You take a nap," I advised him. "I'll do the rest. I'm beginning to enjoy this."

He tried to thank me, but I'd been thanked enough already. As I said, I'm a terrific sucker for romance. I thought to myself that the supreme irony of all lay in the fact that it was the liar, his strongest adversary, who had come closest to finding the true Woodruff, inadvertent though it was. It was the liar, of all the Woodruffs, who had most demonstrated the real Woodruff's ability to understand people. He had been a really amazing psychologist, that liar. He had wrapped himself so completely in his borrowed personality that he had written with absolute conviction. He *had* been Woodruff. One had only to read the manuscript, to search the long passages of introspection, to appreciate how hellishly clever he had been.

And, for that matter, each of the four Woodruffs had done him a remarkable service, if only in that they revealed Woodruff to himself...

I took Ann home and then I headed out to Seaside, I made short work of the rest of it. Woodruff the liar was waiting impatiently for me; Chicago had told him I'd taken the plane. I went over the manuscript with him in some detail, watching his reactions.

I even spoke to Mahoney. Somehow Mahoney seemed spiritless, but he answered my questions diligently. Sometimes we could hardly hear ourselves talk—the party was wilder that night than it had been the night before, granting that the description of the night before had been accurate. Dorothy Dykstra floated by me, favored me with a smile when I was introduced to her. Robert mixed me a French .75, and it was great.

The hell of it was that this Woodruff was a completely real person, rather charming, too—but let's not get back into that again. I expressed the proper astonishment at the story, and in a convincing way I let myself be convinced. Then I agreed that it was time we went to the city apartment, where, Woodruff assured me, my previous disbelief would be a petty thing indeed beside what he would show me.

I held out for only one small exception. I wanted him to take Professor Jenks along with us, in case, I said, I wanted to check on one or two minor points that troubled me the least bit. I could have asked for anything and gotten it. Woodruff got Jenks to come with us by saying that the drive would do Jenks a world of good. He could have thought up a dozen fancier reasons if he had needed them, I thought.

We drove back to the city together. When we stopped in front of the house I borrowed five dollars from Woodruff and gave it to the doorman without a word. I wondered if he would say anything that might disturb Woodruff, but he was too dazed by then to open his mouth.

Woodruff let us into the apartment. He excused himself from Jenks and took me into the library. He closed the door softly and pointed to the real Woodruff. "Well," he said, addressing the real Woodruff, "it's over now for you. I've brought the third person here to identify you. I ask only that you control your cowardice without making any outcries...Mr. Palmer—I give you the coward!"

"We've met," I said, dryly. "I stopped over here earlier this evening and had a chat with Mr. Woodruff and Miss Hunter. Now then, my boy," I said to Woody, pointing to the liar, "who do you say this is?"

"The liar," said Woodruff.

I cleared my throat. "I don't know how I'm supposed to say this," I said, "but I might as well make it formal."

Then I cleared my throat again, for effect, and I said, "By virtue of the authority vested in me as the third person necessary to break this compact by proper identification of one of the two surviving parties to the aforementioned compact, and fully cognizant of all the whereases and wherefores of the afore-mentioned compact, and acquainted with every devious device used by the party subsequently referred to by me as the liar—" I had to take a breath at that point. "I do hereby attest and affirm that I agree completely and without reservation in the identification just made—and that I call you the liar."

HE HAD been there the instant before...and now...well, he just wasn't. That's all. Not even a sound, not a bit of lightning or anything you might think suitable for such an occasion. But if I live to be a thousand years old, I will never forget the look on his face when I went into that speech. There's no use trying to describe it. Maybe one of my good writers like Don Wilcox or Dave O'Brien or Bill McGivern, or even Frank Patten, could handle a description like that. Not me. Just the same, it seemed to me that I could see that expression hanging in mid-air for a few seconds after the rest of him disappeared. Yes, sir, it was that frozen!

By the same token, there's not much more that I can tell you that Clyde Woodruff couldn't tell better. And according to his promise, he had to finish the story, so suppose we let him...?

CHAPTER EIGHT
As the Editor Ordered

IF YOU will glance back at the explanation with which I began this story, it should make some sense at this point. I wrote it just before I began this last chapter, and I mean what I say in it. I have protested to Palmer that I don't want any of this to appear, but he won't let me off. He calmly says that he has a printing press for a heart and ink instead of blood in his veins.

Having said the worst about him, perhaps I should tell you there is another side to him. I've read his Chapter VII, which he says will appear just before this last chapter, and I can see what he means when he says that Ann said he had been dancing with elves in the moonlight. You'd have to meet him to understand that. I'm afraid, though I wouldn't have said elves. I'd have chosen the little men who bowled and drank beer with Rip Van Winkle up in the mountains.

But since I must finish this, I must. I intend to hurry the job, so bear with me and hang on, because I don't pretend to have any style and I never was much of a writer except on checks...

When Palmer arranged for the liar to disappear, he instantly got busy. We had Jenks outside, you remember, and Palmer had promised me the motive. He insisted that I already had the whole thing solved myself, but I was too blind to see it. He asked me a dozen questions and dragged answers out of me. I'll try to quote him as best I can.

"The main thing," he said, "is that Jenks both appears guilty and doesn't. He certainly lied. He certainly was outside the garage with one of the men who wore a carnation. He was also, if you recall, with Dorothy a good deal. Where was he shortly after the fight in the pavilion, when Bancroft and you figured out he must be missing? He showed up and confounded you, and by his own admission, he had been with Dorothy.

"And where was he when you got mixed up in that thing at the pier? He had been comforting Dorothy again! Now, you hadn't seen Jenks in years, and even in the months since you gave him that laboratory, you said yourself that you had only seen him once or twice. Assuming even then that Jenks had met Dorothy every time you did, didn't you think it strange that he should be on such intimate terms with her? Wasn't it odd that he was always on hand to comfort her?

"Sure you did—though you wouldn't admit it to yourself. Just like you wouldn't admit the sneaking suspicion you always had that your Dorothy girl was marrying your money. She had no use for your friends, for your habits, for your cutthroat business sense. And you hated her friends and everything she stood for. She drove you to drink. She was the unconscious reason for every escapade you had with women—you were always hoping you could get out of it, but you never quite were able to make it. Somehow you always wound up engaged to her again. That wasn't your doing—it was hers. She had you on a string, and sometimes she let the string out a little. It's apparent in every line in the story, even though it was written by a liar. I guess you can lie successfully to anyone but a liar, huh?

"But to return to Jenks. That case that the crafty one in you outlined to Bancroft wasn't a bad case. Bancroft tore it apart, but the parts could have been made into an excellent pattern to fit Jenks—if you could find that master pattern—*a motive.*

"All right. Now what you've just found out about Jenks and your Dorothy is the beginnings of a motive. But before you can begin to understand the motive, you must understand Jenks. Ask yourself the question Bancroft asked—if Jenks is guilty, then why did he call in the F.B.I.? It's a damn good question. You might say that maybe you could show that it wasn't Jenks who had called them in. If you could show that, you'd have something. Unfortunately, Jenks did call them in, but the theory behind the question is still a good one.

"What you are doing with that theory is trying to separate the Jenks who is guilty from the Jenks who called in the F.B.I. Right? Do you see it now? You still don't? There we must demonstrate!"

We went out and took Jenks with us. We drove to the laboratory. I watched Jenks and I saw he was shaking as if a fever had gotten into him. He could hardly walk when we got to the lab. Palmer said, "Now, whatever happens, hold on to Jenks. Hold his arm. And don't let go."

We went through the lab, and just before we entered Jenks' private office, Palmer took a deep breath. Then in we walked. There was nothing there. Palmer, nothing daunted, led us back to the cab. "We'll go to Jenks' home," he said. "I sort of counted on the lab, but I see I was wrong."

Jenks grew worse. He spoke in little meaningless snatches, and he was evidently paralyzed with fear. We stopped before his place and went up. I took hold of Jenks' arm and held it tightly while Palmer opened the door.

And there, standing against the window was a second Jenks!

I don't know if I've made it appear as dramatic to you as it was in real life. This other Jenks had seen us coming from the window. He had a terrible smile on his face.

"How does one do it?" Palmer asked him.

The Jenks who had been in the room said, quietly, "Anything will do. The compact could have been broken at any time by Woody's violence. We need that violence now. Kill him!"

I held the first Jenks firmly. Palmer said to me, with a little gulp, "I guess you'd better strangle him."

"What?" I said, feeling faint.

"Strangle him," said Palmer. "He's no more real than your liar was!"

I'd rather skip over that part, if it's all the same to you. I didn't really have to strangle him, though. He died at the first touch of my hands because the *intent* to kill was in them. He died and there was nothing in my hands. Just...nothing...

And then Jenks broke down and wept like a baby. There was no consoling him. He poured his heart out to us. He told us everything, and the story spilled out of him like a disease.

He had been in love with Dorothy and she with him from the first time they had met. Genuine love it was, too. But there was nothing he could do about it. He wanted to tell me but she had refused. He had no money and she would never marry him. Her youth had been marred by the constant spectre of poverty. But they had continued to see each other, though they knew it was a hopeless love.

And then he had discovered this drug. Like many a scientist before him, he had experimented with it upon himself. It was too late when he realized what had happened to him. It had separated him into two beings—one who was him, the other who was evil. And because his will was thus divided, as many a man's is between his conflicting desires, he had been forced into a compact with his evil self.

For several days his conflicting wills had fought for possession of his being, until, half crazed, he had agreed to a compact. They would alternate in controlling the man who was Jenks. Each, while he was Jenks, would have freedom of action. The contest would be fought to a finish, and the prize would be either the attainment or the loss of what Jenks wanted most in this world—Dorothy. If, by four o'clock that Sunday she had married me, the evil Jenks would lose. If she had not married me, if she declared that she was to marry Jenks before that hour, the good Jenks would lose.

For it was the good Jenks who had tried to tear her out of his heart and mind, believing that I had loved her. He could not help his love for her, but he fought against it. He wanted to stop seeing her, but his other self drove him on. And then, with the drug, that other self, the evil self, had come to have an equal share in what he had. If that evil self allowed the other to renounce, or in any way lose Dorothy, then the evil self was doomed.

The terms of their compact were simple. Neither could tell the truth of what had happened to Jenks. They could not communicate in any way this monstrous thing that had befallen him. But within those bounds there was freedom. One might try persuading Dorothy to run away with him. He might do anything to gain that end. The other could do the same to attain his end. But—if the evil was recognized by *me*—and if there was thus violence, as they expected there would be, then the evil was doomed.

The evil self, in control of Jenks, had undertaken to sell the drug to the German government. It would provide him with money enough, and quickly enough to win Dorothy. The good, for his part, fought the arrangement until there was such chaos between their mixed plans that they had agreed to extend that duel until four o'clock on Sunday. The foreign agent was instructed to contact Jenks at four o'clock. By then it would be apparent who had won by seeing whether or not the wedding went through.

It was the good self who called in the F.B.I. It was he who told me the truth of the compound, for he could tell me that much, but he could not say anything more. It was the bad who had left the rum bottle filled with the compound, knowing that Jenks was going to call me to the lab, as he had already wired me to come to him that morning. And so the evil Jenks had prepared a characteristic pitfall for me. It would be Friday afternoon and I would be drunk, and the bottle of rum would be irresistible to me.

He had been right in his calculations. The good Jenks had hidden the bottle in his desk, but I had found it in the few minutes he had been gone with Bancroft…

We left him then. He was too broken to speak, and there was little left for him to say. Palmer worked out the rest of it.

"It was the evil Jenks," he said, "who came to your apartment when you found the four men in your library. He wanted to know what had happened to you, so that he could use that knowledge to further confuse you. He told the truth when he said he didn't know what it would do to you—you had taken so much, remember. So he tried to frighten you by telling you that you would die unless it had changed you.

"Unfortunately for him, he was dealing with the killer, and the killer didn't frighten easily. Meanwhile, he had contacted his agent again and notified him that the F.B.I. was in on the case. He couldn't change his plans, much to the confusion of the Nazis, because that was part of his compact with the good Jenks. But he could try to throw the F.B.I. off the trail. So he had them send in a dozen men with phony F.B.I. badges. He lured Mahoney into a trap and planted false notes on Miller, using the woman and confederate.

"But he had slipped, just a little.

You knew the notes were false, and you said so. Then the evil Jenks came in and said they were real. He almost sewed up the case for himself then, but there was another hitch—his agents had hidden Harrison, as Jenks told us a little while ago, in one of the underground lockers in the boathouse, and Bancroft wouldn't leave. Meanwhile Bancroft discovered the ruse of the white carnations, and he began rounding them up.

"At this point, the Nazis, afraid it was going to slip out of their hands, unable to understand Jenks' refusal to change the appointment for four o'clock Sunday when he himself had told them the appointment was known to the F.B.I.—the Nazis decided to take matters into their own hands. They knew that Jenks knew the formula by heart, so they decided to kidnap Jenks and force the formula out of him at their leisure.

"Here again, Bancroft forestalled them. He knew they wanted to kidnap someone, but he didn't know whom, and he sent Holmes, hoping that he might get the Nazis to reveal it inadvertently. They had no luck with the Nazis, but you, under the pier, heard enough to make you sure that Jenks was involved in it.

"You confronted Jenks with your questions—but *this* was the good Jenks! If you will go back to that conversation, you will see how he tried to lead you to make the right conclusions. He really was trying to help you then, as he had been all along.

"He told you that it wasn't always possible for one to explain what was going on in one's mind. What was he driving at? You knew he meant something, but you couldn't quite grasp it. Then he told you that he had known all along about you. He then as much as told you, though he was speaking through the fourth Woodruff, that there was something for you to work out. He couldn't know which Woodruff he was talking to, but what he was trying to do was demonstrate that *he not only knew what had happened to you, but that such a thing had also happened to him!*

"That is what he meant when he said he hoped the real Woodruff would understand—for how else could he *know* what had happened to you *unless it had already happened to him?*"

There was only one other question I had to ask.

"How did you know when we went to Jenks' house that the Jenks we had with us was the evil one?"

"Because," said Palmer, "the good Jenks would have been delighted when he saw that you finally understood, but this one was terrified."

And that's about it, I guess, though there are still some details that may interest you. Palmer says a writer owes a debt to his readers; when he introduces characters and talks about them, he just can't run off and leave them in the lurch. So here's the dope, done up swiftly and in statistical form.

The Nazi boat came back that following night, and it was trailed and caught. You'll hear about it one of these days in the papers.

Jenks went to a sanitarium for a month (Palmer recommended his own private one) and after that he and Dorothy were married. I did a nice thing by signing him a cool million, which I can easily deduct from the taxes I am paying to beat the Axis, but I won't. Oh, yes—he tore up and burned every vestige of the notes, and he says he is forgetting the formula little by little. I hope so.

Ann and I have been married a month and twelve days now, and yesterday I got my induction notice, so I'm off to Fort Jay in three days. Ann says she'll follow me around the country and I love it.

Mahoney is still drinking coca-colas with eggs.

Bancroft didn't believe our story when we told him that the notes had showed up safe and sound in the office, after all, but he was less skeptical after finding out Dave was in a sanitarium.

Seaside is now one of Long Island's biggest USO headquarters.

For all I know, Alonzo is still in that closet, crying out his little heart. I haven't seen him since I left on my honeymoon.

Robert is in the pantry, making a French .75 this very minute.

Finally, Palmer says that a story has to have I happy ending. I think this one has a fine, hysterically happy ending. Don't you?

THE END

If you've enjoyed this book, you will not want to miss these terrific titles…

ARMCHAIR SCI-FI & HORROR DOUBLE NOVELS, $12.95 each

ARMCHAIR SCIENCE FICTION CLASSICS, $12.95 each

ARMCHAIR SCI-FI & HORROR GEMS SERIES, $12.95 each

www.ingramcontent.com/pod-product-compliance
Lightning Source LLC
Chambersburg PA
CBHW030312180626
46810CB00003B/1037